Other books by the author:

LOVE'S WILDERNESS
GOOD TO HER
A BETTER MAN
CRASHING

VOICES

ENID HARLOW

Livingston Press
University of West Alabama

Copyright © 2025 Enid Harlow
All rights reserved, including electronic text
ISBN 13: trade paper 978-1-60489-384-7
ISBN 13: e-book 978-1-60489-385-4

Library of Congress Control Number: 2025930411

Typesetting and page layout: Kelly West
Proofreading: Kelly West, Scott Robinson, Brooke Barger,
Savannah Beams, Kamille Clark, Maribeth Gray,
Jake Bius, Josie Rollier, Kaylie Lake,
Mahkayla Young

Cover art: Kelly West

6 5 4 3 2 1

VOICES

For Michaelis Odysseus

Contents

Henry's Wife

In front of her were her women friends—Lyla, Ursula, Brandy, and Marianne—publishers' or editors' wives all of them. Except for Marianne who was recently divorced and not presently known to be attached to any particular man.

"Fabulous, isn't it!" Lyla exclaimed, referring to tonight's celebratory party for Ben's first publication.

"What a sendoff," Brandy added.

"Lovely party," Gracie agreed, nodding emphatically. "So happy for Ben."

Behind her was the elegant but inoperable fireplace. Like many old apartment buildings on Manhattan's Upper West Side, this one had an elegantly scrolled fireplace that had functioned in the distant past but was sealed up now and served a decorative function only. These old New York City apartments were typically large—spacious entryways, dining and living rooms with high ceilings and parquet floors, two- and three-, even four-bedrooms, oftentimes duplexes. Anna and Ben Landowski, their hosts this evening, had two bedrooms, a formal dining room, and an enormous living room, perfect for giving parties such as this.

Henry had left her there, safe and protected in this corner of the room, her friends surrounding her, the elegant but inoperable fireplace at her back. How good of Henry to have done so. How kind. Ever thinking of her welfare, always protective. He'd gone off to have a chat with someone across the room.

"Great crowd," commented Ursula. "Great food."

Gracie smiled and nodded again. (How she despised that habit of hers: head bouncing up and down inanely, subserviently.) Especially when she'd had too much to drink. Not that three glasses of wine were too much. And this one wasn't even finished. Yet there she was, inanely, subserviently nodding her head, now at Ursula's comment about the crowd and the food, now at Marianne's remark about the book: "Can't wait to read it. I hear it's awfully good."

Nodding again (how she wished she'd stop that), Gracie said Henry had vigorously sung the book's praises. "Not that he could do anything less," she said. "Being its editor."

The women laughed as one and said, of course; Lyla adding, "Don't we know how our husbands tout their books?"

"Don't we, indeed?" Gracie replied, nodding (*yet again!*).

"Ex," said Marianne.

"Sorry?" Lyla seemed genuinely not to know what she meant.

"Husbands or ex-husbands," Marianne clarified.

"Oh, right," said Lyla, chagrined.

An awkward pause ensued, and Gracie took the moment to slip away.

Walking a bit unsteadily, the wine remaining in her glass sloshing silently from side to side, she made her way across the room. Her balance was definitely off, but it was a party after all. A mid-March celebration in honor of Ben Landowski's publication of his tell-all about a prominent Washington politician. "The Ides of March," Ben had earlier quipped, referencing the evening's date. "An auspicious day to celebrate a book about a famous politician." The sloshing of the wine and that slight imbalance in her gait (no more than a barely perceptible favoring of one side over the other) might very well go unnoticed in a room as crowded as this. And with so many people standing about eating, drinking, laughing, shouting (some of them) to make themselves heard. She hardly thought her imbalance or the teetering of the wine in her glass would warrant a second glance.

Now passing near to an end table (almost too near) she attempted to put her glass down on its cluttered surface, but its circular base gave her trouble. "Oh, excuse me. Sorry," she said as the stem of her glass knocked against an edge of a plate, then against another glass. "Thank you kindly," she said as the glass was taken from her and settled in a spot hastily cleared for it by another guest.

Nodding (*once again!*) to show her gratitude, Gracie walked on across the room. Now and then she caught sight of the book of honor's title—**Accountable** (available at a substantial discount to tonight's guests)—peering up at her in enlarged and bolded red and blue letters. How pleased Henry must be to see the finished product of his work (hard, painstaking work, conducted over three drafts and eighteen months' time) scattered about this living room. It lay on various tabletops and between cushions where people sat on sofas, talking convivially. Even here and there the title could be seen glaring provocatively from the floor beneath tables and chairs where the book had been carefully laid aside, allowing for the better use of hands in holding drinks and plates of food. (Cheese and crackers, crudités, and fat boiled shrimp were in abundance this evening.)

Gracie was on her way to have a quiet word with her husband, standing there by the bookcase on the far side of the room, talking in what seemed his most carefree manner to Elizabeth Parsons, an attractive, tall, slim, young (maddeningly young) woman with soft brown hair falling loose half-way down her back. Gracie loved that about Henry. How he could seem carefree in the most serious of circumstances. Not that tonight's circumstances were particularly serious. They merely involved her husband talking to his other woman in a crowded room and in full view of his wife.

How lovely she is, Henry thought the first time he laid eyes on her. He was walking along the promenade above the Hudson River. She was approaching the balustrade's cutout (made for easy viewing of the river), and he was approaching it from the opposite end. There seemed to be someone with her, but distracted by the woman's loveliness, Henry hardly noticed. Elizabeth (as he would later learn her name) was wearing purple shorts (very short shorts) and a sleeveless white T-shirt. She was slim and tall, had inviting thighs and lovely soft brown hair falling half-way down her back.

It was a humid Sunday morning in mid-August.

As they drew near to their chosen spots, converging upon each other face to face, Henry felt a flash of something like recognition pass through him. *I know her*, he said to himself. *I have always known her*, he insisted improbably. Quickly Elizabeth looked away. But she had looked, Henry would swear to that. She had noticed him. And almost immediately looked away. Then gazed down affectionately at a child she was pushing in a stroller. (It was a little girl in that stroller, Henry saw now, who was accompanying this unbelievably lovely woman). He judged the child to be about five, and felt instantly, preposterously, jealous of the affection the woman was showing her. Upon reaching the cutout, this Elizabeth in the purple short shorts and soft brown hair took the child from her stroller and placed her on the flat stone ledge from which she might enjoy an unobstructed view of the Hudson.

How lovely she is, Henry thought again. *How lovely her hair.* He watched her wrap her arms protectively around the child and felt the same preposterous jealousy of the protected child. Placing her chin on the child's shoulder, this Elizabeth murmured something to her which Henry could not hear but felt its murmur. Then she raised one lovely slender arm and pointed to a sailboat (he guessed it was) out on the river, or perhaps it was a distant cloud or low-flying seagull. *How lovely that arm*, he thought. *How lovely that pointing finger.*

Henry took up a position along the ledge not far from the woman and the child from which he could study them. *Not her child surely.* She was far too young to have a child that age. Blazingly young. Mesmerizingly young. Not a single line marred her face. Her arms and legs were smooth as porcelain. An older sister's child conceivably, for he noted a strong family resemblance between this woman and the child that could easily extend to an aunt. It was there in the eyes: intense and dark in the woman, the same intensity and equal darkness in the eyes of the child. It was there in the chin which came almost to a point in both woman and child. And in the hair, soft brown, worn long by both, falling loose half-way down their backs.

I want to know this woman, Henry said to himself, captivated by the liveliness in her face, by the evident delight she felt in simply being where she was—on this promenade, looking out over the river, the last of the summer's sun in her eyes, the humid city air ruffling her hair. *I will know her*, he vowed, envisioning some future time in which he might. Almost he raised a hand in greeting. *Not yet*, warned a voice, and he stayed his hand.

Gracie knew the woman's name, having asked Henry when first she noticed her and something about her at Jennifer Strom's New Year's Eve party.

"Elizabeth Parsons," Henry told her. "Jenny introduced me. You, too, I think."

"No. I must have been getting champagne."

What Gracie noticed about Elizabeth Parsons at that New Year's Eve party was first of all her youth. Startling. Almost shocking. She might have been a teenager dressed for the prom. Next, she noticed the way her dark eyes immediately fastened on Henry as they walked in and how, in almost the same instant, glanced away. A moment later, when Gracie looked for her again, Elizabeth had vanished.

She knew at once. Or thought she did.

But she had known even before that. Before the New Year's Eve party. Before January 20th. Before the sighting in the post office last December. Since the coffee shop in November she had known. Instinctively, intuitively. Or thought she had.

No, certainly not. She told herself. She was mistaken. *Not Henry.* Not Henry to whom she'd been married for twenty-four years. *Not her good dear kind Henry.* With whom she'd had two children. She pursed her lips and shook her head, allowing herself the consolation of doubt.

She trusted Henry. Trusted him completely. So completely she oftentimes left her diary (a thing whose privacy was sacrosanct) out on her bedside table—where Henry might easily find it and read it—instead of tucking it away securely in the drawer. But he hadn't found it, or if he had, hadn't read it. Never would Henry do such a thing. She hadn't left it out to test him. It was simply a mistake. Careless but harmless. Probably she'd nodded off after writing in the diary, as she did every night, and neglected to put it back into its drawer. Drowsiness and carelessness were the culprits, not a test. She'd never be so cruel as to put her Henry to a test.

Yet the very first time she saw the woman—before tonight, before the New Year's Eve party, before January 20th, before the post office—her stomach sank. It was last November outside the coffee shop. The woman was descending the steps as she and Henry were ascending. Henry and the woman (to come to be known as Elizabeth Parsons) hadn't spoken. Hadn't even met the other's eyes. But something took place between them. A message passed. A signal given. And Gracie's stomach sank. She knew. Or thought she knew. She tossed off the thought, calmed her stomach, allowed doubt (again) to offer its consolation. A moment later the steps were cleared, the woman gone. She and Henry were inside the coffee shop, being shown to a table. She put the incident out of her mind (or almost). It had never happened (or not quite). Until the post office in December. Until Jennifer Strom's New Year's Eve party. Until January 20th. And then tonight.

Coming now to where the two of them were standing, approaching near enough to see the sparkle in the woman's dark eyes and hear their lowered voices—absurdly lowered, as if they could be heard above the clamor in the room—Gracie wondered. She stood between them and wondered. She remained there a moment, directly between the two, not saying anything, only wondering and thinking she was foolish to wonder, then wondering again. She stood close enough to Henry, her hips grazing his, her breasts actually coming into contact with the buttons on his shirt, to make him stop speaking. Why shouldn't she stand between them? Why shouldn't she interrupt their conversation?

Who is that man staring at me? Elizabeth raised a hand to shield her eyes from the sun and took him in. Tall. Handsome. Serious face. Khaki shorts. Navy T-shirt. Do I know him? He seems to know me. Seems to have met me before. Or thinks he has. He's raising his hand, retracting it. A flicker of embarrassment crosses his face as if he'd been about to commit some social error but stopped himself in time. Wide chest, broad shoulders. Probably works out. She wonders what he would be like in bed. She often wonders that, glancing at men (the attractive ones, of course) sitting on park benches, reading or taking the sun, or jogging toward her while she walks the promenade with her child. Not that she was in any way dissatisfied with the man she had, the way he performed in bed. Just curious. She truly loved her husband, loved the way he made love to her. But her experience was limited, her husband the only man with whom she'd ever made love. Inexperience left her curious. Probably other women who had married young as she had (barely twenty) and had no one to compare their husbands to, wondered about it as well. Did other men do it differently? Favor certain positions? Have special techniques? It would be fun to find out. Like a game she could play. In her mind only, of course.

Elizabeth turned away from the man with the serious face

who'd been staring at her all this time. Feeling a sudden flush in her cheeks, she parked the stroller and lifted the child out.

Gracie meant merely to remind Henry of the lateness of the hour and to suggest they should be leaving shortly. But that would be a mistake. Any mention of the time or suggestion about leaving would only call attention to the age difference between herself and her husband's other woman, would infer that she was tired, needed to go home and rest. Would make Elizabeth wonder (though not maliciously, Gracie detected no callousness in the woman's youth) if the older woman's back was giving out, if she'd had her fill of standing around making small talk, of smiling graciously and endlessly nodding her head. This Elizabeth, it was evident from her youth and the sparkle in her eyes, could make small talk, smile graciously and nod her head until the cows came home. Gracie declined to give her the advantage.

But in fact, the advantage was hers. For she knew about Elizabeth and Henry (even knew where the woman lived, knew the actual number of her brownstone), although Elizabeth and Henry didn't know she knew. She hoped for Henry's sake that nothing she ever did, no remark ever made or look let fall, would reveal the knowledge she possessed. And had possessed with certainty since that cold early Monday morning on January 20th. (She couldn't be absolutely certain about the coffee shop in November, the December encounter in the post office, or the fleeting glance at Jennifer Strom's New Year's Eve party, but that morning in late January left no doubt.)

Henry had claimed to have an obligatory early board meeting, and she, unable to sleep after he'd left, had showered and dressed and gone to the health food store on the corner of 82nd and Broadway to get a head start on her weekly shopping. Chancing to turn her head as she exited the store, she saw him there—her beloved Henry—raising the collar of his overcoat against the chill and slipping out the vibrant green front door of a brownstone on the south side of 82nd Street between Broadway and West End. The building's number, oversized and in shiny black paint, stark against the green, was large enough for her to see from where she stood: Number 304.

She had known at once. Then automatically, as wives do, she'd made excuses for him in her mind. Possibly he knew someone else in that building. A bed-ridden board member requiring an update on this morning's meeting; a sick friend he was visiting out of the kindness of his heart to see how she (or he) was doing and provide a little company. That would be so like Henry. He was good in that way. Kind. But it was no use. She knew. The last shred of doubt's consolation fled from her.

Preposterously then, as if betrayal's guilt were hers to bear, as if she were the one who needed to make reparations, she went into a nearby furniture store and bought Henry the expensive brown leather recliner he'd been pining for for years but considered too immodest an act to purchase for himself.

January 20, she noted in her diary. *Bought Henry his recliner.*

Henry saw her again early one morning in September. At the bus stop on Riverside Drive and 81st Street. Without her child this time (if it had been hers). From a distance she looked like a child herself, and Henry sensed a reason—ridiculous, he conceded even then—for that feeling coursing through him of having seen her before. He'd always wanted a little girl. How wonderful, he'd often thought, to have a girl after his two boys. It was not to be, but perhaps he'd buried his wish for a daughter so deeply beneath his delight in his sons that the wish itself (improbably) became a reality (fleeting, of course) upon seeing this young woman at the bus stop. There she was before him, waiting for the Number 5: the child of his dreams.

Already, he was in love. If he'd had a car, he would have pulled over and offered to take her wherever she was going. No place would have been too distant, no location too remote.

"I'm taking a cab," he called out, impulsively hailing one. "Can I drop you?"

She looked up at him baffled, taken by surprise. Then in an instant seemed to consider his offer and all its ramifications and accepted.

Gracie had seen the woman four times before tonight. Once in November, coming out of that coffee shop as she and Henry were entering. Her stomach sank; she had an inkling. But only that. Something seemed to flow between the woman and Henry as they passed one another on the steps. The pause, the quick intake of breath. Although no breath was drawn by either of them, no pause taken,

Henry's Wife

the sinking in her stomach was definitive.

The second time she saw her husband's Elizabeth was at the local post office two weeks before Christmas. They hadn't spoken (Elizabeth had never even met her eyes). Both had been filling out customs forms for parcels they were sending abroad. Gracie had glanced over surreptitiously and caught the return address Elizabeth was supplying on her form: 304 West 82nd Street. And then the third time, just briefly, at Jennifer's New Year's Eve party when Elizabeth had appeared and in almost the same moment disappeared.

The fourth time, on January 20th, the day of the fictitious board meeting, she hadn't actually seen Elizabeth but had seen Henry coming out of number 304 and had drawn the only possible conclusion.

She hoped nothing would ever show on her face or be heard in her words to hint at what she knew. She wouldn't want that for Henry. For it would be in his nature to feel badly on her account if he knew she knew, fearing to have her gossiped about in private or humiliated in public. It was his way to be concerned when he sensed her feelings were hurt. He was good in that way. She didn't want him ever to know. But Elizabeth and Henry must have known there would come a time (like tonight at the Landowski's) when chance would throw the three of them together, living in the same neighborhood and sharing as they did largely the same circle of friends.

It's bound to happen, Elizabeth might say.

We'll handle it, Henry would reply.

He took her to the Sherry Netherlands that first time because it was one of the nicest hotels in town. Also, he didn't have the key to the company apartment on his person. Afterwards, he kept the key with him, and that tiny third-floor walk-up on West 59th Street with a view of Central Park became their special place. Their *hideout,* they called it. It was rarely used by the publishing house, but maintained for their best-selling out-of-state authors who were passing through New York on book tours or stopping over for meetings with editors or for media interviews. Now it was theirs. Three days a week. Lunchtimes: Monday, Wednesday, Friday. The cleaning service was called (instructed to send their invoices directly to Henry); Elizabeth was given a key. Their meetings were easily dismissed at Henry's office, if even noticed, as long business lunches (sometimes conflicting with actual business lunches that had to be rescheduled). Occasionally, Elizabeth called to cancel (using his cell phone as he'd requested, never his home or office phone) if her child (it was indeed hers) was sick and had to stay home from kindergarten. Only twice had that happened; both times Henry felt bereft.

So distraught was he the first time Elizabeth canceled that he said he'd come right over. It was mid-morning, he pointed out when she objected, and her husband (she'd confessed to having one straight off) would already have left for work.

"No," she said. "Don't come. I don't want Clara to see you."

"She won't see me, kid," he assured her, having recently taken to calling her kid. "I'll be like a shadow. I'll be invisible."

Elizabeth laughed. "We could play hide and seek. But no… please don't come."

"I'll be there in a minute."

He thought he'd won their first quarrel. But no sooner had she opened the front door to her brownstone and led him up the stairs, did Elizabeth confirm her original objection. "I can't," she said. "Not here. Not in his house. His bed."

Henry glanced at her husband's things thrown about: a brown leather-trimmed sports jacket slung over the back of a chair; a pile of button-down white shirts tossed onto an ottoman (presumably awaiting a trip to the laundry). He glanced at her child's toys left in her mother's room. (*Clara's* toys. He now knew her name.) A soccer-sized red and white striped ball, two or three stuffed animals on the floor. *Her child. Her husband. Her life away from him.* Suddenly he didn't want to be in that house. Both were relieved when he left.

The apartment on West 59th Street (minuscule), soon decorated by Elizabeth, positioning potted plants and flowers to make it distinctly theirs, became for Henry an idyllic place. A place in which he could forget himself, lose his bearings, his equilibrium, become a different man. A younger man. A reckless man. In this idyllic place a spell came over him. It was a whole new world; he went about as in an altered state. Her body drove him mad. He forgot the wife he loved, forgot the sons he adored. They didn't belong to his new world. Only he and Elizabeth belonged. Only he and this amazingly young woman with the porcelain-smooth skin and buttocks firm as tennis balls, belonged. She was the only woman in the world. He was in love.

Yet, his other world remained. Hovering close, never entirely banished from his thoughts. He was in love in that world also. Gracie was his wife. They had been married for twenty-four years. He didn't want to be married to anyone else. Gracie had given him two sons (athletes, both) adolescents now: James, a freshman at the University of Michigan; Peter, a junior in high school. He shouldn't be here in this apartment with this woman. He knew he shouldn't be. Yet he couldn't help himself. She had stolen his heart. He was in love.

"God, you're young," he said.

"Not so young," she replied. She'd married at twenty, had her baby at twenty-one, the baby was five now. "You do the math."

They set up house. Bought new dishes for ordering lunch in (often they dispensed with lunch altogether). Bought new glasses, new cutlery. That was mandatory, Elizabeth said. She wouldn't have them eating off plates, drinking from glasses, using knives and forks other people had used. New sheets, new pillowcases. Elizabeth insisted on those too, and for the same reason. New wash cloths, new towels.

"It's like playing house," she declared, and giggled. (*Giggled! Oh, he did adore her.*)

Through September into October, through November and December, January into March, that place was theirs. Throughout the fall sunlight poured through the bedroom window. Snow fell early in December, leaving a thick drift on the windowsill in which they scratched their initials. They were like children playing at life. Snow again, sporadically, in January. February was cold and rainy. March made them think of spring. Only twice in all that time (once for four days in October, again for a week in December) did they need to evacuate the premises and return to the Sherry Netherlands for out-of-state authors were coming to town. Otherwise the place was theirs. They were lovers, secret lovers, in their hideout.

"Like bandits," she whispered in his ear. "Like outlaws."

He might have been a bandit, an outlaw. He'd play any role she devised. Oftentimes he didn't know who he was. A spell had been cast.

He hadn't made it happen. It had happened because of the spell. No more could he give her up than break that spell. He was happy. Love had hold of him. He was captive to its power. A new man living in a new world. But he remembered the old world—that world of wife and sons, of home and happiness—where love had also exerted its power. He had treasured that world (treasured it still) but tried gently now to shove aside. His old world, however, wouldn't be so easily dislodged. It defied him. It laid its claim. *What do you think you're doing?* it taunted him. *Are you crazy?* it demanded. Crazy, yes, he was. Demented and in a trance. He was a different man. Altered, transformed. Young again, embarked on a new life. He loved his new life. He loved his old life. Shamefully, arrogantly, he wanted both.

Every time Elizabeth unlocks the door to their cozy apartment on West 59th Street (their *hideout*, they call it), her heart leaps to see him there. Always, Henry is the first to arrive. "I love waiting for you," he says. "Knowing you're on your way, love hearing your key in the lock."

She, in turn, basks in his love. Revels in it as if it were her due. Always, he jumps from the bed or chair (the apartment has only two—straight-backed, cane-seated) where he'd been sitting. Often, he gets to the door before she's fully opened it. Always, he is smiling, his arms thrown wide to receive her, his hands coming up to run through her hair. She's amazed by the size of his hands; his forearms seem like branches of trees. The scattering of hair on his chest delights her—how soft it is, how it converges into a single line running straight down to his belly button and groin. The hair under his arms is a toy to her. She blows on it, bats at it, makes it ripple. Laughs to see it move.

Or perhaps he hadn't been sitting when she arrived. Perhaps, his patience wearing thin (rarely it does, but sometimes), he'd been pacing back and forth between the front door and the couch. She could see him doing that, pacing back and forth, the expression on his face, serious at first, growing more and more agitated as he makes each turn. "Grumpy," she tells him, seeing that. "Grumpy old man." She loves his impatience, loves taunting him with it. It's like another game to play.

"Ah, there you are!" he says. "Finally!" Her lover welcomes her. His voice gruff at first (though she's never more than five minutes late), then joyful. His serious expression vanishes in an instant.

It doesn't matter that the place is small—no more than a bedroom, bath, tiny couch, tinier kitchen—he picks her up like a doll, swings her around.

Her lover. It blows her mind.

It doesn't matter that they rarely go out. "This is our world," she says, pointing to the bed, the table, the two chairs. "It's all we need." They can play at being shut-ins, brittle, bedridden. She mops his brow, pulls the covers up to his chin. She's a fabrication of herself. A woman she hardly knows.

A woman with a lover. It makes her giggle.

Their hideout is an enchanted place. A place in which she smiles constantly. The corners of her mouth pull up like a puppet's mouth with strings. She moves as if her feet don't quite touch the floor. She is happy in this place where a man anxiously awaits her, jumps up when he sees her, makes her smile, loves her. Not that she hadn't been happy before, hadn't had a man who made her smile, loved her (loves her still). Of course she had. And has today. But in a different place, with a different man. When she's in this place, their hideout as they call it, she pretends to forget that other man ever existed. Pretending to forget. It's another game she plays.

Everything is different here. She's a different woman in this place. Looks different, feels different. Has different desires, different needs. Her husband and child wouldn't recognize her if they saw her here, for she bears only a passing resemblance to the woman they think they know. She might have been born from different parents, formed by a different history; possibly had no parents, no history at all. She might have slipped out of her former self like a blast of air and been transported to a different world. Different but parallel to and never intersecting with that other world in which she also knows happiness, knows love. A parallel universe in which she smiles in a different way, is happy in a different way, is loved by a different man, and (almost) loves back.

Even after twenty-four years of living with Henry in this apartment on Riverside Drive, Gracie can't imagine living anywhere else or with any other man. She wouldn't want another man, feels no desire for one. It is Henry she loves. No one else. And this apartment suits her perfectly. She loves its shiny parquet floors, the trim on its walls, the inoperable fireplace. She loves the living room with its comfortable if faded blue silk couch, loves coming home to that couch after an evening out, as they have done tonight, loves sinking into it next to her husband. And there in the corner of the room, a standing reminder of a continuing infidelity (known, so far as Henry is aware, only to him and to Elizabeth), the expensive brown leather recliner she'd bought for him on an impulse. She loves even that.

"Drink, darling?" she inquires, already pouring his usual nighttime Scotch and a glass of white wine for herself. The fourth of the evening, she notes, and promises herself to take only a sip or two.

"Thanks," Henry replies, reaching for the drink with one hand and with the other drawing her down onto the couch.

"Hungry?" she asks. "I could fix us something. It wasn't much more than hors d'oeuvres at the Landowski's."

"No need," he says. "That was enough for me. But you go ahead."

She doesn't feel a need for food either, having consumed more than her fair share of shrimp at their friends' party.

March 15, she will write. *Saw her again.*

He is a delight in so many ways. She could tell him anything, she thinks. Yet there are things she longs to tell him and cannot. Things about Clara especially. What she did or said that morning, the adorable gestures, the clever remarks she'd made. How she folded her arms, tilted her head, pursed her lips while waiting for an answer to a question. *Like a little old woman,* she would say, and he would laugh. But of course she won't say any of that. She'll spare his feelings. For he would have heard it, seen it, all before: the clever remarks, the adorable gestures, the folding of the arms, the tilting of the head and pursing of the lips while waiting for an answer to a question. So alive are her child's words and gestures to her, so precious, so dear, they would but constitute the past for Henry. All that brings her joy in her daughter would be a redundancy for him, repeating what he'd known and treasured with his sons. Her present is his past. She won't bother him with it.

"Listen," she says, and stops, holding back.

"What?" he asks.

"Nothing," she replies, and goes on to something else.

But isn't that wrong? Isn't holding back a denial of herself?

Still, Gracie considers five months a long time for any romance. And it might have been longer. Much as she hates to think, their liaison might have begun weeks, even months before the five she knows about. Would Elizabeth not now be tiring of things as they currently stand? Would she not now be suggesting they move to the next level? My God, five months! Gracie clasps her hand to her mouth, stifling a cry. Five months would have overlapped with February 14th. Their wedding day. Of course it would have. Obviously, it did. How could she have forgotten that? Being young as she was then, romantic and madly in love, she'd suggested they choose that Hallmark holiday for the day they would marry. (How trite! How vapid!) Being young also and equally in love, Henry had acquiesced. Year after year, for twenty-four years, they'd celebrated their anniversary on the same day much of the Western world was observing Saint Valentine's Day. Did Elizabeth know what February 14th meant to Henry? Had he told her? Was it possible? No, certainly not. Some things were private, Henry would respect that. But in a moment's reckless urge to be forthcoming with his other woman, might he have let it slip? Then Elizabeth would have been there in the restaurant with them on that very night. She would have witnessed all they said and did, the promises made, the tender remarks exchanged.

Un, Deux, Trois was her favorite restaurant in all of New York City. Henry had booked a table without telling her. He'd bustled her into a cab without revealing where they were going. He'd held his hands over her ears while conveying the address to the driver. Would he have told Elizabeth that? Putting her there in the cab with them, later in the restaurant? Certainly not. Not her Henry. He ordered champagne. *The best you've got*, he'd said. How flamboyant. How dear. He clinked his glass against hers. Would Elizabeth have heard that clink? Would she have smiled? He leaned over the table and kissed her, right there on the mouth not caring who might see. *Twenty-four years*, Gracie said, and Henry had replied, *The best of my life*. Gracie detected tears in her husband's eyes. Right there in the restaurant. Kind Henry. Sweet Henry. Tears in his lovely dark eyes. Had Elizabeth seen them too? Had she witnessed their kiss? Overheard the promises they'd whispered to one another? Had she swooped in, slight as a shadow, to hover over them and silently observe the celebration of their love? God, she hoped not.

She tries to recall if there ever had been a time when Henry's feelings for her had changed. When he in the smallest measure had betrayed a suspicion that she had failed him, giving him cause to seek someone else. She can think of none. But surely, she had failed him in some way. Wounded him. Disappointed him. Leaving him free to turn elsewhere. Or perhaps he hasn't fully turned. Has merely made a small side-step, a pivot, allowing space for another's love to seep in. It wasn't surprising that with a man as good as Henry another woman would love him also. She only hopes it is a fling. An infatuation that will quickly run its course. She could bear it, she tells herself, so long as he loves her best.

But five months! (And maybe more, heaven forbid!) Wouldn't Elizabeth, now into the sixth month (seventh? eighth?) of her affair with this good man, might be asking (gently, ever so gently) if he'd be willing to leave his wife, his family.

I can't, Henry would reply. And Elizabeth would understand.

His eyes are dark as ebony and deep as wells. Elizabeth peers into them, looks away, peers again, pretending she can read his mind. Now she can, now she can't. It's a game of make-believe. Another game she loves to play.

"If I look hard enough, I can see what you're thinking. If I look away, I can't."

"You're such a kid," he replies. "Always playing games."

He is a marvel to her. When he speaks, she marvels at the words he chooses, where he places his emphasis. She marvels at his eyes, his eyelids. How long the lashes are! How they flutter when she kisses them. She marvels at his hands, the size of them, how gently they hold her breasts. She marvels at his breath itself, plays at catching it in her fists when it comes out of his mouth. He is passionate yet tender in bed. Now she has her answer to her question about how other men do it (one man at least), now she wonders why she'd thought it important to know.

It doesn't matter, she tells herself, that he's so much older (*Forty-nine, if you must know*), has read so many books, knows so much more about everything. He could be a chance acquaintance, a distant relative, a kindly doctor or professor. She plays at assigning him roles, family positions (uncle, brother-in-law, older brother or nephew, never father). To each she plays a corresponding role. It doesn't matter that he's so far ahead of her in knowledge and experience. So far she can never catch up. *Hey, Henry!* she hears herself calling. *Wait up!* All that matters are his arms around her, his fingers running through her hair, cupping her breasts, stroking her belly. All that matters is hearing him say he loves her. The way it makes her smile and feel she (almost) loves him back.

Gracie leans forward to put her wine glass on the coffee table. Her fourth that evening. It is empty. She has broken the promise she made to herself. No matter, she tells herself. Henry, too, has broken a promise. Leaning back against the couch, she closes her eyes and in the sudden darkness sees the woman again before her. Early twenties to her forty-five. Slim, dark eyes. Pretty, certainly. No stomach bulge beneath her one-shouldered, tight-fitting black dress. No stretch marks either, Gracie would wager. A world lies between them. A churning ocean. She has borne Henry two children, raised them with him into adolescence, suffered through their illnesses, their heartbreaks, cheered their academic accomplishments and their victories in sports, commiserated with them when they lost. Basketball, hockey, soccer, baseball: their boys played them all. She and Henry watched with pride. *The two of us. Side by side.* This young woman, this Elizabeth Parsons, with the soft brown hair falling alluringly over one bared shoulder might have given her husband (if she had a husband) a child. One at most. Unlikely she'd had more. She wouldn't have been able to handle more than one, Gracie is certain. Too young, too inexperienced. When she noticed her that first time descending the coffee shop steps as they were ascending, passing Henry without a glance, yet sending a message of some sort, a code she had yet to break, she wondered if she wasn't seeing more than there was. *Was there more?* No, foolish woman, there was not. They were just two people passing one another on the steps. No message. No code. The averted eyes, the intake of breath, all in her imagination. But tonight, in the way this Elizabeth stood speaking to another woman's husband, betraying no wish to have him for her own, she knows she is seeing only what is there. Surely there's a wish. A man as good as Henry.

Yet, there are concerns, disturbing thoughts that gnaw at Elizabeth. Had she married too young? Had a child before she was ready? And that feeling of being forced to hold things back, clapping her own hand over her mouth. It was worrisome. *What?* he asks. *Nothing*, she replies. It worries her. Aren't they meant to tell each other everything? No matter what. Silly things, goofy things. Things about Clara for instance. Her clever words, her endearing gestures. Longing to tell him, having it there on the tip of her tongue, yet holding it back. Shouldn't that be a cause for concern? Wa*sn't it wrong?* Having to watch her words with her lover.

Pretty, Gracie concedes, closing her eyes and leaning back against the couch. *Pretty, certainly.* She can't help but see it in the woman's flashing dark eyes, skin as smooth as silk, in the slimness of her figure. And her youth, of course. Though she'd expected that. Men rarely choose women for lovers older than their wives. But for a wife of twenty-four years, a woman of forty-five, she, too, is pretty. Attractive at least. Skin still uncreased. Blue eyes clear as ever. *Five-foot two, eyes of blue,* to this day Henry is prone to humming that tune. Her hair, shorter than his other woman's, lustrous still, and requiring only a minimal touch up once every six weeks. And she's slim as she'd ever been; happily she'd match the interloper's weight any day. Twelve pounds was all she'd gained with either of her sons, had lost almost at once and never gained back.

And Henry loves her. That's the thing. That hasn't changed. Never will. Neither will her love for him. *Darling*, they call to one another, returning home in the evenings. *Sweetheart! I'm here.* That's the same. As is their pleasure in bed. (Less frequent now, perhaps, but still the same.) The way they converse, laugh, argue occasionally but never hurtfully and always making up before going to sleep. *I'm sorry, sweetheart. Forgive me, darling.* All that is the same. The comfortable silence they settle into when seated side by side on the couch, that hasn't changed. And the breaking of that silence—*Oh, let me tell you,* he might say; *You'll never guess,* she might begin—the two of them speaking at once. All that is the same. Reading each other's minds, finishing each other's sentences. All that is as it ever was. They are suited. They are happy.

Henry's Wife

Something is off with Elizabeth. Something's definitely bothering her. Henry senses it, can almost see it. She's hiding something from him. Has something she longs to say but will not. A secret, perhaps, she is loath to reveal? No, not a secret, for there's excitement in her eyes as she's about to say it, then does not. She opens her mouth, shuts it firmly; the excitement fades from her eyes. Something about Clara, he would guess. For that's the topic closest to her heart.

"What?" he urges.

"What?" she repeats.

"What were you about to say?"

"Nothing," she insists.

"It was something," he counters. "Something about Clara?"

"Nothing," she says again. "Nothing about Clara. Nothing about anything."

Yet he knows there's something. Is this another game? Does she want him to guess? He sees it in her eyes, senses it there on the tip of her tongue. Yet she holds it back. Today he has no time for games. He's expected back at the office for a three-o'clock video conference call.

"Tell me," he commands, his tone too harsh. He might be disciplining an unruly child. She pouts and closes herself off from him. *Pouts?* Had he truly involved himself with a child? Was this his tariff to pay?

Now Gracie removes her shoes and slides (the room sliding with her) to the far end of the couch. She stretches her legs, places her stockinged feet in Henry's lap and gives herself up to the pleasure of his deep massage. Surely no provocation on her part, no anger or reproach ever expressed or implied had caused Henry to stray. She is certain of that. Certain, too, he loves her still. That's never been in question. The proof (if proof were needed) is in his hands on her feet and in the gentleness of his voice from his end of the couch as he asks, as now he does, absent any innuendo (but how could there be innuendo since he doesn't know she knows?) if she enjoyed herself this evening.

"Lovely party," she replies. "So happy for Ben."

Elizabeth did not come again to their hideout on West 59th Street. Somehow Henry had known she would not. He waited as he always waited, eager to see her face, hear her key turn in the lock. He waited an hour, then two. He grew impatient, finally hopeless. He knew there was no point in waiting longer. He got up from where he'd been sitting, first on the narrow couch, then on the bed, then on one of the two cane-backed chairs, then on the other. He had known all along it couldn't last yet had hoped it would never end. He went to the fridge, threw away the food that was left. Threw away the potted plants and flowers though he could hardly bear to touch them that Elizabeth had nourished and now would go untended. He pulled down the bedroom shade cutting off the light that was left of the afternoon, blocking the view of the park. He canceled the cleaning service, instructing them to come one last time (sending the bill directly to him) and then no more until requested by the publishing house. What they'd had was a dream. A plaything. An impossible fantasy. Its end was inevitable. And now its fragile structure had shattered, as he'd known it would, and clattered to the floor. He opened the front door, took one last look back, shut the door behind him. He would not see her face again or hear her key turning in the lock.

Gracie moves up from her end of the couch to lie beside him. His arm is draped over her shoulder, one hand hanging down, fingers grazing her breast. His breath blows warmly on her cheek. She could lie forever in his embrace. She closes her eyes. Breathing in, breathing out, she wills herself to see nothing on the backs of her eyelids, nothing of the two of them flickering in her brain. No figures, no images. Nothing intimate. She will not think about her Henry with his Elizabeth. Will not imagine them embracing.

"Henry…," she says, and is about to say more, then does not.

He will never leave her, loving her as he does. She knows this to be absolutely true.

The affair is bearable, she tells herself. So long as he loves her best. A satisfactory arrangement, all in all. Except that it isn't. She will live with it as long as she can. And then she won't.

Henry, she will say. *I'm sorry, I can't.* And he will understand.

Other People's Conversations

There was a time years ago when single women, suspected of being
sex workers in pursuit of their trade, and therefore of attracting an
undesirable element to otherwise presumably respectable establish-
ments, were not welcome in New York City restaurants or bars.

Discreetly, but firmly, they were turned away. But that time
has long since passed, its passing giving rise to Margery's predilection, allowing it to flourish. It isn't a sin. Nor even a vice. A penchant,
she would call it. Harmless. A predilection which over time has
become a habit. A harmless habit of frequenting selected cafés and
bistros on her own. One she imagines is shared by many women her
age (forties, approaching fifty) who live alone and whose social life is
circumscribed, at best. She is not ashamed of it. Far from that, Margery indulges her habit. She has boldly selected a few favorite cafés
and dining places to visit on her own. All within a twenty-block radi-
us of her apartment on Manhattan's Upper West Side, for usually she
walks and doesn't wish to wander too far afield at night alone.
She doesn't always go at night. Often, she goes in the late afternoon
or early evening, approaching darkness, and she prefers for her walk
home to take place well before dark. She is not a courageous person,
nor has she ever thought of herself as such, and solitary walks on
darkened streets frequently provoke feelings of anxiety, even dread.

Margery's custom is to rotate among her chosen spots, visiting one or two (sometimes as many as three) several times a week.
Her purpose is simple: to listen to other people's conversations.

Oftentimes as she walks, she feels a stone pressing on her
heart. A burden. Sliding from side to side and pressing down. If she
is lucky (which so far she has not been) she will find in one café or
another a place to rest her burden.

It is sometimes easier, she has found, to talk to a stranger than to someone close. A foreigner in particular. The language barrier providing an extra layer of protection, should she choose to bare her soul. The right foreigner, of course. She must choose carefully. Therefore, upon entering her evening's chosen establishment, she will seek out a table next to one occupied by two or more persons and listen to the language they speak. If she hears English, she will make some excuse to request a different table, (The light here is too bright, or, This table's in a draft). If she hears the parties next to her new table speaking in a foreign tongue, she will listen quietly to determine if they are the ones to whom she might relieve her heart of its burden.

She will settle back in her chair and meticulously examine the menu when her server brings it. She might look up with an expression of surprise, perhaps annoyance, by the speed of his (or her) return. Has the management advised the young man (or woman) that a single patron, clearly contributing less to the evening's take than a party of two or more, should be hurried through her meal as quickly as decency will allow? Nevertheless, Margery will respond courteously when asked for her drink order.

"A glass of red wine, please. Beaujolais, I think."

She curls her fingers around the stem of the glass when it arrives, takes her time surveying the room. After a moment or two, she will permit her eyes to drift toward the adjacent table. Surreptitiously, she will examine the occupants. Tonight it is a man and woman, elegantly dressed. Elderly. Kind eyes, hazel in the man, blue in the woman. Sympathetic faces. People to whom she might indeed unburden herself. She sips her wine and listens (unobtrusively) to the talk that flows between the two, priming her ears for accents or dialects. Oftentimes, her neighborhood being popular among the city's foreign visitors, these conversations are conducted in languages Margery does not speak, or only minimally, but whose gist she understands. Tonight, it is Italian. She studied it briefly in high school long ago. Predominantly now, it is the woman who speaks. The man listens, mostly in silence, nodding or shaking his head when appropriate. He is compassionate. The woman is sympathetic. Margery is pleased to think she has her couple.

Her table is situated alongside a bank of windows on her right, fronting the street. To her left, and close by, is theirs. The elderly man is tall, with a clenched jaw, wavy black hair (tinged with gray) and something like anguish in his hazel eyes. In his silence he seems to be imploring the woman opposite him (his wife, very likely) to do … what…? let him speak? Listen to what is troubling him? The woman is just this side of stout, with jaunty red cheeks and glinting blue eyes. She wears a neatly tailored black silk suit over a white blouse with lace at its cuffs, and a cherry-imprinted scarf around her neck. Sporadically, she fidgets with the scarf. Nerves? Distress? Now Margery observes, as they raise and lower their hands, the matching wedding bands. Yes, she was correct. The woman is his wife. She does not respond to what the man is in his silence attempting to say, but in a stream of swift Italian talks cheerfully straight through it.

Made in Italy, those wedding rings, Margery would guess. And by a skilled artisan. Softly beaten gold, wide bands, inscribed, no doubt—a *mio amore* or *per sempre* or some other fond endearment. Rings exchanged some thirty-five or forty years ago, judging from the look of the hands they now adorn—careworn, wrinkled, finely veined. This couple would have taken their vows in a double-ring Catholic ceremony, attended by perhaps two hundred family members and friends. The men in shiny black suits, polished shoes with pointy toes, she sees them before her, the women in calf-length, floral-patterned dresses, low heels. An outdoors ceremony in the early evening it would have been, at about the time of year (late summer) they now find themselves in. A lawn of lush well-manicured grass at their feet, rimmed by vines of succulent tomatoes and groves of slender olive trees.

Still oblivious to her husband's silent importuning, the wife chatters on. About a film they'd just seen or a play they were about to see. Margery can't be certain which, but judges it likely to be the film, for they are in an area where movie houses proliferate, particularly those showing foreign films. Yes, a film. Now Margery's hearing acclimates to the cadences of the language spoken by the couple. The wife has read several reviews (*molti recensione*), and those reviews are now the subject of her discourse. She wants her husband to know they will not be disappointed (*non deluso*). Slowly, uncertainly, the words come back to Margery, emerging through the fog of years like distant memories. The reviewers have agreed unanimously, the wife continues, that the cast is marvelous (*meraviglioso*). She goes on about

the costumes, the sets, the music, smiling, fidgeting with her scarf, the
direction, and what Margery presumes to be the cinematography,
although the technical term is beyond her grasp.

Perfecto! There is no mistaking that. Nor the radiant look on
the wife's face, cheeks highly rouged, periwinkle blue eyes glinting.

If only, the husband says now in that language Margery has
barely mastered. If only. What? *Cosa*?

That she would look at him? Stop talking? Listen to what he
needs to say?

The couple's server returns, bringing their meal. (The same
server who had attended to Margery.) Chicken Fra Diavolo for the
husband, Veal Francese for the wife. Green salads for both. Margery
is close enough to smell the food's delicious aroma, to hear the clink
of their knives as they press against the overturned prongs of their
forks. Now she notices a slight trembling in the man's right hand,
which she had not noticed before, as he cuts into his chicken. She
would help him if she could. She would steady his hand, listen to
him.

Temporarily then abandoning her Italian couple, Margery sips her
wine and lets her thoughts drift to a long-ago university lecture hall.
A professor, delivering dryly and at eight o'clock every Monday,
Wednesday, and Friday, obligatory remarks on the history of the
world. A prerequisite for any subsequent course in history, whatever
the country or the era. One hundred or so undergraduates seated in
tiered rows before the podium. Herself two rows from the top. The
boy whose name she does not yet know, two rows down from her,
slumped in his seat. It is very early in the morning, and they would
all—all one hundred or so of them—prefer to be still in their beds.
Margery remembers gazing at the back of the boy's head, remembers how his long black hair fell to his shoulders, thick and dark.
Remembers how it curled up at the ends. His ears are the color of
pearls. Already she adores him. Now his head drops forward, now
it jerks upward again. Valiantly then and with considerable effort, it
maintains an upright position. Momentary. Precarious. Then it drops
again, that gorgeous head (already she thinks of it as gorgeous), and
lolls helplessly from side to side. She would plunge her hands into
that thick black hair, let it seep through her fingers like a rushing tide.

Again, the head jerks upright and as if awakened by that sudden movement, the boy's fingers twitch on his chair's fold-up desk. Margery had seen him raise his desktop as he entered his row. She had watched him drop his stack of books onto it, watched him place a lone three-holed notebook open on top of the stack. All through the ensuing lecture, day after day, that notebook has lain open and unused. Now again the boy's head falls forward. A pen, stuck useless in his fist, drops to the floor. The shiny black hair fans out, spreads across the empty notebook. Margery envisions that hair spilling from the notebook, falling to the floor, becoming a carpet of lush black grass. Envisions herself cavorting in the grass. Naked, of course.

When the class ends, she makes certain to be the first one from her row into the aisle and scurrying down the steps. She must hurry to keep up with her beloved (already he is that) as he lopes ahead, bounding from the bottom step and exiting quickly through the double doors at the back of the lecture hall.

It has taken her two consecutive Wednesday mornings to find the nerve to speak to him, and when she does, "Boring, right?" is all she can think of to say.

He'd felt her staring at him from her row above, he confesses sometime later, the two of them in his bed, in his dorm, in his spectacularly messy room. "Felt your eyes poking through my scalp," he tells her. "Like something hot and sharp." He was aware, he continues, that she'd scurried down the steps to keep up with him, that it had taken her two full weeks to speak to him. If she hadn't done it by that Wednesday, he says, he would have done it for her.

His hair was soft and silky in her hands, just as she'd imagined. His skin like flowers against her flesh. And the tenderness of his touch was beyond anything she had yet imagined.

Now, between dainty stabs at her Veal Francese, the Italian wife fingers her scarf, sending the cherries flying. She wears it, Margery assumes, to conceal the flab beneath her chin. She cannot, Margery also assumes, tell her husband how dreadfully she abhors that flab, or how lately she has begun avoiding mirrors, passing them by without a glance, disowning the face she would see if she looked, looking back.

Despite that little flab, despite the trivial weight gained over the years, it is evident to Margery the woman was a beauty once.

The height of her forehead, the prominence of her cheekbones, the gleam in her periwinkle blue eyes attest to that. The color has not faded from the tresses of her auburn hair, piled high this evening like a crown atop her head. Her mouth retains its perfect bow shape. Like her husband, she is tall, unstooped, and tonight bears a distinctly regal presence, reinforced by the hair piled crown-like atop her head. There's lace—antique Belgium, it would be—encircling her wrists. She has borne him children, certainly. Four would be Margery's guess, their language having identified them as Italian, their religion, logically following, would be Catholic, indicating a preference for a large family. No, five, Margery reconsiders. The first-born, a boy, four weeks premature and weighing a mere two pounds, having died shortly after birth. His brief existence never revealed to the suc-ceeding four. Margery deduced the loss of a child from the ceaseless movement of the woman's lips and the continual fingering of her scarf. A personal tragedy—devastating in its scope—that would shadow her heart until the end of her days. A devastation this Italian matriarch doesn't know she shares with the woman seated at the table next to hers.

Now Margery's server returns to take her order. She requests another glass of Beaujolais and, for the meal, exactly what the Italian wife is having. It pleases her to think they have so much in common it extends to a preference in cuisine. The server nods, places her empty glass on his small silver tray, and walks away.

    The old couple, as Margery has come to think of them, would have three daughters, married now, with grown children of their own, and one son, younger by five years than his nearest sibling, married as well. That child's birth, to replace the son they had lost (as if that were even possible), had been achieved after many attempts. He is living now here in the States and is the reason for his parents' visit. Happily ensconced upon a second marriage, with children from both (his divorce having come as a shock, a sin, if you asked his mother), he has invited his aging parents to meet his new wife. American-born, she would be, and considerably younger than he. Or so Margery pictures it.

    The wine the old couple is drinking is darker than her own. A Pinot Noir, Margery would guess. She had noted it on the menu

Other People's Conversations

and considered it briefly, but needing to stay within a retired school-
teacher's budget, had selected instead the slightly cheaper Beaujolais.

The son would be in finance, Margery decides. Tall, like both
his parents. Broad-shouldered like his father, with wavy dark hair.
At his office now, working late. The American wife, also engaged in
business, working in some other part of the city. Children in private
school, dropped off and retrieved by nannies. Visiting grandparents
enjoying a day on their own. They had been…where? *Dove?* To a
museum? *Quale?* The Metropolitan or Whitney? Or to see (or about
to see) that film the wife is going on about. Tired now and flagging, as
tourists tend to do in the early evenings, they'd come to this restaurant for a bite to eat and a bit of a rest.

It was the hair that drew her to that long-ago college lover—long,
shining, pitch black. When she learned his name, she couldn't stop
saying it. Over and over, turning it round and round in all its permu-
tations…Ted, Teddy, Edward, Theo, Theodore. He balked at Theodore. No, he had insisted. Not Theodore. She tried Edmund. Better,
he said. Names were so important, choosing the right one. Gustavo?
Might that be the name of the Italian gentleman at the table next to
hers? And Helena, his wife? Eddy was the name the college boy preferred, so she settled on that for the love of her life. Eddy, her Eddy.
My Marge, he would reply. My own. Eddy and Marge for ever and
ever. Boyfriend/girlfriend, then husband and wife. The leap seemed
instantaneous, though it had taken several years to achieve, requiring
first their graduation, then procurement of their parents' blessing.
The blessing was a necessity for her, a formality for Eddy.

Never would Gustavo and Helena have encountered obstacles in
obtaining parental blessings, Margery was certain. Their fathers and
mothers would not only have sanctioned the marriage but possibly
arranged it.

Gustavo and Helena would have known one another since
childhood, possibly since birth, having grown up in the same village—a small one, Margery saw it, in the north of Italy, near Genoa,
perhaps. It would be fifty or sixty years ago now since the two were
betrothed. Gustavo not yet sixteen, Helena no more than fourteen.
They would have loved one another at first sight (as she had loved her

Eddy). They would have believed life without the other was insup-
portable (as she had believed it to be without Eddy).

Initially, so Margery's musing continued, Gustavo and Helena's time alone would have been severely guarded. Dutifully overseen
by a family member—a parent, grandparent, aunt or uncle, cousin or
neighbor. They would have played sports, which would be … what?...
cosa? in those days in a small Italian village? Soccer? *Bocce?* They
would have been assigned chores, of course. Sweeping floors, she
imagined it, weeding gardens, picking tomatoes when ripe from the
vine. Dates. Olives. Grapes. Figs. Helena washing and drying dishes,
Gustavo laying coals on the hearth. When they were older—eleven
and thirteen, she would guess—they would be permitted one night a
week in the summer for dancing at the square outside the village tav-
erna, still under the watchful eyes of family members or neighbors.
Once formally engaged, Margery sees them escaping all supervision
at last, and chasing one another through the vineyards, racing down
the rows of grapes and tomatoes ripening on the vine, shouting,
laughing, Helena in front, long billowing skirts rising above ankle
boots; Gustavo just behind, careful to keep his beloved always in view.

And the lovemaking! Married lovemaking. How splendid it was. Margery and her Eddy. How different from the lovemaking they'd known
before. Freer, somehow, more abandoned. The first night, sharing a
bed as husband and wife in a drab motel near the airport. Scheduled
to catch an early morning flight for the Bahamas and begin their
eagerly awaited honeymoon. Eddy removing his tux, unhooking his
cummerbund (it had been the excessively extravagant wedding of her
dreams, provided by her father). Eddy stepping out of his trousers,
dramatically ripping at his bow tie, tearing it apart with vengeance.
All the while smiling at her mischievously (how she loved that mis-
chievous smile). Eddy, her Eddy, opening the buttons of his absurdly
ruffled shirt, pulling off his black patent leather shoes, his dress socks.
She flashes back to them dancing earlier in the grand hotel's ball-
room. Eddy reeling her in, swinging her out, reeling her in again. She
resting her cheek a moment against his chest—that incredibly hard
male chest—when they came close. Then, back in their drab motel,
Eddy dropping his shorts, revealing his body—a husband's body—
new to her. Boldly, she stares. Allows her eyes to linger on his hips, his

Other People's Conversations

gorgeously muscled thighs, that wild nest of pubic hair and beneath the nest, his hanging penis, already partially erect, straining toward her.

My Marge, he whispers. *My own.*

Two years later a son is born to them. Perfect in every aspect save that of life. They looked into his face, the porcelain-like features. Stillborn, frozen. They gazed in tenderness and disbelief. Their gaze had seemed to pull them through the surface of their child's skin and down into his very center. They would say so afterwards that it had been like that—their gaze pulling them down into the center of their son.

She thought about their perfect lifeless child every single day (as must Helena). She would never stop thinking about him (as Helena surely would not).

Night after night, for weeks and months afterward, she and Eddy plunged into one another. Assuaging the guilt they both felt, never spoken of, neither ever blaming the other. Wordlessly, savagely, they plunged. And then they stopped. Inexplicably, and by mutual consent, they stopped. Three years remained of their marriage. During that time, they were civil to one another. Courteous, respectful, but barely spoke, hardly met the other's eye.

Would you like more coffee?

Would you care for more wine?

They never had another child, although they tried, and when Eddy left, as she had known he must, the emptiness was complete. Could she tell them that, Gustavo and Helena? About the emptiness, the guilt, about the stillborn face they knew so well? Many years later, she heard through a mutual friend that Eddy had remarried, moved to Chicago, and was the father now of four. Choosing his life, she saw him doing it. Getting it right the second time around. She was happy for him. She was.

Now, at the table next to hers, Helena continues talking. Fingers fluttering at her throat, Belgium lace waving at her wrists. Gustavo listens, hand on chin. Letting his eyes settle a moment on his wife's, then looking away.

Oh, Helena, oh, Gustavo, we have more in common than you can guess.

Suddenly Gustavo leans across the table, grasps his wife's hand. The unexpected movement shocks Helena into silence. Now he will speak. Now he will offer his halting confession. What will it be? A long-concealed affair? A plea for forgiveness? Margery holds her breath, awaiting his words. But no words come, no confession is offered, no affair revealed, no forgiveness sought. Gustavo sits silently, his wife's hand in his. Their eyes search one another's. Neither speaks. Then Gustavo leans back, and Margery sees the anguish vanish from his eyes. *È possibile?* Had that simple touch, that clasping of his Helena's hand in his, been enough?

It is late in the evening now. Margery has finished her meal. She has stayed longer than she'd intended. Turning toward the window, she watches the people walking by. Turning back, she surveys the other couples in the room. Some are engaged in conversation; others, oblivious, absorbed in cell phones. *Take care*, she would warn them. *Don't waste time. It goes faster than you think.*

Now a party of six enters. Three couples. All, Margery estimates, in their early thirties. They are greeted by the Maître D', presumably asked to wait while two tables are pulled together to accommodate them. The six stand about awkwardly. One man draws a woman close and out of an oncoming server's way. Another man says something to the group Margery cannot hear, but understands his remark is made in German, a language she does not speak.

With the two tables firmly conjoined, salt and pepper cellars centered, utensils snugly cocooned in cloth napkins laid at each plate, the party is invited to be seated. Their voices are loud. She would beg them to lower them for their table is near the one at which Gustavo and Helena sit, and Margery has something important to say to them and requires silence to gather her thoughts. When sufficiently composed she will go up to the elderly couple, apologize for the intrusion, ask if they would be so kind as to hear her out. *Per certo*, they will reply in union. Of course. *Sì, sì*, they will say. She would be so thankful for just a few minutes of their time, she explains. *Per favore*, they will tell her, motioning for her to pull over her chair. *Grazie*, she will reply, her mouth going dry as she prepares to speak. They'll order her another glass of wine—their superior Pinot Noir—and she will thank them and begin.

                                    Other People's Conversations

Perhaps she'll address the husband first, finding him alone, the wife having repaired to the ladies' room. She will talk and he will listen, a growing look of concern on his face indicating the meaning of her words is becoming increasingly clear to him. He will show tenderness and sympathy. Lifelong grief, she'll say, and he will understand. The dreadful loss, she'll continue, they unwittingly share. A loss compounded, in her case, she will tell him, by the loss of a mate. He will nod his head gravely. *Capisco*, he will say. *Per certo*. No greater loss than the loss of a child.

Or perhaps she will accompany the wife to the ladies' room and tell her as they make their way down the hall. She will admit she'd guessed about the son Helena had lost; Helena couldn't guess it was a loss they shared. Grief would be their bleak companion for the rest of their days, Margery will say sadly. Sadly, Helena will agree. Margery will confess she'd shut her Eddy out, knowing no other way to do it at the time. Grief had filled her up, she will explain. It had consumed her, leaving no space for Eddy. Helena still has her Gustavo. And her other children, and her children's children. Margery is so very thankful that is so. Helena will place a hand on her heart. They'll speak as if they're friends, sisters, even. There'd been no man since Eddy, Margery will confide. No other marriage, no children. Helena will shake her head over that. *Che peccato!* she will exclaim and, relieved to have a woman finally know, Margery will answer, *Sì, sì*, she is right. The pity. The terrible regret. The impossibility of there ever coming another time she would be a mother, hear a man whisper in the darkness of a room, *My Marge. My own.*

Or perhaps she'll address them as a couple. *Grazie! Molte grazie*, she will say, leaning back in her chair, having spoken at length. Even if not fully understood, she will feel at last relieved of her burden, the terrible weight lifted from her heart. *Grazie. Molte grazie*, she will say again. She is so very grateful to them for having listened to her, for having understood. *Non c'e`diche*, they will tell her. Don't mention it. She owes them a debt she can never repay.

But they are rising now, Gustavo and his Helena, having finished their meal, the coffee afterwards. They are gathering their things. The woman her handbag, the man an umbrella he has brought along out of a preponderance of caution and that Margery has not noticed till now, lying there beneath the table. They are turn-

ing their backs to her, walking across the room. His hand laid lightly
on the small of her back. Her head inclining in his direction. It is
better, Margery understands, seeing them approach the exit, that she
hadn't burdened them with her story. Better, she tells herself, signaling for her check, to have kept it to herself.

Mistaken Identity

In a corner of the room sits an old man with sparse white hair, face of chalk, and fixed blue eyes. Body as thin as a cadaver's and eyes that stare out into the room as if they would seize everything in it and take it down into themselves.

The baby at the breast cannot see the old man sitting in the corner. The white slope of flesh is all she can see. And maybe, an awareness of the surrounding dark areola as the nipple slips from her mouth and is gently re-inserted.

But the old man in the corner sees her. His fixed blue eyes drink her down as she drinks down her mother's milk. Later, she will wonder at his absence.

"Did I know him? What was he like?"

"He was a musician. He played the piano."

"Did he love me?"

"He loved you."

The boy's room can be reached from his parents' room by a path that runs through their closet. A secret path. He likes to think of it that way, secret, although he knows his parents know about it. They never use that path, but they know it exists. In fact, they were the ones who pointed it out to him. "Look," his father had exclaimed, upon opening the door to the closet when they first moved into the old house. A house new to him but so old it creaked. "You can reach your room through our closet." "Or through the door in the hallway," his mother had added, always liking to give him alternatives. "You'll have two routes," she said. "One through our closet. The other through the door off the hallway." His parents never mentioned the path that led through their closet to his room again. They forgot all about it. Or seemed to. And the boy allowed them to seem to forget. He went back to thinking he was the only one who knew about it. His secret path. His choice to use or not.

A path through a jungle, it might have been. Barefoot, he follows it. An ancient, overgrown path, old as the house itself. Dense foliage all around, shoes rough as stones beneath his feet. His father's trousers hanging sideways like the edges of sheets. His mother's skirts sweeping down to brush his face as he passes through. Wisps of cloth on his skin. Filaments of ghosts. Scrawny witches' fingers reaching for him in the dark. In his sleep, gnarled branches come for him, twisted vines snatch him away. He dissolves in the tendrils of the overhanging brush. But as the baby's older brother it is his job to protect her from such fearful things.

"What was he like?"

"He played the piano."

Thin fingers white as bones clattering on the keys.

"His eyes were blue."

And wide as the sea.

The boy would stand behind the old man when he played. Articulated bones running up and down the keyboard. Notes like demons screaming. He could grab his bat, step forward, take a swing. The white head would fall. Blood would splatter on the keys. The music stops, feet come off the pedals, scrawny hips slide on the slippery bench. The chalk face sways like a lantern, bottomless blue lights within. Too late, the boy looks away. Magnets at the backs of his eyes drag him down into the sea.

"What are you doing there, Boyd?"

The voice is like something dying.

"You want me to teach you? Would you like that, Boyd?"

Something that has already died.

"For me to teach you?"

A hand reaches out. He jumps back, but not far enough. Bony fingers clasp his face.

"Answer me."

His face is compressed. His lips pucker. The tender flesh inside his cheeks is forced against his teeth.

"And look at me when I'm talking to you."

The old man's eyes are drowning places.

Looking into them he felt something of what he would feel later when he let hookers—not girlfriends, not women he dated, only those he picked up and paid for a few hours of their time—suck him off. A fear that something essential in him, something he thought of as his essence, would be sucked down through the tubes of their tongues and pass out of him and into them. Just so had he been sucked down into the sea of the old man's eyes.

He has no trouble looking into other people's eyes. His father's, which are pale and brown and not a place to drown. His sister's, which are small and new and have no power. His mother's, which, like the old man's eyes, are blue and wide, though not as wide. It's natural, he supposes, for his mother to have eyes like the old man's, for he is her father.

He would have thought his mother's eyes, like her father's, would be drowning places too. But that turned out not to be so. He would have thought that because she is his mother his eyes would be like hers as hers are like her father's. But that also turned out not to be so. His eyes are like his father's, pale and brown. He can look into his father's eyes and into his mother's and his sister's without fear of drowning. But not into the old man's eyes. He'd had to turn away from him as soon as his brain made the connection between the old man's eyes and death by drowning. His mother saw him turn away and took it as an insult. She looked at him differently from that moment onward.

The old man has been living with them in the old house for as long as Boyd can remember. He is always there, in the house, in him. Sometimes he has a horror of coming upon him in the closet as he passes through. Midway on his journey, the skin will pull tight at the back of his neck, the flesh over his heart will shrink, and he will stop dead in his tracks, certain the old man is lurking there in the dark, thin enough to be concealed even by the sideways fall of his father's trousers spilling from their hangers. Cautiously, he will assess his jungle, the sway of the vines, the density of the foliage, the curvature of the rocks beneath his feet, and only when he's finally convinced he is alone, will he move on, keeping to the secret path that leads him to his room.

His sister sucks at their mother's breast and he, not quite three, has been newly ousted from his mother's lap by the baby's arrival. He circles their mother's chair, seeking a way up into it. His sister sucks first at one breast and then after an interval—during which she is made to sit up and be folded over herself and have her back rubbed and patted, and people in the room wait anxiously for the sound of a burp and exclaim in delight over it when it comes and sigh in dismay when it does not—at the other.

All during the time of the sucking at one breast and the interval of rubbing and patting and burping or not, and the sucking at the other breast, Boyd circles their mother's chair, seeking and neither finding nor being offered a way up into it. With each revolution he makes, an explosive feeling grows inside him. It rises and rises within him, reaching now to the walls of his chest, now to the top of his head, now to the tips of his fingers, seeking escape. Blocked at every turn by skin and cartilage, bone and hair and muscle mass, the feeling grows desperate. Eventually, the force of its desperation shoves him up against a table in the center of the room. From there it propels him against a chair with thick wooden legs. He kicks at one of the legs, kicks again. Steam releases through his foot.

"Don't do that."

The voice like something that has already died comes from behind him.

He goes to another chair. A squat, fat one with upholstered arms and silly white things on the ends of them. He passes by one upholstered arm and then the other and dislodges the silly white things as he passes, shoving them to the floor.

"Pick those up."

He walks on as if he hadn't heard.

"Boyd!"

The voice reaches out for him from beyond the grave or wherever it went when it died. He turns and walks back and picks up one of the silly white things from the floor and returns it to one of the chair's fat arms. He leaves it there and walks away without caring if it is facing up or down or is in the same spot it had been in when his mother put it there.

"Now the other one."

The voice is losing strength, but he knows his mother is watching him over the slope of her breast, so he turns and walks

                                        Mistaken Identity

back and picks up the other silly white thing from the floor and puts it back on the chair's other arm.

Already at not quite three Boyd knew there was no escape. Not from the terrible voice. Not from the fixed blue eyes or sparse white hair. Not from the bones of the man himself. His form—the hair, eyes, bones, cadaverously thin body—was the last form of man on earth. The form he and all men and women too would acquire shortly before the end. He knew this even then, at not quite three, and took it as a premonition. Not of something to come, but of something already present. Sitting there in the corner of the room, living with them in the house. living in them, in him, inescapable.

Fate, he would later call it. But at the time he didn't know what to call it. He could hide himself in his closet jungle for hours, once for nearly a day, but he would have to come out eventually. He would have to eat, shit, piss, sleep, perform his human functions, and then there it would be: the thing he would later call fate. There was no escaping one's fate. He knew that all the things he would have to do—eat, shit, piss, sleep—simply to sustain life were the very things that would drive him from the closet to confront its end. Already at not quite three, he knew that.

The knowledge provoked a feeling of violence within him. He wanted to smash things, to be cruel to people, to make them suffer. What did it matter if he broke everything in the house, if he told his mother she was ugly, and his father he was stupid, and his baby sister she was an abomination? What did any of it matter if there was no escaping one's fate?

Boyd was not quite four when his baby sister discovered his secret path. She had just learned to walk and had wandered from their parents' bedroom, where he and she had been playing, into their parents' closet. The door had been left ajar, but he hadn't seen her go in. He was busy trying to make his red block balance on top of his yellow one. A tricky operation, for the blocks were slippery, being made of plastic, and the yellow block was balanced precariously on the green one below, and the green one was balanced just as precariously on the blue one below, so it required all of his attention to get the red block to sit on the yellow one without falling off. By the time he had achieved this difficult feat and looked around, his sister, who had no interest in his blocks, was gone.

He knew immediately where she was. He ran, but by the time he reached her, she was already on the secret path and halfway to his room. He could not let her proceed. He could not let her leave this place and take the knowledge of its existence with her. He stops her where she is, her body half concealed by their father's trousers and belts and their mother's skirts and dresses and long hanging sleeves of her blouses. He tells her she cannot leave. She is the goddess of the jungle, he says, and it is her sacred duty to stay and keep guard over it. He can see she likes the idea. Her chin lifts abruptly and her head jerks from side to side on her neck like a chicken's, so he tells her he will help her to stay where she is and perform her sacred duty.

"Hold your arms out like this."

He says he knows it will be hard for her to remain in the required position, arms out, keeping guard over the jungle, for as long as she will have to. And so he will help her. To help her, he ties her up.

"This will make it easier."

He takes down a few of their father's leather belts and their mother's silk scarves, hanging like foliage of various colors and density from hooks on the closet walls, and wraps them around his sister to hold her in place. She doesn't resist, for all the time he is doing it he keeps reminding her that she is the goddess of the jungle with a sacred duty to perform and that this is how she must perform it.

"Like this. Like a goddess."

He doesn't know how long she must stay there, but he thinks it must be until the knowledge of the secret path passes successfully out of her and back into him, where it will once more become a thing known to no one else on the entire planet.

He understands it might take a long time for the knowledge to pass successfully out of his sister and back into him. He also understands that because she is essentially still a baby who has only just learned to walk but who cannot yet talk, she might grow tired of her sacred duty or even forget that she has one at all. She might completely blow off her task and try to walk out of the secret jungle and, finding herself restrained, might begin to howl in that infuriating

way of hers that can go on for hours and would be certain eventually
to reach the ears of their parents who, following the trail of her cry,
would be led into the jungle where they would find her, tied on the
secret path. He cannot let that happen, so he takes down one of their
mother's silk scarves and wads up one end of it and stuffs it into his
sister's mouth. He wraps the other end around her head and loops
it through in front to keep it in place. She cannot get at the scarf
because her hands are tied and her wrists attached by other scarves
to nails he has found driven into the walls on either side of the closet,
down low near the floor at about his sister's height. These scarves will
keep her in place, her arms spread in an attitude of sacred protection
over the jungle.

Continuing along his secret path, he came to his room. Once
inside, he shut the door to the closet behind him and walked across
the room and out through the door leading into the hallway. He
walked down the hallway, turned and walked back into his parents'
room. He went to the closet and shut its door. He doesn't remember
exactly what he did next. He may have taken up another block, perhaps a purple one, and tried to balance it on top of his red one, now
sitting more or less securely on top of the yellow one, or he may have
gone out into the kitchen to see what his mother was doing. He thinks
it likely he did both. First, he would have worked with the purple
block, lifting it high into the air and positioning it directly over the
red one, then, having made allowances for the blocks' slippery plastic
surfaces and the precarious angles at which each was balanced on
the one immediately below—the red one on the yellow, the yellow on
the green, the green on the blue—he would have lowered the purple
block increment by increment, cautiously bringing the slippery purple and red surfaces closer and closer together until there was only a
whisper of air between them, and then not even a whisper and they
were joined, one on top of the other, purple surface to red surface.
And then he would have gone into the kitchen to see what his mother
was doing.

She was baking cookies.

"Chocolate chip," she said. "Your favorite."

She pulled them on the rack from the oven and placed the
rack on the kitchen table. Boyd climbed onto a stool and put his
elbows on the table and leaned into them to look at the cookies. His

mother took a spatula and lifted one of the cookies from the rack and placed it on a plate before him. He loved the way the cookies came warm from the oven, and the way when he pulled one apart chips of chocolate turned long and fluid as threads and the threads hung in loops from one edge of the cookie to the other. He loved the feel of the warm chocolate threads on his fingers and tongue. He loved the soft sweet doughy taste of the cookie between his teeth.

"Where's your sister?" the old man said from the corner of the kitchen where he sat.

Boyd went on eating his cookie.

"Go, bring Alma," his mother said. "We'll give her a little piece."

The first thing he noticed when he went back into the closet and pulled the scarf out of his sister's mouth was a bit of froth like baby spit-up in a corner of her mouth. As the scarf popped out, the howling came with it. He put his hand over her mouth to shut her up. It revolted him to touch her mouth because he didn't want to have to touch that frothy piece of spit-up in its corner. But he went ahead and did it anyway, shoving his hand right down hard into the spit-up to shove the howling back down his sister's throat.

"Cookie," he said. "Chocolate chip. Mommy baked cookies."

At the word "cookie" or maybe it was "mommy," the howling ceased. But only for an instant. Then it started right back up again, gargled now, muffled as it was by his hand, and he thought what it would be like to shut his sister up for good.

He saw the tears in her eyes, the look of absolute terror on her face, and didn't care.

"Cookie, Alma. Want one? I'll take you to mommy. I'll get you a cookie."

He looked straight down into the terror on her face, and didn't care. All he cared about was keeping her quiet.

"But you have to be quiet. You have to stop howling. Will you promise to do that? Will you stop?"

But of course she couldn't answer. She hadn't yet learned to talk.

"If I take my hand away, will you stop?"

He could do what he liked, and she couldn't tell a soul because she couldn't talk.

"Will you, Alma? Will you stop?"

All his life he would be safe because his sister hadn't yet learned to talk.

And by the time she had learned, she would have forgotten. The scarf in her mouth, her arms spread wide, wrists bound, her terror, his heartlessness, all would be forgotten. For her it would be as if it had never happened. All she would remember of their growing up would be the big brother who taught her to play soccer with a balloon and come down a slide without holding on and to ride a bike and later drive a car and who gave her her first taste of weed and held her head over the toilet when she came home shit-faced from her senior prom. It would be as if she never knew him. The secret of what he has done in this moment in the closet, revealing more or less exactly who he is at his core, will be forever irretrievable to her, buried in the folds of her faded memory. But right now, in this instant, she knows.

"Nod your head if you'll stop."

She glares at him over the hand he has clamped down hard on her mouth and for this one rapidly receding instant, knows him for who he is.

"Nod, and I'll take my hand away."

She nods, and he removes his hand, peeling it back from her mouth like he's pulling off tape, but keeping the flesh of his palm close to her lips so he can press it down again quickly, should the howling resume.

Once his hand is free, silence reigns over the closet. She has succumbed to his will. He unties her wrists, smooths her hair, tugs at her shirt, straightens her baby shorts that have been pulled to one side. He throws her a smile, suggesting she's the one in need of forgiveness, and takes her hand. He walks her off the secret path back through their parents' room, out through the door leading into the hallway, and down the hallway to the kitchen.

"What happened, Alma?" the old man says the minute he sees her. Boyd follows his sister's eyes into the old man's and sees the knowledge of what he did transmitted from her to him. The old man looks at him, and Boyd knows he knows. But he'll never be able to prove it, for already that knowledge has begun to fade from his sister's mind.

"Come to me, my pretty," their mother says. "Why such a sour face? Here's a cookie, Alma. Will that make you smile?"

And it does. She reaches out, grabs the piece of cookie their mother has broken off for her, and no sooner does her fist close upon the clump of dough and transport it to her mouth than the terrible, unspeakable knowledge of who her brother is fades forever from her memory.

Boyd was not quite five when his grandfather finally left the house. The piano playing ceased. The fixed blue eyes and terrible voice vanished. The fingers white as bones, the pressure on his cheeks were no more. Yet he remained, a not-quite-five-year-old trapped in the certainty that the old man has seen into his center. He would have overcome that certainty in time, he imagined, and would have come to understand, were he given the chance to know the old man, that one mind cannot read another. But he was never given the chance. For one day the old man was there, the next day not. There was no time to adjust to his leaving or come to understand that he could not see into his heart. No time for the knowledge of the scarf in his sister's mouth, her arms splayed, her wrists bound, to fade from the old man's eyes where it never had been, as it had faded from his sister's eyes, where, in actuality, for the briefest of instants, it had been. For years, Boyd would be haunted by the old man's eyes and the knowledge he mistakenly believed them to possess. Those eyes and that presumed damning knowledge followed him through the house when he went from being five to six and from six to seven. They followed him from room to room at eight and nine, ten and eleven, twelve and thirteen, rousing him, trembling, through all those years from sleep.

Even now, today, when he looks into the sad, mute eyes of animals, the black orbs of chimpanzees he sees in zoos, or the dark glazed eyes of deer he now and then comes upon dying in the road, the knowledge he believed to lie at the bottom of the old man's eyes leaps up at him, and nothing else in all the world but himself, heartless and uncaring and stone-cold cruel, is returned to him in their reflection.

Would it always be this way?

There was no one he could ask. The old man was gone. His parents, too. He could ask his sister, he supposed. But it was not quite dawn, and she lived in a different time zone and long ago had forgotten all about it.

But had she, really? Could he be absolutely certain of that?

It's a bad idea, he knows, but once it's in his head he can't get it out.

"Hello? Alma?"

"Do you know what time it is?"

"Yes. I'm----,"

"Here, I mean. Do you know what time it is here?"

"I was just wondering----,"

"At this hour, you're wondering?"

"Yes."

"About what?"

"If you remember the closet."

Arms splayed. Wrists bound. Scarf stuffed in mouth.

"What closet?"

"In the old house. I still live there."

"You called to tell me where you live?"

"Same house."

Goddess of the jungle. Howling in the closet.

"You think I give a shit you still live in the same house?"

"Do you remember?"

"What?"

"The closet. It had a secret path. From their room to mine. Nobody knew. Except them, of course. But then they forgot. And I thought, maybe, you."

"What's it been, Boyd? Seven, eight years? Not a word. And now you're calling about some closet. Who the hell do you think you are?"

"Nobody. Your brother, I mean."

"I don't have a brother."

"So, you really don't remember?"

"I'll tell you what I remember. You were a stupid shit all your life. Didn't give a damn about anyone except yourself."

"Okay, let's leave it at that. Me, a stupid shit. You, a saint."

"I never said saint."

"So long, saint."

"I never said saint."

"Maybe goddess is more like it. I was right the first time. Goddess of the fucking jungle."

"What are you talking about?"

He could tell her. He thinks for a moment he might. It would help her get her facts straight. She has his identity essentially down. He never gave a damn for anyone except himself. She's got that right, but there's a fundamental mistake in her assessment. It's worse than she thinks. He never cared if she lived or died. If anyone did, really. Not mom or dad or the old man. But it's worse even than that. He actively wanted her dead. All of them. Dead and out of his way. That's the god's-honest truth, and why shouldn't he be truthful now that he had her on the phone and wouldn't live to see another day? He'd already picked out the bridge. All his life he'd wanted them gone, himself left alone. That's who he is. She should know. And here he's almost got what he wants, himself the last one standing. Except for her. She's still standing, even if she's lying in bed, the phone in her fist, out there in the fucking golden state. The only one between him and his desire to be alone. He could come out there and put an end to her. Fly out and drive a stake through her heart.

"What, Boyd? What are you trying to say?"

"I tucked your hair behind your ears to keep it out of the vomit."

"What? When?"

"You don't remember, do you?"

"No."

"My mistake. I thought you might."

The flight from the bridge's railing would be steep. He'd be unconscious before he hit the water. A good thing, because he couldn't swim. But maybe the bridge was a mistake. He was making lots of them lately. This phone call, his guess as to what she'd remember, his idea of identity.

He lays the phone down then picks it up again and holds it to his ear. He listens to her breathing. "I'm sorry," he says in a voice so low he knows she cannot hear.

Stalking

Through it all, Bella remained her friend. Even the sun, now bearing down upon her, reaching for her skin, said so. Whatever else, she could look back upon the experience and call herself a friend.

She will walk through the park and stop at the end of the path to gaze at the building under construction across the way. She won't live to see it completed. But for now where she walks no buildings compete with the line of the trees. No construction rises to cut her off before her time.

She saw them together. The pretty new art teacher, Adele Williams, and the boy. Art, that would be her subject. Young and pale, tall and slim. Like a candle, she had thought the instant she saw her. Masses of untamed golden curls dancing around her head, flickering like flames. And around her neck, fastened in that trendy way, looped with the two ends passing through the loop, a scarf. Blue-green, long and silk. Sea colors winding nonchalantly about her throat, falling like seaweed onto her chest. So trendy. So arty. Of course that would be what she taught. Her subject, as she put it.

"Art. Tenth, eleventh grade. Seniors, too, if they're interested."

If they're interested. Why wouldn't they be? A woman like that, so pretty, so young. But the student Bella saw her with wasn't even a senior. Sixteen years old. Tenth grade. New to the school. Hadn't yet made friends.

To remain her friend through it all. It was a solemn vow, and she had kept it. Her supporter and comforter. And when the time came, she would help her find redemption. For she would hunger for redemption. Bella knew it the instant she saw them together.

They were smart. So early in the school year to have found Paddy's place. Between the two buildings, down a narrow street, then a short flight of stairs, and there in the back, off to the right, the empty room. She followed them. She couldn't help herself. An abandoned storeroom, probably. Paddy had set up an old cot inside, a cardboard table he'd found on the street and carried in. He used the place for breaks from his janitorial duties, to nap and have his lunch. Then Paddy was fired. He wouldn't be back. Adele must have seen him go in there one day and, never suspecting she in turn would be followed, had gone in later, already seeking a lair, already realizing she would need a place. How long had she planned it? Since the moment she set eyes on the boy? The child. Friendless. New to the school. An easy mark.

"I love him," she insisted.

Love.

"I cannot stay away from him."

"You must end it," Bella told her.

"I will," she replied.

But she didn't. Couldn't, if you listened to her. She was drawn, obsessed, compelled.

Matching bra and panties. Trimmed with champagne-colored lace at the legs and waist. Bella had watched, eyes half closed, her own skin tingling as to a phantom touch. Again and again, she had followed them and watched. That flat stomach, those full breasts. That glorious, taut skin, those golden tendrils wild as flames about her head. The boy—Franco Marconi was his name—would find it daring. Italian father (out of the picture, Bella had checked the school records), Ukrainian mother. The boy would think himself brave to put his hand in those flames, to reach out and stroke that skin. And him only sixteen, a loner, not yet part of a pack.

Bella wanted to slap her. This Adele. This teacher of art. A boy like that. Fatherless. Vulnerable. A child. No, not slap, she didn't mean that. She would caress her, comfort her. For she would require comforting when she was discovered, and she would be discovered, no doubt of that, and who better to provide comfort than herself, a woman of experience, an older woman.

"You think you're pretty, do you?" Bella's mother had demanded the day she turned sixteen. "You think we gave you that name because you're pretty?"

Bella, the Italian word for beautiful. So, she had something in common with the boy. An Italian name. Although he had earned his, Franco Marconi, by right of birth. And she had come by hers through a word whose sound appealed to her mother, though its meaning didn't apply. But what good did it do the boy to have an Italian father? The man had deserted him, abandoned his mother, returned to the land of his birth. Franco and Bella. Two people with Italian names that did them no good.

"You were pretty when you were born," her mother said. "We thought the name was apt. But when you turned three you changed. Your face took on flesh. It swallowed your eyes, and we knew we had made a mistake."

Bella understood that she and the boy had done nothing to be so mistreated—he abandoned, she irrevocably divided from the meaning of her name. They were innocent and misused. United in innocence.

"Don't worry," she said to Adele. "I'll help you. But you must do as I say."

"I promise."

Promise.

Adele had finally agreed to come home with her after school one day for tea.

"Make yourself comfortable," Bella had said.

She was so happy to have her in her apartment. A bright, clean, studio apartment in White Plains. The Clayton Park Apartments on Canfield Avenue, just off Main Street. Half an hour by train from Manhattan via the Metro-North Commuter Railroad. She took it every day to and from school. "Takes no time at all," she had assured Adele, and finally, after weeks of cajoling, begging almost, and being repeatedly put off, when Bella was about to give up—*Who do you think you are to make me beg? Do you think you don't need a friend?*— Adele had agreed to the visit.

"Yes, thank you. It sounds lovely."

Lovely. Yes, it was. To have her close, moving about in her space, touching her things, her books, to feel the graze of her shoulder, her hip, as she passed by. "So many books. You must read a lot." Touching the little doilies Bella had placed here and there to protect the furniture from water marks. "Oh, how pretty." Picking up a doily she had bought on the street in China Town. "I just love those colors." Yes, she would. Chinese reds and yellows and blacks. An art teacher. An artist. With a predilection for frilly, colorful things.

How nice to have her in this apartment that hardly ever saw a visitor. Though Bella was not unfriendly, not, as she had heard herself described by some of the other teachers, a loner. That Camilla Carson, in particular, the English teacher. Loner. And what did she know about it? Camilla Carson with her husband and four boys, *My boys*, always referring to them like that, like possessions. Children are not objects or pets that can belong to one person or another. *My boys.* Not hamsters running around a wheel in a cage brought home from a store. Not small objects let loose to run around their parents' apartment. A loner. How dare she? As if she with her husband and four boys knew anything about being alone!

But now with Adele here at last in her cozy apartment, drinking her tea, fingering her things, she would keep her safe. She would never let anything bad happen to her.

"You could lose your job. You could go to jail."

"I know. I promise."

But Adele had not kept her promise. She had gone back to the boy the very next week. Bella had caught them at it again in the same place, the same embrace. No, the embrace was not quite the same. They were progressing. Bella now and then had to stifle a cry as she watched from her vantage point, that filthy little window high in the wall above them, so high and streaked with dirt they probably didn't even know it was there. But all Bella had to do to ensure herself an unobstructed view from that window was to hop up on the Dumpster beneath it. She had seen Adele lifting the boy's shirt from his pants, unbuttoning its buttons and lifting the shirt, exposing his delicate skin and heartbreakingly flat chest. She had seen Adele kissing that chest, and her own lips had pursed as if in preparation for alighting upon it.

Week after week, she followed them, careful to keep her distance, staying well back as they went down that narrow street, that short flight of stairs. Pierced by excitement as she watched, Bella would sometimes feel her fingers drawn to her own skin. She might allow them to pass through that opening in her blouse where it buttoned in front and the material parted as she leaned forward for a better look, and to graze the swell of her breast. If she was wearing a skirt, she might, almost without knowing she was doing so, run her fingertips lightly, ever so lightly, along the inside of her thigh. Adele's hands were in constant motion, unbuttoning the boy's shirt, helping it to billow out loose as gauze, as if all she had to do was tug it free from his waistband for the wind to take it, although Bella knew there would be no wind in that room, no air to speak of. It would be close and dank and smell of old bits of sandwiches and pieces of fruit left long ago by Paddy to rot in the corners. But Adele was unaware of all that. Both she and the boy, unaware. Adele's lips moved on Franco's hairless, flat chest, kissing his torso, sucking at his nipples as at the sweetness of berries.

"I can't stay away from him," Adele admitted.

How well she understood.

"I can't keep my hands off him."

How well she sympathized with the impossibility of keeping away from the boy, keeping her hands, her lips, off that luscious young skin. She would be obliged, as was Adele, to implant a line of kisses down that flat, thin, vulnerable torso to the boy's navel and beyond, drawn as by a plea that cannot be denied to that place below, that enticing bulge, that gleaming nest of hair.

From the moment Bella saw the champagne-colored lace at the legs and waist of the panties, the woman's flat stomach, the boy's hard, hairless chest, his nipples like berries, she knew she had to bear witness. A companion, an accomplice, invisible to them, yet indispensable. As if without her eyes to document it, her flesh to respond to it, their act would have no meaning. Goosebumps rose on the backs of her arms; a gentle tugging took place at her groin. Her heart beat a rapid, mocking pattern as if to say, *You? At your age?*

Yes, why not at her age? Her body was not immune to touch, not frozen to feeling. She remembered what it was like. His skin against hers, his fingers on her flesh. The shock of it, there at the quick of her. The sweet sensation and unfamiliarity, the longing unleashed, that deep, almost compulsive need to pull, to fill herself up, to leave no space inside where he was not. And then the sudden, exquisite release, the spasms, almost but not quite painful, the muscle fluttering there like a moth trapped inside her. It was more than thirty years ago now, but she had never forgotten the feel of it, nor been entirely freed from the yearning to feel it again. Why, especially in light of the grim diagnosis she'd recently received, shouldn't she have it again, if only once more in her lifetime? Even if vicariously and hidden behind a filthy pane of glass and from a distance that precluded contact? She had been young then. Almost as young as Adele at the time. Almost married, almost happy. Naked in the arms of her fiancé. They were never formally engaged and no marriage ensued, nor did she ever meet any other man whom she might wish to marry, but it was as close to becoming a wife as she would come, and all these years later she still liked thinking of him like that, *her fiancé*.

Watching now from her vantage point, fearful of making some inadvertent move, some small sound that would betray her presence, she recalled his touch. If you can see them, they can see you. Her best friend in eighth grade, Allegra Scott, had pointed that out, so wisely, so accurately, when they were peeking through a cabin window at camp, spying on the counselors making out.

If you can see them, they can see you. It had remained with her through the years, Allegra's voice and that wise, true statement making itself heard whenever she found herself the outsider, looking in. Ninth grade: crouched on the stairs, peeking between the balusters, her parents in the living room below, both on their feet, moving about, dangerous, threatening. "Who is she?" her mother screaming. "You don't know what you're talking about," her father screaming back. "Who? Just tell me who!" She saw them clearly … then they can see you. But only if they're looking, only if, as in the movies, the eye of the spied-upon travels the room, moving across furniture, across books on shelves, paintings on walls, until it comes to a crack in the plaster, moves on, then quickly back, alighting on that crack again and landing in extreme close-up on the eye of the spy. But in their rage her battling parents looked only at each other. Their warring eyes did not seek her out and so, crouched there on the stairs, Bella could see without being seen. And she saw with an acuity she didn't know she possessed, not only her present life crumbling before her, but also future unions inevitably dissolving, an unofficial engagement unraveling, a marriage never to be, subsequent marriages fading from all possibility, and herself, an unwanted third party, crouched in other hiding places—here atop a Dumpster—witnessing other disasters in the making and unable to prevent them from happening. Then her father was gone, her mother was what she called an abandoned woman. "Both of us," her mother cried. "Abandoned. He threw us away."

Bella began to keep a close watch on the boy at school. She learned his schedule, kept track of his activities. She had to raise herself up a bit on her toes to look through the glass at the top of the school-room door to see if he was in class. George Banks, tenth grade geometry, that's where he belonged at this hour. She lingered there a moment, pleased to find Franco in his seat. A tall, thin, olive-skinned boy, dropping a book on the floor, bending a little and blindly searching to retrieve it, one arm making great sweeps along the floor while his head is kept up, his eyes resolutely forward. For George Banks was at the front of the room now, calling the role, looking down at the names in his ledger, names he would check off as soon as he heard a reply and looked up to confirm that the face of the boy or girl actually corresponded to the name being called. He would not check off a name until he saw the corresponding face, for he knew from experience that these children were not to be trusted. They lied and cut class, and the boys especially, but sometimes the girls as well, sank to bribing a friend to call out "Here!" in response to his or her own name being called when they were nowhere in the room, nor in the school building for that matter, and George Banks, who had been caught in that scam once, would not be caught in it again. So Franco kept his head up, listening attentively for his name and prepared to answer smartly, "Here!" and to look Mr. Banks in the eye as he did so, so the teacher could see his face and check off his name and record him as present.

"Everything all right?"

The bitch, Camilla Carson. Coming up stealthily behind her in the hallway, to spy on her as she looked in through the school-room window. How foolish she must look, skirt hiked up in back and having to stand a bit on her toes in order to see in.

"Everything's fine."

"Good. I just wondered----,"

"No need. All's well."

Swiftly, Bella turned away. She would not meet Camilla's eyes or even glance in her direction. She hastened back down the corridor to the teachers' lounge. She didn't have a class for another forty-five minutes, so she could sit in the lounge and recover herself over a leisurely cup of tea.

In February, the next time Adele consented to come to her

apartment in White Plains (*consented*, Bella felt it like that, as if she were being done a favor), Bella understood that the boy had Adele in his power.

"You haven't stopped, have you?"

Adele's lovely pointed chin trembled. "I can't," she confessed. "It's like a compulsion." Her golden curls shimmered as she looked down into her lap.

Sitting across from her at the table, a pot of geraniums between them, Bella saw Adele's shoulders shake and she thought of the loveliness of those shoulders as she had seen them naked, and of the gracefulness of her arms reaching for the boy and of the boy, also naked, coming to be wrapped within them.

"I taste him even in my sleep," Adele told her.

"Trust me," Bella said as she had said to her so often since this terrible business began. "I will help you."

She knew then she must do what Adele herself could not do. In such situations the stronger party must act for the weaker. Action by proxy was how Bella thought of it. She was only doing what Adele herself would do if she had the strength. But since she did not, since she freely admitted she was in the grip of a compulsion, of something that came over her and guided her hands and lips and tongue to the boy, to Franco Marconi, to his eyes and mouth and down his glorious, frail, hairless chest, since she tasted him even in her sleep!— how well she could imagine it—Bella knew it was up to her to act where Adele could not.

After she made the phone call alerting Alma Myers, the principal, to the situation—"There is something you should know...," made the statement in her own name and her own voice, "A student's future is at stake...," for it was only right that she take responsibility for what she was doing—Bella began to feel better than she had since receiving the diagnosis. She awoke each morning with energy and hope. She looked forward to the end of the school year when she would take the "early retirement" that had been offered that would enable her to pursue, as the official word was, "other interests." That's how Alma, with her big teeth fairly chipping away at the words, put it at the retirement party she threw for her in the school lunchroom. Camilla Carson was there, delighted to see her go, and George Banks, too. Also Regina Phillips, the Phys. Ed. Teacher; Burton Lawson, Marianne Gilman, and Howard Caskran, who taught, respectively, geography, world history, and social studies. Sylvia Glickenhaus, the guidance counselor, was there as well. Adele Williams was not present, of course. By that time Adele had been let go and was awaiting trial.

"Bella is retiring," Alma announced to the assembled group, her pinched lips pulling back in her freakishly thin face. A cadaver's face almost, and her big white teeth gleaming. "To pursue other interests." When Alma said that, "other interests," in that jeering, mocking way, everyone in the room picked up her meaning and nodded knowingly and laughed as they applauded. The applause echoed hollowly through the room, which normally would seat two hundred children or more and was empty now on this late Friday afternoon except for the seven or eight individuals who had condescended to attend this dreary party. *The lunchroom!* That was the space Alma Myers had chosen for her retirement party. Walls the color of egg-yolk, long picnic-style tables with attached benches set out in stark rows across a linoleum-covered floor. Harsh fluorescent lights, windows crisscrossed with wire as in a jail. Adele would do jail-time, there was no doubt of that. The only question was how much. "For your own good," Bella would say, if Adele ever asked her why she had made the call. "To give you time to reflect, to seek redemption." So in that sense, Bella had kept her promise and remained her friend to the end.

On the final day of the school year, graduation day, Bella sat in the back of the auditorium watching the seniors in black gowns and tasseled caps climb the stage. She watched how they walked up to Alma Myers, some skipping, some hopping, none taking the measured steps they'd been instructed to take, as if they knew they were free already, beyond school control, beyond the control of anyone in that room, and free to walk or run or skip as they chose up to the woman who had been their principal and was nothing to them now and receive their diploma from her hands.

Gradually, Bella's eyes drifted from the stage over to Franco Marconi, sitting three rows in front of her and across the aisle with his class of tenth graders, advancing now to eleventh grade. The boy had filled out. He'd grown a good two inches since the beginning of the school year, and it was easy for Bella to spot his head rising above the heads of his fellow classmates as they sat, nudging and jostling one another, leaning in close to whisper and giggle, emitting waves of restlessness and energy strong enough to stab her skin.

Franco Marconi was no longer a loner. No longer friendless. In the two months since Adele's departure, he had drawn a group of boys around him, attracting them no doubt with tales of his exploits, liberally embellished to be sure, and today these boys were seen everywhere in his company. His posse, Bella considered them. Some of the students at school shunned him, appalled by what he had done, for though the papers kept his name out of it, they knew. Everyone at school knew. The girls had been warned by their parents to stay away from him, and for the most part, they did. But should they happen to come rushing out of a classroom, gathered in a clique as girls tend to gather, and find him there in the hallway, his full-on, astonishing presence close enough to touch, they would pull back and gasp. They would go silent and wonder: what was his power? how had he entrapped a teacher? could he, would he, entrap them?

The boys who did not shun Franco, but who went with him everywhere, regarded him as an object of wonder. A hero, an idol. To them, Franco Marconi was The Man. More than a man. A superman. Having done what they could only crudely fantasize. They cleave to him in the hope that some of his supernatural power, that very power the girls so fear and desire, will rub off on them.

How well Bella understood. She watched now as Franco elbowed the boys on either side of him as he pointed out certain girls, making what were undoubtedly blunt, crude comments about them, comments, it seemed to Bella, that were likely to be given more credence than they deserved in the minds of Franco's posse, based on their hero's notoriety and what the whole school now knew about his escapade with Adele Williams.

Franco had not been expelled. Disciplined, yes, as was only fitting, suspended for ten days, but not expelled. And now he could not wait to spring from his seat at the end of this interminable ceremony and shove his way out of his row and up the aisle and into the freedom of the streets. He was bursting to begin his life as someone who would enter eleventh grade in the fall when he would be among the elite, the upper level classmen on their way to college and a privileged future. Bella had given him that. She had given him his future. For had she let it go on, who knows if all that was locked away inside

that boy, those brave, fiery impulses and misguided thoughts that had
led him to believe it was somehow all right, somehow appropriate
even, for him to behave in such a fashion with a teacher, an adult,
might not have erupted and swallowed him whole? His life would
have been ruined. Bella had prevented that from happening. The
teacher was awaiting trial and almost certainly would be sent to jail,
and the boy had been saved. Bella had spoken passionately, as had
George Banks and several of his other teachers, though with less passion, to prevent his expulsion. "Not an exemplary, but an earnest student," Bella had declared him. "Full of potential." It was not his fault
that in his youth and the fervor of his emotions he had been seduced
and led astray by a young and beautiful, though clearly unbalanced,
woman. Bella had stood up before the school board and said in a
fearless voice: *Clearly unbalanced*, and by so doing had secured Franco's
hopes for college and handed him his privileged future. Perhaps one
day he would thank her for it. Perhaps he would come to her and
express his gratitude for his life.

Now, finally, it was over, the diplomas given out, the speeches
made. The doors were opened, the students free to go. Bella watched
the swift, agile way in which Franco Marconi rose from his seat,
positioned himself ahead of the others, and pushed his way out into
the aisle. There he encountered a jam, for students and parents in
the rows ahead of him were swarming into the aisle, and Franco was
forced to slow his pace. Bella observed the impatient way in which
he pulled off his jacket and rolled his sleeves up past his elbows, the
way he took in his breath to avoid spewing his frustration out into the
crowd. She saw how the bodies of his posse gravitated toward the
wonder of him, how they strained their necks to see how far ahead of
them he was, to judge the distance they would have to travel to catch
up. She has seen them in the lunchroom, racing to find seats at his table, one or two of them quickly jumping up and running back to the
line to get him another glass of milk or a second dessert, and in the
school hallways she has heard them shouting, "Hey, Franco! What's
up?" their hands reaching out to slap him on the back as he passes by,
to give him high-fives or fist bumps as he approaches. Only to feel his
skin against theirs. Only for the touch. How well she understands.

Now the jam clears and Franco is coming toward her. What
a marvel he is, this boy, this almost man. His eyes sparkle like the sun

on choppy ocean waves. He is exploding with life, with the desire to hurl himself into it. She will soak him up, permeate herself with him. How fortunate she has worn a sleeveless dress today, despite the disgust she feels for the loose flesh hanging from her upper arms. Today, at fifty-nine, she fully understands the scope of Franco's power and what would have caused an adult woman to prostrate herself before it, willing to risk arrest and jail, public humiliation, all that she has in the world to subject herself to that power. Franco is approaching. Moving toward her up the aisle. Bella moves to the front of her row, angles herself toward the boy. She basks in the glow coming off his face, his arms, bared now to the elbows, his hands brushing back his hair, those inexplicably beautiful teenage hands that are still slightly too large for his body. His beauty pierces her heart. She will know it skin to skin.

Bella times it perfectly. She steps out into the aisle at the exact moment that Franco reaches the front of her row. She forces her arm against his. Naked, they touch. She drinks in the sensation of his hot, young flesh. The wonder of it will last her the rest of her days. Oblivious, Franco pushes past her and runs out into the street.

Bella walks through the park, alive to the memory of his touch. Malignant cells have reached the peritoneal lining. Lymph nodes, they told her. Fourth stage, they said. The building under construction across the way has reached its fourth story. At the end, bricks and flesh are even, four apiece. But the advantage is hers. The marvel of the boy burns within her. The arm he has grazed is on fire. She lifts her eyes and in the glare of the sun is blinded to the building's height. Only the hot-skinned beauty of the boy overtakes her.

L'Oiseau

Alan didn't know.

No one knew except her sister.

Why hadn't her sister told? It was good that Alan didn't know for Alicia suspected he might leave her if he did. No, she corrected herself. Alan would never leave her. He would understand. For Alan was a lovely man and always understood. Her sister would never tell. For she loved her. Both her husband and her sister loved her. More than she deserved. Alan understanding, carrying her up the stairs at night whenever necessary. Her sister, elderly now, maintaining her silence. Still, her sister might yet tell, if she remembers. Probably she won't. It has been more than fifty years.

Alicia recalls the look of astonishment on her sister's face when the pitcher struck. *What have you done? To me, your sister?* She remembers how her sister lifted one hand to the spot, just there toward the back of her head above her left ear, searching for a lump, feeling for blood. She remembers how her sister held her fingers there a moment, pulled them away, put them back, inspected for blood. She remembers the look on her sister's face. Incredulous, confused. *Blood? You've drawn blood?* Had there actually been blood? Alicia can't quite remember now; it was so long ago. Vaguely she recalls something red, possibly wet, glistening on the tips of fingers. Was that blood? And were those hers or her sister's fingers?

The sun was extremely hot that day. She remembers that. That's why they were wearing bathing suits—hers, two-piece, bare midriff, her sister's flashy pink. That's why they had made lemonade. Or she had made it. Sliced the lemons, a dozen or more. Sliced each one in half. Some were slippery and difficult to hold while passing the knife through the thick skin. She had to dig her nails into the slippery ones and hold them firmly while she sliced. She was the one who had done all that—slicing the lemons, digging her nails into the slippery ones, holding them firmly. She was the one who had twisted the halves of the lemons back and forth, pressing down hard on the cone of the juicer. So hard that twisting motion hurt the center of her palm and made her wrist ache. She remembers some of her cuticles were torn. She had a habit back then of biting her nails, pulling at the cuticles with the tips of her teeth, leaving bloody places on her fingers where the skin pulled away. She remembers the sting of the lemon juice as it found those places. Her sister had done nothing. Just sat in her chair, filing her nails. Bare feet crossed at the ankles, propped on the kitchen table. Alicia was the one who had sliced the lemons, squeezed the halves, added the sugar, the water. Stirred and tasted. Added more sugar, more water. Stirred again. Tasted again.

Her sister sat there, filing her nails. The file made a sound like a tiny saw as it moved around her sister's fingernails. Alicia remembers how that sound had set her teeth on edge.

She took the heavy glass pitcher down from the cupboard, removed the tray of ice cubes from the freezer, ran it beneath hot water. Quickly back and forth so the cubes would loosen but not melt. She had done that, not her sister.

Her sister sat there, bare feet crossed at the ankles, propped on the kitchen table, filing her nails. She began with the pinky finger of her left hand. She ran the file along the inside edge of that nail, forming an ascending slope, ending in a point. She filed across the top of the pinky nail to round the point, then brought the file down along the outer edge, forming a descending slope.

Alicia held the ice-cube tray across the mouth of the pitcher, pressing down on its back to free the cubes. Like breaking the spine of a book. The tray was longer than the pitcher's mouth, and a few cubes at either end missed the opening, bounced off the rim of the pitcher, and scattered to the floor. Seeing them scatter, her sister looked up from her nails and laughed—her laugh crawling out of her throat like a snake from its hole. Alicia remembers thinking how easy it would be to reach out, grab that snake, and shove it back down her sister's throat.

Then her sister recrossed her feet and moved from her pinky finger to her ring finger. From there she moved to each finger in turn. With each one she drew the file first along the inside edge of the nail, forming an ascending slope and ending in a point. Then she filed across the top of the nail to round the point and brought the file down along the outer edge, forming a descending slope. She corrected then for any miscalculation that might have occurred, resulting in either the ascending or descending slope veering more steeply in one direction or the other.

Alicia picked the ice cubes off the floor.

"Rinse them before you put them back."

Of course she would rinse them before putting them back. What did her sister think? That she was so stupid she wouldn't rinse ice cubes that had fallen on the floor before putting them back into the pitcher?

Alicia refilled the ice-cube tray, returned it to the freezer. She inserted the long iced-tea spoon into the pitcher and stirred the lemonade. The stirring caused the sugar she had added to rise up and circle in a cloud and the ice cubes to swirl around inside the pitcher.

Having finished with her left hand, her sister went on to her right. The veins on the back of her hands moved like thin blue worms.

Alicia took the oversized red lacquered tray from where it sat on the counter and placed it on the kitchen table across from her sister's bare feet. She took three stacks of plastic cups (six to a stack) from the cupboard and placed them on the tray. She picked up the pitcher of lemonade, finding it so heavy she had to rest it a moment across her stomach for balance. The sting of the cold on her bare skin was shocking but thrilling. She carried the pitcher over to the tray and set it down beside the plastic cups.

"We'll ask a dollar a glass," her sister said.

"That's too much," Alicia answered.

She used both hands to carry the tray out the kitchen door and across the front yard to the edge of the sidewalk where she had already set up a card-table and two chairs. She put the tray down on the card-table, removed six cups from their plastic wrapping, arranged them in a row in front of the pitcher, sat down in one of the chairs, and waited.

"We need a sign," her sister said, coming out of the kitchen and sitting down in the other chair.

Alicia got up from her chair, went back into the kitchen, and made a sign: "Fresh lemonade, 25 cents a glass." She brought the sign out and placed it in front of the pitcher.

"That's too little," her sister said, picking up one of the

plastic cups and pouring herself a glass. She sat back in her chair and sipped her lemonade.

Alicia paced up and down the sidewalk, looking for customers.

"Lemonade," she said to anyone passing by. "Fresh lemonade. Twenty-five cents a glass."

"Like they can't read," her sister said, getting up and refilling her glass.

Alicia felt the heat of the sun on her bare shoulders, felt the straps of her bathing suit digging into her flesh. A man leading his dog—a snub-nosed pug with sorrowful brown eyes—was coming toward her down the pavement.

"Lemonade?" she said. "Twenty-five cents a glass."

The man drew his dog over, placed a quarter on the card-table, picked up the cup of lemonade which Alicia poured for him, and drank it down.

"Good," he announced. "Not too sweet." He gave her a wink, tugged at his dog, and walked away.

The sun glinted off the glass pitcher, the ice melted inside. Her sister poured herself another glass.

"It's watery now," she said.

Alicia poured the rest of the lemonade out onto the sidewalk, watched the yellowy water seep through the cracks. Then she walked around behind her sister and hit her over the head with the empty pitcher.

More than fifty years ago. She still remembers it. How her sister had reached up, touched her head just there above her left ear, feeling for a lump. How she had held her fingers to the lump a moment, pulled them away, put them back, inspected for blood. A streak of something red glistened on her fingertips. She looked at her fingers, looked at her. A look of astonishment crossed her face. *Have you struck me? Me, your sister? Have you drawn blood?* Still she remembers it.

Alicia knew about Alan's other woman. She had known about her for weeks. Three weeks exactly. Sometimes she thought Alan wouldn't actually have another woman, so this woman must be herself, younger, of course, and in disguise.

Listen to her, Alan, her husband's sister, who was easy to confuse with her own sister, said. *She makes no sense.* Whispering as she said it. To this day Alicia often thinks when she hears people whispering in doorways or on the street that they are whispering about her.

Honestly, Alan. She needs help.

Her husband turned away from his sister then. His sister, or hers? It was hard to say. They'd been standing behind the kitchen door (their kitchen, hers and Alan's) when the whispering began. The door was partially opened. Alicia was on the other side. She heard the woman whisper, saw her words curling like smoke pass through the door. *Needs help, Alan. Makes no sense.* She saw the strained expression on Alan's face as he turned away from his sister. Alan was a lovely man. He always understood. They'd been married for nearly thirty years. Remembering that—how lovely he was, how long they'd been married, how he always understood—Alicia thought she could forgive him his other woman, for her presence in Alan's life made no difference in the life they shared. It neither affected Alan's feelings for her nor his behavior toward her. He still kissed her goodbye every morning, came home every night, kissed her again, lifted her, when necessary, from the couch and carried her upstairs to bed. It wasn't always necessary for him to carry her for, contrary to some people's beliefs—her sister's or Alan's sister's in particular—she could keep from taking a drop when she chose.

Help? She needed help? Who was she to make such a suggestion? And what was she doing in their kitchen? That sister or sister-in-law, or whoever she was.

Alicia found out about Alan's other woman by mistake. Not hers or Alan's, but the postman's. A mistake easy enough for a postman to make. It was a flat square envelope addressed to Alan, purple in color and small enough to have stuck between pieces of mail addressed to their neighbor and placed in his mailbox by mistake. Bill Maxwell was the neighbor's name, a man close to ninety. The very next week, police responding to a call at his address about a missing person—Bill, it was believed—found him curled on his attic floor as if asleep. People whispered about that. Particularly the women. Whispering like hissing cats. And from the way they whispered, Alicia considered it likely they thought she had killed him. *Ridiculous. Preposterous.* If she was going to kill anyone it would be her husband's other woman, or his sister, or her own sister, or even her lovely husband himself. Not a harmless old man like Bill Maxwell.

"Apologies," Bill said, having knocked on her door three weeks ago as she was leaving for work. "Got mixed with mine." He handed her the envelope addressed to Alan.

Purple paper it was, and cheap. Instantly, she recoiled from its touch.

"Yours," Bill said, insisting she take it. "Not mine."

With two fingers, Alicia accepted the envelope and carefully slipped it into her purse.

A note on cheap purple paper. Addressed to Alan. For the woman to have written to her husband at his home, to have taken the chance of her note falling into his wife's hands (as indeed it had, through the postman, then through Bill), was remarkable. Laughable even.

Alicia laughed. She got into her car, drove a mile or two down the road, laughing all the way. Without ever taking her eyes off the road, she dug into her purse and found the envelope. As if by instinct, as if by smell. She ripped the envelope open, pulled out the note, glanced briefly at its message, then tore the cheap purple paper into tiny pieces and tossed them, fluttering, out the window onto the road. Purple paper flying like confetti down the road. She laughed, seeing that. Clutched the steering wheel and laughed out loud. Her laughter following her down the road like someone else's laughter. Someone attached to her left rear tire or to her bumper. Once she even glanced in her rear-view mirror to see who it was.

And why this woman had not used email or Alan's cell phone, or even his office phone (though surely Alan would have dissuaded her from doing that) to deliver her insipid message was beyond her. But to write to his home address! Stupid. Utterly stupid. For such stupidity the woman deserved whatever she got. But all she would get, so far as Alicia could foresee, was the annoyance or bitterness or frustration she would undoubtedly feel in never having received a reply to her silly note. Palpably silly. Written while the woman who signed herself *Oiseau*—*Oiseau*, of all things! Bird in French—was drunk. Had to be. Alicia knew the signs. Wiggling penmanship, unsteady hand, sentences nearly indecipherable. Telling him, Alan, her husband, as best Alicia could make out, that she couldn't stop thinking about him. That she loved the way he twisted a rubber band around his ponytail, pulled it to the top of his head, let it dangle free.

Love the way you do that, she wrote. *Can't stop thinking about you. Here's love flying into your heart.* Just that. Nothing more. Signed *Oiseau*. No return address. The postmark indistinct. Stamp askew, obviously affixed in a state of inebriation. Perhaps the woman hadn't meant to mail the stupid thing. Had simply given into a momentary compulsion to jot the meanderings of her silly mind down on paper—not even good paper, cheap, ordinary stock, purple to boot!—and would think better of it when she sobered up and toss the thing into the trash. Alicia could understand that. Could empathize even. She, too, often felt compelled to jot things down. When she worked at the architect's firm, for instance. The number of phone calls she answered in a day, the number of renderings recorded and filed, the number of packages received and sent—she'd count them all, make note of the count, and jot it down. More recently, working at the flower shop here in town, counting the number of flowers that passed through her hands in a single day, the number of stems. Counting them stem by stem, remembering the count, jotting it down. Just as *Oiseau* jotted down her silly thoughts. The difference being that Alicia threw her calculations in the trash, not put them in the mail. Certainly not mail them to somebody else's husband. And at his home no less. This *Oiseau* might have regretted it in a sober moment, but by then it would have been too late. She would already have staggered to the mailbox, dropped her message in. Alicia could empathize. She, too, sometimes staggered. Sometimes regretted things.

Alan had always worn his hair long. Even before the ponytail, it had reached to his earlobes. There was a lock of hair he loved to curl about his ear, always the right ear. Shiny hair. Black as night. Curling once, almost twice, about his ear. Alicia loved seeing him do that. But she had never told him so. Then came the ponytail, streaked now with gray, the tip of it dangling loose like a tassel, his fingers caressing the tassel, abstractedly, pensively. She loved seeing him do that, too, but had never told him so. About the same time the ponytail appeared, Alan began going to the gym, lifting weights, running, trying to lose weight. He said all those things, especially the ponytail, ushered in the new man he was becoming. A man with a new attitude, new affiliation with the youth of the day. (Young, female

youth, Alicia would discover.) Eventually, he gave up running and
the gym and attempting to lose weight, but the ponytail remained.
She had ample opportunity—thirty years, at least—to tell him how
she loved seeing him twist that rubber band around his ponytail, pull
it to the top of his head, abstractedly, pensively caress the end of it,
hanging loose like a tassel. But she never had.

There was something sexy about it. Something intimate. She
could have told him that, but never did. Now *Oiseau* could tell him.
She didn't say anything in her note about the way Alan handled his
ponytail being sexy or intimate. She said only that she loved seeing
him do it, that here was love flying into his heart. But Alicia knew
what she meant. Intimate and sexy, that pulling of the hair through
the twisted rubber band, that tassel dangling loose, that abstracted,
pensive way of caressing its end. She'd had all those years to tell
him, and never had. That was a mistake. One she would correct.

In the evenings now when Alan came home from work and
they were sipping wine in the living room and would soon enjoy the
lamb chops or steak she'd grilled only until pink as Alan preferred,
and the asparagus or green beans, steamed only until tender as he
liked, she'd say the words the other woman had written in her note.

Love the way you do that. Can't stop thinking about you.

Alan looked up from his glass of wine, startled as a bird. (The
bird from the note he never received? The bird of his dreams?) Had
his *Oiseau* once said the same? Not only written it in a silly note he
never received, but actually said it to his face? Was it *déjà vu* he now
was feeling? (If it was French he wanted, she could give him French.)
Was he hearing tonight an echo of his other woman's remark? Did
confusion fly about his mind like a maddened bird? Alicia said it
again: *love the way you do that.* And again: *love flying into your heart.* But
not so often as to make him uneasy about hearing two women saying
it—if two women had. Perhaps only one had actually said the words
aloud, the other having merely jotted them down, drunkenly, carelessly, on a piece of cheap purple paper and mailed the note against
all common sense to his home address where it had fallen, by way
of a postman and then an elderly neighbor (now deceased) into the
hands of his wife, who tore it into tiny pieces and tossed it, fluttering,
out the window onto the road.

Signed, *Oiseau.*

Oiseau! A bird of all things. Did it have a small, beating heart? A sparrow's heart, a Robin's perhaps? Beating with love for her lovely Alan? She saw it flying about his head. Saw it preening its feathers. Saw the chicks it would have.

She and Alan had never had children. No fault, medical or otherwise, laid to either of them. Simply a decision they'd come to mutually. They were enough for each other. (Or so she thought.) They had their routines, their jobs—Alan in advertising; she, an architect's assistant. For much of their married life, Alicia worked in an architect's firm in Manhattan, Smythe and Archibald, on Greenwich Street. She answered phones, filed renderings, sent and received packages—and it was for this job that she left her house on Martine Avenue in Westchester at 7:10 every weekday morning and got into her car. (Alan would leave some ten minutes later, opting for Metro North.)

"You're crazy to drive," regularly he told her that.

But she loved that drive. South from White Plains, past Dobbs Ferry, Ardsley, Hastings-on-Hudson, Yonkers. Then crossing into Manhattan, picking up the West Side Highway and continuing south to the architect's building on Greenwich Street (which housed a garage, so parking was never a problem). Greenwich Street, not Avenue, she frequently had to clarify for delivery people.

Besides, she had a horror of trains. The enforced enclosure, the uncontrollable speed, the distastefulness of being seated next to a stranger. Alan understood, as he always did, and eventually stopped saying she was crazy to drive. Had she told him how her heart began to race when she sat behind the wheel of her Toyota Camry (*Most popular car in America*, the dealer had assured her upon purchase), Alan might have understood that as well. But she never told him. It seemed prudent to keep the racing of her heart from him, and that she drove in her stockinged feet, and that her blood throbbed in her veins as the car's vibrations traveled up through the gas (or brake) pedal and into her naked (but for the stocking) foot and along her spine. It was her secret pleasure, which also seemed prudent to keep from Alan, for he was not above jealousy. He would not have liked to know how she looked forward to the car's vibrations traveling through her body, how she allowed her all but naked foot to hover an instant above the pedal (gas or brake) before pressing down in exquisite anticipation of what was to come. He would not have liked to know how the blood throbbed in her veins, how happy she was in that car on that drive to and from work. So, out of consideration for her husband, she kept that knowledge to herself.

Now, still laughing at Alan's other woman's silly note, she began to feel that she was not alone in her car. Someone, some other woman, was lurking in the shadows of the back seat. Someone who knew about her secret pleasure. Some woman whispering condemnations from where she sat. *Slut,* she once heard the woman say. *Whore,* another time. Then *Bitch.* Then *Worthless woman. Unworthy of Alan. Unworthy of love.*

She snapped her head around to confront her abusive passenger. But the woman, whoever she was, vanished the instant Alicia turned her head.

Not long after that, driving past Dobbs Ferry and Ardsley and Hastings-on-Hudson, she found it harder and harder to tell the towns apart. The landmarks that previously had distinguished one from another began to blur. Every town she passed had a firehouse or a church on a hill. It was difficult, frequently impossible, to tell the hillside firehouse or hilltop church of one town from that of another. Over years of taking this drive to and from work, she had identified certain clusters of trees (white oaks or hickorys or sycamores) or defining highway curves (sharp to the right, going; wider and more gently to the left, coming back) to alert her to which exit to take. But all the trees came to look alike, all the exits grew indistinguishable one from another. Often, she had to brake abruptly and look around to find her bearings. At times narrowly avoiding an accident, invariably causing a deafening blare to sound around her, or a curse or finger to protrude from the window of a passing car. Increasingly, she grew convinced that the person in the car's back seat, calling her a slut or whore, saying she was unworthy of love, had slipped into the driver's seat and taken the wheel. She'd look at her hands and fail to recognize them. Sometimes, they disappeared altogether, making it seem the car was driving itself.

Very soon after that, she gave up driving to and from work, gave up work altogether. *All the towns look alike,* she said to Smythe by way of explanation for her hasty departure. *The landmarks blur,* she said to Archibald.

Within two weeks, she had found a part-time position in a flower shop on Main Street, close to home.

"That's important," she informed her new employer. "Being close to home." And of course she did love flowers.

That last wasn't entirely true. Alicia had never had much feeling for flowers. But she learned to manage them, to cut and trim and sort, to arrange them artfully in vases, to staple them in glossy white paper that ripped off with a scream as she tore it from its roller. That scream filled her with an uncanny pleasure. The staples delighted her. Less than a quarter of an inch in length, so sharp and shiny, so bright. The way they shot out from the head of the stapler with just a slap of her hand. She would already have torn the glossy white paper from its roller, laid it flat, gently enfolded the flowers. Then a slap of her hand on the head of the stapler and a bright, shiny staple would shoot out. Then another slap and another staple. She'd affix them slantwise in a row close to the stems. But not too close, for well she knew how such bright, sharp instruments could injure fragile stems. And make them bleed. She saw them bleeding in her dreams. She saw the sharp, shiny splinters of metal piercing the stems. Green blood flowing. Flowers bleeding. She saw herself handing the bleeding flowers to her customers. And later, she would count the stems. Count the number that had passed through her hands that day (as before at the architect's firm she'd counted the number of renderings recorded and filed, the number of packages received and sent). Now at the florist's, she counted stems every evening before returning home, jotted the number down on a piece of paper, never failing (unlike *Oiseau*) to toss the paper into the trash before leaving the shop.

One night after Alan had carried her up the stairs and she was later lying in bed next to him, staring at the ceiling, she heard herself say: *Love the way you do that. Here's love flying into your heart.* In the shadows crossing the ceiling she saw the bird flying, saw it pecking at the tissues of his heart, saw its busy beak carrying her love like food into Alan's open mouth.

The only light in the room came from the lamp on the table on her side of the bed. Alan reached across her to turn off the lamp. And as he did so it seemed to Alicia she could feel his ponytail brushing her cheek. Feel its tassel drawing blood. She put her fingers to the spot, inspecting them for blood. But in the darkness of the room she couldn't see.

She was grateful for all the years she'd had with Alan. Grateful, too, that over time his *Oiseau*, like everything in life if you waited long enough, would become a thing of the past. As with the violent swing of a heavy glass pitcher, its contents emptied onto a pavement, yellowy water seeping through its cracks, blood on the tips of her sister's fingers. After a while she would barely be able to remember any of it.

Special Needs

The girl came back from summer vacation with no legs. She was older than Peggy, first year of high school to Peggy's seventh grade. Peggy didn't know her, knew only her reputation on the basketball court. The girl was the school's high scorer. Its star female player. Quick and agile with sure hands and long legs and feet that could race down the court and pivot on a dime. In every game she was the one who sank the most baskets, scored the most points. Now here she was, returning to school late in the school year, the week before Thanksgiving, with no legs. Peggy knew it wasn't possible. It couldn't actually have happened the way they said it did. That must be some fake girl she was looking at now, walking into the gymnasium, the site of her former triumphs, on wooden crutches.

Prosthetic legs encased in white cotton stockings. Plastic feet in shiny black leather sneakers. Eye-level to Peggy, sitting cross-legged on the floor as the middle school and upper school kids, who had been ushered in before the girl, had been told to sit. The girl clomped her way around the shiny, highly shellacked floor. Head down, leaning heavily onto her crutches, she thrust the hard plastic legs awkwardly before her, first one then the other, upper body following as an afterthought. Her mother was on one side of her, the gym teacher, Ms. Leonard, on the other side, neither one touching her, only there for that other kind of support. *Moral*, Peggy figured. She came into the room, the legless girl, entering this place where she had been a star, and the room exploded in loud, brutal, forced applause. Peggy applauded along with the others, all those rows of middle school and upper school kids seated cross-legged on the floor. Later, they would be told it was a motorboat accident. *See what can happen if you're not careful?* The girl having dived off the back of the boat and come up too close to the blades.

But of course that could not actually have happened.

The girl was steady, if awkward, on her crutches, presumably having received months of training (which would account for her having returned to school from summer vacation so late in the academic year) in how to handle them, how to thrust the plastic legs before her, one after the other, how to lift up and put down the shiny black plastic feet. She walked into the gym and stopped at the applause and lifted her head. It wasn't like real applause, showing appreciation for a thing well done, but more like a drum beat or a dirge, loud and slow and forced and hard.

It was whispered that the legs had been severed right there in the water, contaminated by lake water so they couldn't be reattached. But Peggy knew that could not really be true. The blades of the propeller shearing off her legs. The blood in the water. The severed limbs. Such things were the stuff of horror movies. They were not real. That girl on those crutches before them was not a real girl. The real girl, the high-scoring basketball star with two good fast legs, existed somewhere still. They'd taken the real girl away and brought in this fake girl, this freak with plastic legs, in her place. This girl not like other girls. From her seat in the front row on the floor of the gym, Peggy tried to look up under the fake girl's skirt when she passed in front of her. She wanted to see where the hard plastic legs encased in white cotton stockings ended and the soft fleshy stumps began. But the girl's skirt was too long, and she couldn't see.

Peggy didn't feel sorrow or pity for the legless girl. She didn't feel anything for her. Why should she, when she didn't even know her? When she didn't believe what had happened to her was real?

The thing that had happened all those years ago by the river wasn't real either.

They brought in that fake girl with the plastic legs and let her clomp around the school for awhile, and then she was gone. She never came back to school after Christmas break, and they forgot all about her.

Peggy and Ritchie Myers had begun hanging out regularly after school the year the girl with no legs returned and then disappeared. They spent most of their time in the park, for they liked trees and rocks more than people. Mostly they liked the river.

The Hudson River on that day was gray and choppy. Peggy and Ritchie liked to walk along the river, right down next to it. Peggy had noticed Ritchie Myers leaning against his locker one day. Just leaning there, staring out across the hallway as across a battlefield. The bell had just rung, and the hallway was teeming with kids scurrying across it on their way in and out of classes, and Ritchie looked like he might be picking them off with a rifle. He glanced up and Peggy caught his eye—like pale blue stones they were—and something clicked between them. "It's all bullshit," Ritchie said to her from where he stood, leaning against his locker, and she immediately knew what he meant. They'd been running down to the river most afternoons after school ever since. On the day it happened, they'd run through the little tunnel and down that narrow strip of concrete, the dangerous sweep of cars coming up the underpass from the highway so close they felt the air pushed off the fenders and into their faces as they passed. They'd run along the skinny path by the river past the tennis courts, the bicycles manacled to the fence, the people waiting on benches for their turn on the courts. They'd run up to where there was a break in the chain-link fence and they could slip through and race down the embankment and get right up next to the river. *We could jump in. We could swim away,* Ritchie had said. But of course they never did.

Ritchie was a couple of years older than her, and big. Big hands, long arms, big feet. Peggy thought he might've been held back a year, but she never asked. He had a big face, too. Broad and smooth, with a high forehead and wide nose and those pale blue eyes like stones. He never said much, but what he did say usually had a "bullshit" and "crap" in it. There was something kind of desperate in the way Ritchie looked at things. Like he was always trying to get to the bottom of them, and always failing. Peggy felt that way, too, that at the bottom of everything where you'd expect to find something, things just fell away and turned to bullshit.

It was almost like a strip of beach in that place where they went. A river beach. All that fall they'd been going there. They stopped going for a while after it happened but started up again in the spring. They didn't go at all in the summer when school was closed and families like Ritchie's went away like they'd disappeared. Years later, Ritchie went away to fight the war in Iraq and disappeared for good. Peggy was the only one left alive then who knew what had happened.

Sometimes the river was blue and placid-looking and almost, but never entirely, still. The sun setting low in the west cast a golden watery path over the water as it crossed from New Jersey and reached almost to their feet. At such times the river might appear calm, with just a few ripples cutting through. But then the sun would catch on those ripples and they'd leap like flames right out of the water.

On the day it happened the river was gray and choppy. The turbulence beneath held in check, the river clutching to keep it in the way Peggy sometimes clutched with her body to keep things in. Making tight places like fists in her stomach and between her legs. Her mother saying, *Why are you like that, Peggy? What gives you the right?* Her mother's skinny fingers on her shoulders. Bird claws digging in. And she herself a mother now. A wife and mother. Never, no matter how they provoked her with their sassy remarks and hateful bickering would she dig her fingers into her girls' shoulders like that. It was best to let it go. *Shut up!* she might say. *Just shut the fuck up!* But most times she let it go and let life cover it over.

The river lapped at the shore like a thirsty animal. It took out the natural debris, the tiny stones and twigs, the clumps of leaves and bits of broken tree limbs, and the human detritus as well, the melon rinds and corners of uneaten sandwiches, the used condoms, the soda and beer cans. Making no distinction between what humans and nature left behind, the river took it all out, covered it over.

She was eleven back then, that day on the river. Twenty years ago that would make it now, for here she was today, a thirty-one-year-old married woman, mother of two small girls. Not so old, but old compared to then when she'd been lean as a boy, not an ounce of fat on her anywhere. She felt like a different person, a stranger to the person she'd been back then. And of course she was. She and Ritchie Myers, thirteen at the time, dead in Iraq now, had run down the street after school, running past the statue of Joan of Arc on her horse, and cutting over to Riverside Drive. They'd entered the park and run down the steep, winding hill, Dead Man's Hill, it was called, and up its far side and across the plaza where the benches faced inward and the gardens came to an end. They'd run down another hill, a smaller one closer to the river, and passed through the tunnel next to the underpass, Ritchie going first, then out its far end and past the tennis courts to that place where they could slip through the fence and get right down to the river's edge. *No one will ever know. We are the only ones.* Only the two of them alive to tell. Then only her. But of course she never would.

Peggy had sensed someone following them that day, running behind like a shadow and always disappearing when she turned her head to look. It could have been anyone. It didn't have to have anything to do with them.

"That didn't really happen," Peggy had said to her fifth-grade world history teacher, Ms. Manheim, the day she told the class about Joan of Arc being burned to death at the stake. "Yes, it did, Peggy. It happened," Ms. Manheim replied. "But she didn't actually feel it," Peggy insisted. "The flames burning her feet, her hands. She didn't feel that." Ms. Manheim had looked at her as if the words coming out of her mouth were not in English and therefore could not be understood by her or by any of the fifth-grade children in the room. And then Ms. Manheim's eyes had passed over Peggy and gone on to focus on someone else, and it was as if Peggy had ceased to exist.

Even today when she comes home from the beauty salon, her hair in some elaborate do, and neither Harry nor the girls notice, something inside her drops away and she ceases to exist. As if the whole afternoon spent in the salon didn't exist. Her neck aching over the hard metal rim of the sink didn't exist. Her hair being carelessly yanked while wound into curlers didn't exist. Having to listen to the stylist going on about her new boyfriend, his cute spiked hair and dragon tattoo just like in the movie, as if she should care, didn't exist. And afterwards, sitting under the hot dryer, the world only a roaring in her ears, as if all that didn't exist. And then at home, seated at the dinner table with her family, her hair—her beautiful hair, shiny as platinum and still as glass, having been sprayed into immobility—going unnoticed, she herself didn't exist. But she would let it go. She would let life cover it over. She was trying to be a good wife, a good mother.

They couldn't see them from above, for she and Ritchie Myers were backed up tight beneath the embankment. Anyone who might happen to look down over the fence would fail to see them and what they did. Mostly they didn't do anything more than throw crap back into the river. Bend down and pick it up and throw it back in. Stones and beer cans, pieces of broken glass, melon rinds, sometimes a bottle cap, a penny. Bending down and picking up what had been left on the shore and throwing it back into the river. Used condoms, too. They'd pick those up and throw them back, but not with their hands. They'd get long twigs and hook the condoms on the points of the twigs and hurl them both, twigs with used condoms attached, back into the river. Shouting with each thing they threw, *Crap! More crap!*

The shadow following them that day turned out to be a kid they didn't know. They'd seen him around school—*Yes, you have too, Ritchie. He's one of them*—in the lines of special needs kids walking through the halls on their way to special classes. A species apart. Not like them. Not like regular kids. They would learn later that this particular kid often wandered off alone after school, disappeared for hours at a time, sometimes well into the night, and the police had even been sent after him once or twice, so at first no one worried.

"Don't know him," Ritchie claimed. "Never seen him before in my life."

But of course he had. Peggy knew he had. She wasn't the only one. They didn't know his name and didn't care. Peggy thought he was probably around Ritchie's age, but kids with special needs often looked older or younger than they actually were. Fatter, too, the ones people called obese—*Disgraceful*, her mother said, *to let a kid get like that*—or thinner than other kids, the ones with eating disorders. Blank eyes that slid away when you tried to see into them, the ones with autism. The shadow kid had eyes like that. Blank as BBs. He came up behind them that day. Just stood there, silent on the riverbank. His eyes slid away when Peggy tried to see into them. You knew something wasn't right inside his head. He wasn't like them. No connection between him and her and Ritchie, or only a sliding connection. An accident of place and time. There was nothing between them. They didn't know him. She let it go, let life cover it over.

Peggy knew that the most horrible events get sucked right down into the depths of life and covered over. The horrors of war, of family. Social and cultural horrors. She read about them. Bride-burnings, honor killings. Fathers stabbing their own daughters to death. The world absorbed it and moved on. People graduate from high school, never see one another again, or if they do, only by accident. Peggy was already married, had recently given birth to her first child, when there by accident was Ritchie Myers on the subway platform at Times Square. Stockier than she remembered him. Heavy jaw. A large, light-colored mole on his left cheek she didn't recall having seen before. Hair cut short and slicked down in a way she didn't associate with him. Khaki shirt, pseudo fatigues. Already he was appropriating army dress. This was a month before he enlisted and went to Iraq and got killed by an IED, leaving her the only one alive with actual knowledge of what had happened all those years ago by the river. In another country, she, a recent bride harboring such knowledge, might have been burned to death to protect her family's honor. But here in her country, people move on. She and Ritchie Myers locked eyes on the subway platform and moved on. *Do I know you? Is there something between us?* That was the last time she ever saw him.

The shadow boy was thin, with scrawny, rounded shoulders and a caved-in chest. He had pasty-white skin, almost like an albino, but he wasn't that. Albinos had blue eyes milky as mucous. Peggy had seen a photograph of one in a magazine once. First albino she ever saw. Even looking into the eyes in that photo had given her a sickish feeling in her stomach. The shadow boy stayed well away from them that day, but he watched everything they did. After a while, he crouched down and picked up one of the used condoms with his bare hand. *Hey, don't!* Peggy cried. *Not with your hand!* He ran his finger around the condom's thickened rim. He poked his finger into the center of it, making the slimy latex stick up like a tent. *Don't touch it!* Peggy cried, but Ritchie said to leave him. *He's got nothing to do with us.* The boy kept running his finger round and round the rim of the condom and sticking it up into its center and staring down into it like it was the most fascinating thing in the world. It was a mechanical movement, hypnotic. Round and round with his finger, and then that poke into the center, and Peggy began to get sleepy watching it. She thought she might just nod off right there on the riverbank, the river gray and choppy, the water lapping at the shore, the boy's finger going round and round the latex circle.

    "C'mon, let's go," Ritchie said after a while.

    And they moved on.

They heard that the boy's body had been found the next day further down the river, washed up on the bank. It was bound to happen, people said. A kid like that, always running away. "Did you know him?" her mother asked. "He went to your school." No, Peggy replied. She didn't know him. She had seen him around, maybe, but she didn't know him. He had nothing to do with her. What had happened to that boy didn't touch her in any way.

To this day it didn't touch her. It would have to go down a very long way to touch her, like to the bottom of a well, and it didn't go down that far. When later she heard about the thirty-three Chileans trapped in a mine she thought it would have to go down that far—two thousand feet into the earth at least—to touch her, but it didn't go down nearly that far. Not then when it happened and not in all the years since. She watched the footage of the rescue on TV. The miners, trapped for sixty-six days, lifted up one by one. Carried out of the earth in a specially built, steel-mesh capsule, capable of lifting only one man at a time. She watched with Harry and the girls. The trip up from the bottom of the shaft took approximately fifteen minutes per man. The capsule was barely six feet high and no more than twenty-one inches across. Chileans are not very tall people, and none of the miners was near six feet, but they would all have to cross their arms over their chests to fit into the capsule. "What if it gets stuck?" her younger daughter asked. "It won't get stuck, stupid," the older one replied. Peggy knew it might. There was always the danger that the capsule would become jammed in the rescue hole. The hole itself was only twenty-eight inches in diameter and didn't go straight down into the raw earth but curved along the way. They'd prepared for the possibility of the capsule getting stuck. Should that happen, it could be opened from the bottom and the man inside lowered back down into the mine by cable. Two thousand feet below the surface of the earth. What had happened to the boy that day on the river would have to go down that far to touch her. But in all the years since no one had lowered a capsule two thousand feet to rescue her. And even if they had, even if someone had thought to dig a shaft and lower a capsule and reach down that deep inside her, Peggy knew that at the bottom of the shaft they would find no one there to be rescued.

What had happened to the boy after she and Ritchie walked away had nothing to do with them. They had already left. They

didn't even know his name. They could in no way be held accountable. And what had happened to him, anyway? *Body washed up.* What
exactly did that mean? How had that boy with eyes blank as plastic
BBs gone from being a boy to being a body? Had he walked into the
river? Or had he simply let the river's great thirsty tongue come and
lap him up? No one knew. No one would ever know.

It was said that his parents should have kept a closer eye on
him. A kid like that. What was he, retarded? And of course that was
right. His parents were remiss. They were the ones at fault, if anyone
was, the ones who should be blamed and punished. No one could say
it was Peggy's fault. She didn't even know the boy's name. And besides, all the time she and Ritchie were there, nothing had happened.
All the time they were throwing stones and beer cans and other crap
into the choppy gray river, the boy's finger going round and round
the used condom, the light still faint in the sky for they hadn't turned
the clocks back yet, nothing had happened. *Spring forward, fall back.*
They hadn't fallen back, so it was still light, faintly light, although it
must have been close to five in the afternoon that day, and nothing
had happened. So there was nothing to tell. She and Ritchie had
walked away. And when they heard the next day that the body had
been found washed up down river, it was almost as if they didn't
know what people were talking about. *What body? Whose?*

It was a mystery to them. Maybe it had not actually happened. They couldn't say for sure that it had because they had
walked away. If anything had happened, it happened after they left.
They weren't there and could in no way be said to be responsible,
or *culpable.* Maybe it hadn't even happened. Maybe it was somebody
playing a joke, making up a thing like that, planting it in the newspapers. And when her own children were born Peggy sometimes looked
at them and imagined them with no legs or with that blank, sliding
look in their eyes so that you knew something was wrong with their
brains. *Miswired.* But then she would know that wasn't real. She was
deceiving herself. Playing a joke on herself.

Her children were normal. She loved her children.

Light hadn't touched the eyes of the Chilean miners for
sixty-six days. While they were waiting for the shaft to be dug, one
of the miners asked the rescuers to send down a picture of the sun.
They had to wear special sunglasses coming out. The world would

look different to them, unreal. Their vision would be altered, they were told, as if they weren't looking out of their own eyes but out of alien eyes implanted in their heads by the special sunglasses. Seeing an unreal world.

"It's like an elevator going down for their souls," Peggy said, watching with Harry and the children as the capsule descended.

"What are you talking about?" her husband asked.

She let it go. So often Harry failed to take her meaning. But it wasn't his fault. Perhaps she had not been clear. What she meant was into her, the capsule going down deep into her, and at the bottom finding no one there.

"It doesn't matter," she said. She loved her husband.

She was holding her younger daughter on her lap, watching the TV. Just the other day, leaving pre-school, that child had run toward her and had fallen to the pavement and scraped her knee. The knee had begun to bleed at once and the child to cry. Horrible, loud, piercing screams at the sight of the blood. Screams that set Peggy's teeth on edge. Her daughter had picked herself up off the pavement and run up and buried her face against Peggy's leg. She had thrown her arms around her leg and refused to let go. It was like a force of nature, the child running to her leg, crashing into it. Something wild, unstoppable. Peggy had been forced to bend over at an awkward angle and clasp the child's back and hold her there against her leg. But of course she loved her. Certainly she did.

Ritchie Myers got killed in Iraq. He got blown up by a remotely triggered IED left in a car at the side of the road, making Peggy the last person alive to have seen the boy. Although no one would ever know that. She had looked back at the boy over her shoulder when Ritchie said they should go. *C'mon, let's go*, he'd said, and the boy hadn't looked up. He was still crouched on the riverbank, still staring at the condom, still running his finger round and round its edge and poking it up into its center when Peggy looked back at him. Because Ritchie was gone now, leaving no one to corroborate or contradict her story, Peggy could change the story in any way she liked. She could put herself somewhere else that day. In the gym, playing basketball. In the library, working on a school paper. She chose the library. How could she know what had happened? She wasn't even there.

Not long ago and for reasons that were never entirely clear to her, Peggy joined an organization devoted to books. The discussion of books, how they were made and sold, the people who wrote them, what was new in the "industry." It wasn't a book-reading club. She would never join one of those. She hadn't told Harry she had joined this organization. When she went to the meeting that night, the first one she had ever attended, she didn't tell Harry or the girls where she was going. It wasn't that she meant to deceive them. It was simply that she didn't want them to know. Couldn't she have something, *one thing*, that was hers?

She told them she was going to her health club and would be back in a couple of hours, in time to put the girls to bed. The meeting was held in a downstairs room of what was called the "Cultural Center" on Columbus Avenue between 79th and 80th Streets. A steep flight of stairs descended into a bare room in which several metal chairs and card tables of various lengths had been set up. At one end of the room was a small table holding a pitcher of water, some plastic cups, bunches of red grapes, some cheese and crackers and clusters of cookies. No plates or napkins had been laid out. Peggy noticed that right away. Someone had forgotten to lay out the paper plates and napkins. There were about fifteen people in the room, mostly women. Peggy didn't know any of them. They sat with their hard, metal chairs pulled up close to the tables, holding loose grapes and cheese and crackers and cookies in their hands.

At the other end of the room, a card table longer than all the others was positioned horizontally across the floor. Chairs were placed behind the table and one at either end, angled away from it, so all the participants could face out into the room. This is where the panel sat. Employees from Random House. The two at either end seemed marooned, cut loose, not having a piece of the table to pull themselves up to. The members of the panel introduced themselves and talked about their specialties. Marketing. Newsletter editing. Subsidiary rights. Production design—the inside of the book, the woman whose specialty it was explained, not the cover. Each page had to fit a specific word count, each book a specific page count. The books had to have a certain look, a look the editors and author would previously have agreed upon. They went around the table, describing what they did, how they had come to be at Random House, how many years or months (in the case of the production designer it was less than three months) they had been there. The man in charge of subsidiary rights spoke of e-books and kindles, how they were changing the nature of the industry. "It's a business, don't forget," he said.

When the presentation was nearly over, a large woman—one of the obese people Peggy's mother found so disgraceful—in brown silky-looking pants pulled tight across her rolling hips and a brown shirt in the same silky material pulled tight across her enormous chest, walked into the room. She was carrying the forgotten paper plates and napkins. She placed them in two piles on one end of the refreshment table and quickly retreated. As in disgrace. Not for her weight, as Peggy's mother would have it, but for having been the one to have forgotten the napkins and the plates. Though by that time people were used to eating out of their hands and no one went up to the table to make use of a belatedly introduced napkin or plate.

Most of the women in the room were young, younger than Peggy. Graduate students, two of them identified themselves as such, having raised their hands to ask questions. They were interested in internships, possible employment. Other hands went up. Other questions were asked. Peggy wasn't looking for a job. Taking care of her children was employment enough for her. She wondered why she was there. She had never come to one of these meetings before. She didn't think she would ever come to one again. She wasn't particularly interested in the book industry. Certainly she would never buy a kindle, never read an e-book. She wasn't like these other women, so passionate to know, so eager to ask questions. She had nothing to do with them, nor they with her. Her husband and children didn't know she was here. She didn't know anyone in the room. No one knew her. If she died here, it suddenly occurred to her, it would take them a while to identify her. They would have to go through her pockets and purse to find her ID. Should that happen, should she have a heart attack and die, unknown among strangers, at the foot of these steps in this basement room at the bottom of the world, she would like Harry and the girls to know that she had loved them. For of course she loved them. She would write it down. She took a small notebook and a pen out of her purse. She would leave it for them to find, for she would want them to know. She loved them, she would write. Certainly, she did.

Strangers

It had happened that once. And never again. Impossible for it to have happened again for, affected by the stress at work and then the alcohol, she hadn't been herself in the original encounter. She'd been a different person entirely and would never be that person again.

"Buy you another?"

It annoyed her. His raspy voice coming up behind her. Shattering her thoughts, commingling with her boss's voice: *I know you didn't know.* What gave him the right to talk to her that way? Boss or no boss. *If I'd wanted you to know, I'd have told you.* As if she didn't have eyes, couldn't see for herself what was lying right there, face up on his desk, in front of her. A request for an interview, résumé attached. Not a single piece of paper obscuring it. Not one of his many neatly labeled manila folders concealing the request. Labels she had typed up and affixed herself. Of course she had eyes. Of course she could see. So, the bastard was recruiting for her position, was he? And then he had the nerve to send her out for coffee. Mocha java, his favorite. From Crosswicks. *Remember, Margaret, Crosswicks. That's the only place near here that has my blend.*

And now this man's voice coming up behind her, raspy, shattering her thoughts.

"Buy you another?"

As if a woman sitting alone at a bar was fair game and had no say about someone coming up behind her, invading her privacy.

She was already a little drunk. Three glasses of wine when two was her limit, and no dinner after work. She'd gone in for the wine, didn't want dinner. Couldn't have tolerated sitting alone at a table tonight, although she generally enjoyed eating alone in restaurants. But not tonight. The business of unfolding the napkin, realigning the utensils, lifting her water, if her water glass had been filled, sitting there alone, exposed, would have been too much tonight. So, the bastard was replacing her right in front of her face, was he? As if she didn't exist, had no feelings about the matter. And then this man, out of the blue. Accosting her.

She'd found a stool near the end of the bar wedged between two taken ones. All she wanted was a glass of wine, and then another, and maybe one after that. This was her favorite bar, her local. She liked its high-backed stools, the comfort of the wood against her shoulder blades after a day's work. She liked that the bartender knew her on sight, always acknowledged her, if he wasn't busy, with his eyes when she came in. And then this stranger coming up behind her. She had almost finished her third glass—a Pinot Noir with a slightly tinny taste—and there he was. His raspy voice: "Buy you another?" mixing in with her boss's voice: *If I'd wanted you to know I'd have told you.* That tone, that arrogance. The angle of his head, the thrust of his jaw. She'd put his mocha java, which she'd gone out of her way to get, down on his desk and scanned the desk for a pin to stick into his eye.

"Buy you another?" the man said again, sliding onto the stool next to her the moment it was vacated.

She cringed at the raspy voice, breathed in the awful breath.

"Didn't mean to frighten you."

"You didn't."

"You jumped a foot. In another world?"

What business of his what world she was in?

"I was just leaving."

"One more? My treat."

He turned into the light, gesturing for the bartender. Broken capillaries in his nose. Patches of flushed skin. Narrow, dark eyes. And there, below the left eye, it flashed. Long and glinting like a silverfish. Electric, alive. Flashing again as he turned back to face her. Long and skinny. Quivering below the eye. Normally, her instinct would have been to pull away. A gut reaction to a disfigured face. But she didn't feel normal tonight, not herself. She felt an impulse to touch the thing. Even to lick it. To let her tongue prod and poke. Certainly, she was a different person entirely this evening. Certainly, it would have happened only that once and never again.

His name was Simon.

She gave her own in return, hesitating a moment before giving it, thinking it might be better to proffer an alias. But the alcohol was having its effect. "Margaret," she said, then said yes to his offer of another glass of wine. He ordered a beer for himself, and when their drinks came, he clicked the neck of his bottle against her glass. He threw back his head to let the beer slide down his throat, giving her a better view of the shiny scar. She imagined hooking her tongue under it, teasing it out.

He knew all the bars around here, he told her.

She had no interest in knowing what he knew.

This one was his favorite, he said.

"Nicer class of women."

She let that go.

"I'm from Ohio."

She didn't care where he was from.

"I like figuring out how pieces fit together. Tunnels, bridges. Thought about engineering once, but that didn't happen."

She didn't care what he liked to figure out.

If I'd wanted you to know----.

How dare he take that tone with her, boss or not?

I'd have told you.

As if she didn't schedule and reschedule his appointments, write down his messages on yellow post-its, stick them to the rim of his computer. As if she didn't get him coffee from Crosswicks. Always mocha java. Always Crosswicks. Even if she was going in the opposite direction. *Remember, Margaret, Crosswicks,* he'd call after her as she was nearly out the door. Where she was going, what her lunchtime plans might be, didn't matter to him. Only he mattered, only his needs, his plans. Still, she'd gone to Crosswicks as he'd requested. And the moment she came out of the coffee shop, mocha java in hand, a little dog ran loose from its collar and was nearly killed by an approaching cab. What a horrible thing to see, the driver slamming on his brakes just in time.

"We're lucky to have a job…any job…dishwasher, jani-tor…,"

The stranger's raspy voice again. His awful breath.

"With the economy what it is. Never thought it'd be this bad this long."

She didn't care what he thought.

"You work around here, Margaret? What kind of work you do?"

He brought his face close to hers; the thin, quivery thing

glistened before her.

So of course it was only that once.

She had high cheekbones and a pointed chin. Her lips kinda quivered when she saw his scar. Her face, as later he would see it in his mind, was not beautiful, but intriguing in a remote way. She had a vagueness about her, about who she was, where she worked (although he knew where and didn't have to ask), even about her name, hesitating before saying it as if she wasn't quite sure. But there was no hesitation about his scar. No vagueness there. It turned her on.

He told her things he thought might interest her.

"Ohio's called a purple state 'cause it combines the red and the blue. You know what they say, 'as Ohio goes, so goes the presidency'."

She didn't answer.

He might have told her other things—his age, that he'd been married once, briefly. Thirteen months it was, just over a year. That his wife, like her, had been turned on by his scar—what he'd come to call his 'shiny friend'. There were women out there who took to it. But seeing her attention drift, he cut out some remarks he might otherwise have made, supplied only the essentials. He'd save the rest for later when he got her out of the bar, which he was confident he'd do without much effort, and back to his place where he wanted her.

"You liking that wine, Margaret? Want another?"

It wasn't exactly that she didn't listen to him, but that she seemed to be listening to someone else. Someone standing just past his left shoulder, where her eyes kept drifting. Sharp eyes, almost black. They were sure to be picking up details about his shiny friend as they strayed in that direction. They challenged him, women like her. That remoteness, that vagueness.

He told her how he'd spent his day, not getting too specific, just providing a general outline. He said he was an early riser.

"Five thirty, I'm out of bed."

She didn't care what time he got out of bed.

He liked the mention of the bed, put it in her mind. He spoke about the day's economy. Skipped over his job, having already made mention of the dishwasher and janitor.

"I'm a walker," he told her. "Good city this for walking. The things you see. Saw a dog nearly killed today in front of Crosswicks. You know Crosswicks, Margery? A few blocks from here? Cabbie slammed on his brakes just in time."

That got her attention, though she didn't respond.

He told her how he liked to look at faces in the street. How he'd set himself up mid-block, lean against a building, watch the people going by.

"Creatures of habit, people are. Same routes every day. Coming and going from their trains, their places of work, their lunch spots." He told her how it pleased him in particular to pick out a face he'd seen before. "Like a friend coming at you."

Now and then she'd move her head like in a nod at something he was saying before he'd come to the place in his discourse where he thought it might be appropriate for her to nod. That drifting of her eyes excited him, annoyed him, too. That glancing past his left shoulder as if seeing someone she knew. It made him want to turn on his stool, confront that person she was seeing coming through the door. No such person there. That and her remoteness, her vagueness, spurred him on.

A tormented man, she saw that from the start and had been drawn to it. Not she herself, but someone else, someone urged on by the wine had been drawn.

It spurred him on but angered him too. Sitting there like a queen leaning against her high-backed stool, looking past him as if he wasn't there. His shiny friend was there all right and it turned her on. He picked up on that right off. Saw it in the way her eyes lit up, in the quiver of her lips. Some women took to it that way. Not many, but some. His wife had been one. His wife of thirteen months. He was doing all right back then and had bought her everything she wanted. Clothes, shoes. Dozens of shoes. She showed her gratitude the way women ought to, sexualized by his shiny friend. Then one night he found empty shoe boxes all over the place, waiting like open mouths to be fed.

"What's all this?" he asked, and she said she'd known all along it wouldn't work, it was a mistake. "It was always there," she said. "A mistake like a lump in my heart."

She didn't know what to do, she said, her father having already laid out the cash, the room for the reception in that fancy hotel already having been booked, so she'd gone ahead with things like they'd planned. But she'd known all along. A lump? A fucking lump? What to do? He'd wanted to slice her up in little pieces, hearing that about a mistake, wanted to stuff the pieces in the open boxes on the floor.

"A mistake?" he shouted. "That's what it was? Me? Our life? A mistake?"

Women like that ought to be punished.

And now this one, drinking wine on his dime. Guzzling it down, all the while pretending she can't quite get him in focus. Her eyes drifting past his shoulder. Looking for what? Someone more interesting? More to her liking? But then he angles his head the way he's learned to do for women like her, and his shiny friend catches her eye.

Scarface, freak, they'd called him in school. When he was young, he'd tried to rip it off, digging in his nails, tearing at the skin.

"That will only make it worse," his mother told him.

An accident. A stupid accident. Nine years old, falling off his skateboard, his cheek coming into contact with a broken Coke bottle. Twenty-one stitches they'd done. A thing like that changing his life. For it did change it. Making him wary, prone to shy away from people, whereas before he'd been a trusting and friendly child.

As he got older, he learned there were women susceptible to his shiny friend, finding it intriguing, mysterious. Women are suckers for mystery. Each one believing she'll be the one to solve it.

This one seated next to him—this Margaret—guzzling wine at his expense, she's one of the susceptible ones. He angles his head the way he's learned to do, presenting his left eye, the scar beneath, so she can have a nice long look.

"Come here often?" he asked, knowing that she did. "Your local, is it?" He knew that it was.

The wine paralyzes her brain, prevents even an attempt at an answer. She sinks her eyes into his shiny friend the way women like her like to do, having their thoughts about mystery. Danger. Whatever turns them on.

"Want to go now, Margaret?" He reaches for her empty

glass, a little wobbly in her hand. She lets him take it. Her eyes are glazed. He didn't know how many she'd had before he arrived, a few for sure. He puts her glass on the bar, pays the tab. Tomorrow she'll blame it on the wine, tell herself it would only be this once. He knows how they think, these susceptible women.

"Come on. We'll go."

Afterwards, she hardly ever thinks of it. Certainly not consciously, not willingly. Yet images intrude. They appear on their own like snippets from a film. His sweaty face, his stubby fingers. She might be performing some trivial task at work—shoving toner into the printer or taking reams of copy paper out of the box, ten to a box, stacking them on the shelf—and right then, through the gaps left in her attention by these mindless actions, fragments of that night would return. The thrust of his jaw, the two of them walking out the door, down the dark street. The glare from the streetlight at the corner illuminating the silvery thing. Herself staggering, not actually staggering, she didn't think, only being a bit unsteady on her feet. Once she nearly tripped, and he pulled her upright. Cars passing. Pedestrians. No memory of getting to his place, what it looked like, if they'd climbed stairs or taken an elevator. No memory of getting home. No memory ever of that.

As the days passed, more unbidden images emerge. Suggestive, watery, soft core. An arm flung across a rumpled sheet. A flash of breast, the nipple raised, tough as muscle. Some woman—not herself but some other woman—on her knees on a bed, straddling a man, hair hanging loose. Not her hair, not her knees. Occasionally then, just before she falls asleep, comes a tongue—not her tongue but someone else's—licking at the thing, prying it loose, nearly lifting it away. With the images comes a feeling of release, being expelled from her body, the freedom she'd felt in that. She was glad to have the wine for an excuse.

He didn't mind being of service to women in that way. To their mutual benefit was how he saw it. What he minded was when they pretended not to know him when they saw him again. When he'd come up behind them in the street, ask how things were going, no more than a gentlemanly thing to do, and they'd turn and see who it was and act like they'd never seen him before. Women like that didn't deserve to live.

A tormented man, she'd recognized that right off. And had been drawn to his torment. She recalls the wine, recalls his bed, remembers the feeling of release. The freedom of that. The astounding freedom. She owes him a debt for that. She can acknowledge it for he wasn't anyone she'd ever see again. There was no history between them. No past, no future. No need to account for herself. Nevertheless, she avoided her local for three weeks.

"Things going all right?"

He was there again, behind her. Then sitting in the seat just vacated.

"Buy you another?"

She heard the raspy voice, breathed in the awful breath. Three weeks weren't enough. She should have avoided the place for longer, for a month maybe. Maybe never gone back. But this was her place. She liked its high-backed stools, the wood against her shoulder blades. Enjoyed stopping in for a glass or two of wine after work, maybe a third. Enjoyed the bartender knowing her on sight. Who was this man to rob her of that?

"Please, leave me alone."

"We had something, I thought."

"You don't know me. You don't know anything about me."

"I like that. Puzzles. Putting pieces together. It's what engineers do."

"You're not an engineer."

"Think you're too good for me, do you? Not that night you weren't. Weren't too good for anybody that night."

He got up and left. Walked straight across the room, out the door, and into the night. He felt her eyes boring into his flesh at the back of his neck as he walked away. He might wait for her on the street, conceal himself in darkness, follow her when she left. He'd followed people in the streets since childhood. But the compulsion wasn't strong in him that night. He knew where she worked, where she went for lunch. He'd been in the same coffee shop and saw her on line. Mocha java was her order. He saw the dog nearly killed by the cab coming out. He'd tracked her back to her place of business. He knew right away she was one of the susceptible ones. He'd returned later, just before five, waited in the doorway until she came out, tracked her to the bar. He had her habits down. Even knew where she lived, having heard her give the driver directions that night he'd hailed her a cab. Act of a gentleman that was, she'd have to say as much. *A mistake?* That's what his wife of thirteen months considered it? How's a marriage a mistake? Like boarding the wrong bus, or taking an elevator and getting off on the wrong floor?

He went to the all-night diner a block away, the woman's eyes still boring into his flesh.

Bacon and eggs it would be, sunny side up. White toast, coffee.

"Fries with that?"

The waitress was well past middle age. Wiggly lines etched as in cement at the corners of her eyes. Short vertical lines along her upper lip. Yellow hair sputtering in the neon lights.

"Hashed brown," he corrected.

He understood he left his mark on them, or his shiny friend did. Afterwards, they'd never be the same. They had him to thank for that. Her, his wife, the others. There were plenty of susceptible ones out there. He knew how to pick them, could snare one whenever he pleased.

She thought about not going to work the day after. Pleading illness, COVID, but decided against it. It turned out she hadn't been re-placed. There'd been no interview. No appropriate applicant for her job. She thought she might quit. Get another job in another part of town, never visit this neighborhood again. Any kind of job. *Dishwash-er. Janitor.* His voice came back to her. His emphasis on the words. *Dishwasher? Janitor?* Did he think those sorts of jobs would interest her? Did he think they had anything at all in common?

It mattered how people spoke. The words they chose. Their tone. She went into work early that day. She liked being alone in the office, having the space to herself, the phones not yet ringing off their hooks. She straightened up, put pens and pencils back in their holders, threw out the disposable coffee cups and half emptied cans of soda left overnight on her co-workers' desks. Never touched her boss's things. Never after that. *If I'd wanted you to know, I'd have told you.* Two months later and still it rankled. Not the words so much, the tone. She opened the windows a crack, turned on the copy machine so it would be ready for use when the others arrived. Four besides herself. Three accountants, one super accountant—him, the boss. She managed the office. Managed it extremely well and didn't deserve to be spoken to like that. He never apologized. Never would.

"Things going all right?"
Behind her on line in the ATM.
"Please, leave me alone."

Another time, coming out of Crosswicks, having gone out of her way once more to get her boss his mocha java.
"How you've been?"
That shining thing under his eye. That silverfish sewn there, skin to skin.
"Please, leave me alone."

Yet another time, behind her in the congested street.
"Things going all right?"
She'd stopped at the corner to wait for the light. And in the lull that oftentimes occurs as swells of people, coming and going on nearly impassable streets stop at a corner to wait—swinging arms coming temporarily to a rest, footsteps momentarily halted, eyes focused on a signal from across the street telling them when to walk—his voice came again.
"You been all right?"
"Please, leave me alone."
"Just checking to see you're all right."
He told her that was only the gentlemanly thing to do.
"Especially in a city like this."
He told her it was important for people who lived alone and could so easily succumb to the indifference of city life to keep tabs on one another. "I see you alone in your coffee shop. And in the bar after work. Always alone. Never a date or a friend. People without friends need to look out for one another."
Looking out for her, was he? Just being kind? That changed

things. Wanting to connect her to her community? That made her see things differently. Hoping merely to raise the store of friendships for someone who could so easily…what had he said?… 'succumb to the indifference of city life.' What was that but a form of compassion, if not love? Perverse, distorted, yes. Nevertheless a form of love in all its imperfections. She hadn't understood at first, but it was that that had drawn her, not the man's torment. And it was she who had been drawn. Not someone else. Not some other woman entirely.

"Please," she said, and started again to ask that he leave her alone. But in a shift of density in the crowd behind her, she sensed that he was already gone. From her immediate vicinity, perhaps, yet the impression remained, he was still out there. And capable of reappearing at any moment, emerging from the swells of people coming and going, indifferent as a tide.

The Walk

His father had suggested the walk, and now he's crying. Never in his life had he seen his father cry. Yet he's doing so now. Right there on the street. Then silence.

"Dad…?"

Something catches in his father's throat. Something stuck and scratching. A carcinogenic substance inhaled off the street?

"Dad…?"

Tears well up, brim over, run down his cheeks. His father makes no attempt to hide them. It is a stunning event, in the sense that he is truly stunned by it, his senses knocked askew. His larynx freezes. He doesn't know where to put his eyes. Certainly not on his father's. How could he let his dry, thirty-five-year-old eyes settle on the red, freely running eyes of a man—his father—twice his age, who has abruptly come to a halt and is standing next to him now, immobile in the street? Broadway, no less. The most famous street in the world. Standing there stock still and clearly incapable of containing…what?…some unbearable grief?…some indescribable pain?

"Dad…?"

More silence. An instant before he heard that catch in his father's throat, he thought his father was about to respond to what he'd just said. What had he just said…? Something about making partner? How it was what he'd been dreaming of, how now that his dream had finally come true it would not only wipe out his egregious and, in his father's opinion, irresponsible credit card debt, but also permit him at last to take Jeanne on that long-promised and long-delayed vacation, which if anyone on earth deserved, she did?

A named partner, Dad, like you. Was that what he'd said, just prior to whatever it was that caught in his father's throat and caused the man to stop dead in his tracks, tears welling up in his eyes? *Named. Like you.* The words, ghostly now, hang in the silence. Stillborn birds on a wire. He thought, because his father would be proud to hear it, that he might say it again, pull down one of those ghostly words, and

after it, another and then another, forcibly breathing life into each so
as to go on with the conversation and make his father hear what he
wanted to say. But he hadn't been able to do it. His larynx froze. He
didn't know where to put his eyes.

He looks away, stares up at the streetlight, thirty feet above
his head, looks back at his father. He cannot walk away. For surely
he must remain by his father's side, bear witness. Everything in him
cries out to run, flee the scene, swear later to the police or anyone else
who might inquire that he had not been there, had not seen or heard
anything. Out of the ordinary. What, tears in his father's eyes? Something catching in his throat? Not possible. His father now ground to
a halt and silent in the middle of Broadway, forming an obstruction?
No way. Things have been established between them. Boundaries set,
styles of being laid down.

"Dad…?"

In this instant and right before his eyes, something altogether
new has entered the universe. His father, Howard Neiman, attorney,
retired, man of means, in apparent good health, immobile beside
him, crying on the street.

He's disoriented, can't say for certain where they've stopped.
Might be on the north-west corner of 49th and Broadway in front of
the old Colony Music Store. Gone now. Boarded up. A place that
had stood on that corner for sixty years. Sheet music. Vinyl records.
His father would have known it as a boy. History now removed. Everything in what he took to be the world, distorted. His father crying
on a public street. The air around him grows thin. The pavement
shifts beneath his feet.

"Dad…?"

Or they might have stopped on Seventh Avenue, not Broadway. They might be standing in front of the Carnegie Deli, not what
was once the Colony, or even over on Sixth in front of Staples. Tears
in his father's eyes. They might be anywhere. That's where he'd like
to be. Anywhere but here. He longs for disguises. Capes, eye masks.
Jet propulsion to lift them off the street and out of sight.

Transplanted families, out-of-towners, four abreast, comman-
deer the street. Gawking, camera-toting tourists. A constant at any
time of year, only the clothing varies. Now, mid-summer, tempera-
ture in the 90s, T-shirts and shorts the order of the day. Sunglasses.

Flip-flops. Risky those. Only the skinniest of padding preventing toes from making contact with the pavement. Shoulder to shoulder, they march. The movement is relentless, yet orderly, except for a gaggle of fast-walking New Yorkers, loathe to have their steps slowed, cutting through the crowd at every opportunity. Sons and daughters born of this city zigzag through the hordes of foreigners at a remarkable clip. They have business in this town, they're in a hurry, they live here, for God's sake!

"Dad, we're blocking traffic."

Silence again. They can't stay here. People need to get by. He nudges his father along. It's like pushing a mannequin. They come to the corner, stop, wait for the light. Bodies pile up behind them. Two people refuse to wait. A man and a woman, indisputably New Yorkers. They break free, make a dash for it. Instantly, the blare of horns, the screech of brakes. The man makes it across. The woman is caught in the middle. Passenger cars and yellow cabs, trucks and bicycles swerve around her, surge ahead. The woman turns, looks back at the curb as if for salvation. He catches her gaze, looks into her eyes. Hers, not his father's. She's panicked, petrified. This is normal. A normal New York City scene. A terrified woman on display, frozen for the amusement of the crowd. No one runs into traffic to save her. No one risks his life for hers. He doesn't run, doesn't risk. He stands where he is, grateful for a place to put his eyes.

Now the cars line up as at an imaginary marker and all but tip their hats to let her pass. The woman makes it across, safe, to the other side.

The light changes in their favor. Still his father does not move.

"What is it, Dad?"

"Nothing."

"Not nothing."

They both are obstacles now. The crowd is forced to move around them. That goes against all expectation, and theirs is a society based on expectation. People are expected to stop at the corner when the light is red, wait for it to turn green, then move on. He and his father should do what is expected. The light is now in their favor, but his father refuses to move.

"You okay, Dad?"

"Yes."

"You sure?"

Desperate question. What would he do if the man answered no?

The crowds are relentless. Wave after wave, they come up from behind, bear down from the front. Encountering the obstacle he and his father have become, they adjust for it with varying degrees of annoyance, curiosity, indifference. Tourists and locals alike, they adjust. Parting to the left and right, they move around the obstruction, merge on its far side. It's New York. People adjust. But this. This is different. His father, stopped dead in his tracks on a crowded street corner, tears running down his face.

"Come on, Dad. Let's go someplace."

"Where?"

"Anywhere. Some place."

He'd whisk him away. Magically transport him to an old folks' home. He's not that old, not impaired, but he'd be off the street. His needs would be attended to. Favorite foods. Newspapers. And he could visit. Weekends. Holidays. Bring him things. Books. Bagels. He'd be safe. Not standing here on a corner, the light turned green, tears in his eyes, refusing to move.

He doesn't know what to do. He looks away, looks back. He doesn't blame him for anything.

"Hungry, Dad?"

His father shakes his head.

"Come on, let's go."

His father won't budge.

When he was a boy, his father took him to see his office. The echoes in the lobby, the murals of laborers at work filled his head. The silence in the elevator as if everyone's holding their breath scared him. Twenty-seven floors up. Through the sky, it had seemed. The corridor on his father's floor, quiet as church. Two sets of doors. One to an outer office, the other to his father's private domain. First time he's seen it. Smells of smoke and leather. His father's desk big as a boat; a green blotter wide as a lake. Glass inkwells. Real ink. Fountain pens, not ballpoints. His father's world. His privilege to have been invited. He thinks he might return the favor now. Show his father something he has never seen. But what? His father has lived in this city all his life. What could he show him he hasn't seen before? His new office? Would he like that? Office for office, world for world. *A corner office, Dad. Like yours. You can see up and down Madison and east nearly to the river.* He would introduce him to the receptionist. *Dad, this is Gloria. Gloria, my dad. He never calls, so you've never heard his voice. But on the off chance that he calls one day, put him straight through.* His father would be pleased to hear the authority in his voice, the ease with which he instructs a subordinate.

People are staring at them. They've become a tourist attraction. He's embarrassed. His father is oblivious. He takes his arm, feels the thickness of his jacket. Old-school gentleman, jacket and tie even in this heat. His father stiffens at his touch. He's a tall man, not yet shrinking. He holds himself erect, except for his head. His head is bowed. He's staring at his feet. He feels a desperation in his love for him. A desperation threatening to leap out of his chest, take on a life of its own, wrap itself around him.

"Okay," his father says. "I can walk now."

The light turns red, then green again, they cross the street. They pass an open plaza, sunken below street level. Short flights of concrete steps on either end leading down to the subway. At the back a notoriously expensive gym. He could take his father there, get him a steam bath, a massage.

They walk on, arm in arm. There is comfort in the walk. The sheer physical movement of it. His arm in his father's. His feet, his father's feet, lifting off the pavement, coming down again. Steady, regular footfalls, moving forward with the crowd.

He remembers being a kid and walking with his father down these streets. Away from his mother, away from all he knew, away from time itself. Just the two of them. His head reaching to his father's hip, his shoulder pressed against his thigh. His inclination to move closer to the man, closer to his hip, his thigh, closer still until his father's flesh parted and let him in.

"Silly old man," his father says, shaking free of him.

"Not silly."

"To let it get away like that."

"Let what get away?"

"We never denied each other. Never in thirty-eight years."

"Mom, you mean?"

"And then I did. I let it get away."

They have arrived at 52nd Street. An African man sells knock-off designer handbags on the corner. The bags are piled high on carts and hang from hooks on a makeshift display. Just beyond, jeans and short-sleeved shirts spill from a metal coat rack outside a clothing store. Maybe his father would like a shirt, a pair of jeans. He could distract him, buy him one. Further down, there's a store selling sofa beds. He could take his father in there, pull out a sofa, dim the lights. His father could lie down, have a nap.

"Why are we walking in this heat?"

"Your idea, Dad. You suggested a walk."

"Crazy, walking in this heat."

"You could ditch the jacket."

Tears again. Voluminous. As if in deference to the sudden downfall, he and his father stop where they stand. They turn toward one another, turn away, tracing arcs on the pavement as they move. They are like large animals pawing the dirt for traction, only there is no dirt and they can't get any traction. Again, his father is immobile. Again, they're an obstacle in the middle of the block. People come up on them from the rear, approach from the front. Parting to the left and right, they move around the obstacle they have become, merge again on its far side.

Next to the store selling sofa beds there's one selling luggage. Black and gray bags on wheels stand in the window, tall as children. Some have shiny metal handles sticking up into the air. Others, shaped like duffel bags, have wide shoulder straps. He could dart in, buy a couple of bags, rush his father off to JFK, fill the bags at airport shops with clothes and toothpaste and aftershave and anything else they might require, and fly off to …where? It doesn't matter where. Los Angeles. London. Dubai. Rome.

"I went crazy," his father says.

"It's okay."

"How is that okay? Going crazy?"

"People do."

He tries to prod his father forward. His father holds his ground.

"Seven weeks, crazy as a bedbug."

"Come on, Dad."

His father will not abandon his spot.

"Seven weeks, for Christ's sake! Me, a crazy man."

"That's okay."

"Okay again? What's okay about it? She deserved better than that."

"Mom, you mean?"

"Of course Mom. Who do you think? The woman's a saint. At my age I oughta be ashamed. I am. I'm ashamed."

Tears again. They muddy his speech. His father stops talking. He hopes that's the end of it. He's got the gist now and doesn't need to hear any more. But his father is resolute. He swallows hard, looks him full in the face.

"Not here, Dad." He steers him toward the corner of 53rd. There's a coffee shop half-way down the block. He could take him in, get him off the street. His father shrugs him off.

"I ended it. Then she calls. Out of the blue."

"Mom, you mean?" He knows it wasn't mom who called.

"No. Not Mom."

He doesn't want to hear more.

The street overtakes them. People from the previous block catch up, converge on them at the corner, wait for the light. The light changes. His father doesn't move. The crowd parts, left and right, moves around, merges again on their far side.

"Out of nowhere she calls."

"Mom?"

"Not Mom! I said that, didn't I? I said not Mom. Her."

Tourists gawk at buildings, shoot photos with their cells, hold animated conversations. They don't see them until they're almost on top of them.

"She called. I took her out. Big mistake."

People stop just short of bumping into them, recover, and adjust.

"It started up again. Like it never ended."

The New Yorkers in the crowd can't let such an inconvenience go without comment, if only with a look. A city look that says this is New York, people here keep moving. Didn't you get the rules at the border? Then they, too, part and move around them, merging again on their far side.

"Then yesterday, in the seventh week…what do I care how many weeks? For me, it was the whole calendar. She calls to cancel."

"She ripped my heart out. Someone that young. Ripped it right out and ran away with it."

"Dad, stop."

"What could I do? I had to go after it."

"Just stop."

"You don't have a choice. Get to my age, you'll know."

Another word, he'll punch him in the face.

"One fucking call, seven weeks of craziness."

He'll wring his scrawny neck, hack off his feeble arms and legs.

"Seven weeks. And I make another date."

"Mom knew?"

"Of course she knew."

He'll cut out his liver, feed it to the pigeons.

"She always knew. But you, you were oblivious."

He'll tear out his guts, chop off his balls. Give the tourists something real to gawk at.

"You live a life. You work, have children. The days pile up, cave in on you. So what? You'll be dead before they crush you. Then a call out of the blue and your heart is seized. You got no choice, you run after it. Don't expect to get it back."

Again, they're overtaken by the street. From the front and the rear.

"Then yesterday, in the seventh week…what do I care how many weeks? For me, it was the whole calendar. She calls to cancel. She's back with her fiancé."

"She's has a fiancé?"

"Before me. They broke up. Now they're back."

They stand immobile on the corner of a street in a city where they'd both been born.

"And Mom knew?"

"I said that! Didn't I? I said she knew."

They stand without moving. One great boulder of stone, of bronze, of iron. The crowds converge upon them, part, and move around.

"So Mom's leaving. Is that it, Dad? Is that what you're telling

The Walk

me?"

He wants to feel his fist against his face. Wants to hear his teeth crack.

Again, they're overtaken by the street. From the front and the rear.

"That what you brought me on this walk to tell me? Is it, Dad? Mom's leaving? You fuckin' bastard. You son of a bitch."

"That's just it … the damndest thing."

Tears again. They wash his face. He hopes they clog his throat and drown him. He hopes a car jumps the curb and mows him down. He hopes a bolt of lightning falls from the sky and cleaves him in two. He'll spit on his body as it burns to hear it sizzle.

Then he looks into his father's eyes and is astonished to see they are shining now, not with tears, but with a look of absolute disbelief as in the presence of some holy thing, and he knows it isn't pain or grief his father is feeling, but pure, inexplicable joy.

"You don't get it. I don't get it. Who could? She's not leaving. She forgives. She's a deity, that's what I say. And me, a dick. Who but a deity could forgive such a dick?" His father's voice starts out low and rises now toward wonder. "Hats off, son! She's staying."

Girl... There Was A Time

He looks at her, and something goes shut in his heart, something else swings open. He sits there in the back of the bus, watching her board and feeling this thing in his heart like a swinging door, opening and shutting. The girl does that. Makes it swing. She's fine. Young. Tall. Slim. A stunner. He's stunned, wholly dazed for a moment, as if a piece of her beauty broke off and came flying down the aisle and hit him in the head. He's seeing stars. Maybe she's one. A movie star, or on her way to being one, she's that pretty. He stares. He knows it's rude. He hates it when people stare at him, but she's not looking his way, so he figures it's okay to go on ogling her for another second or two. Not that he could pull his eyes away if he tried. She's got this smooth, dusky skin and long, thin arms and her legs, bare beneath her breathtakingly short skirt, look like they've just been buffed and polished. Her eyes are almond-shaped and her hair is black and shines like lights are switched on inside it. Like maybe she's a model carrying around her own set of miniature invisible lights, already set up and focused, illuminating her beauty wherever she goes, even here, climbing so daintily, so finely, up the steps of the Number 5. She positions her MetroCard just so above the slot to get it right, dipping it in, pulling it out and, like it's a teabag, giving it a careful little shake. She could be doing a commercial, an MTA promo, maybe, now flashing the driver—today it's Ortiz—a drop-dead, perfect white-toothed smile that's so broad and gleaming he thinks, no, not MTA…toothpaste. She's a toothpaste model or a smile model, if they have such a thing.

He's happy for Ortiz to be flashed that smile, for it's only his second day back on the job after a visit to his family in Guatemala to see with his own eyes what Hurricane Stan, which killed his grandmother, left of their village. "Roads wiped out, houses collapsed like toothpicks," he'd told him yesterday, and a smile like that could go a long way toward wiping that picture out of his mind. He'd give the medal in his bottom drawer at home to see the look on Ortiz's face, but all he has is a view of the back of his head. Still, he'd bet his last dime Ortiz hasn't seen anything that perfect and gleaming and white in maybe his whole entire life.

The girl takes a seat in the row of three-seaters just inside the door, opposite the driver. Ortiz's head does a little double take as she passes by, so he knows he's won his bet. The girl picks the third seat in, which gives him such a good view of her from where he sits he doesn't mind she's taking a spot reserved for the elderly or disabled. She'll get up if a person fitting that description boards, he knows she will, senses it's in her character to do so. Letting his eyes roam over her fine brown skin and lithe body, arms long and graceful in her scooped-low, sleeveless, green cotton T-shirt, expensive-looking legs, not crossed, but held close at the knees beneath her wonderfully short skirt, he can even see her doing it—the naked toes pressing down into their flip-flops, as an elderly man or woman boards the bus, the slim hips lifting, propelling her out of her chair and onto her feet even before the person has advanced from the top step to the fare box. "Oh, please, sit here," he can even hear her saying, the mellifluous voice, the knock-out, drop-dead, white-toothed smile gleaming in the internal lights issuing from her hair, her long, smooth, generous arm gesturing toward the now empty seat, palm upward as if she would physically pick up the seat she has so swiftly, willingly vacated and hand it to the person standing there on that cane or walker or pair of crutches before her.

Girl… There was a time.

And in his heart, that door swings on its hinges to and fro, softly, easily, like it was designed to do and hasn't done in almost forty years. A valve, opening and closing, letting things through like on newly oiled hinges, keeping other things out, and suddenly he can take a breath, an actual, full, natural breath. It's so simple he can't quite trust it, thinking maybe something's slipped loose in his lungs, opened too wide. He's used to having his breath stop just short of full, catching like a thread on a nail, causing him to go back, make some small adjustment, and start again. It's got to do with that time and place. Been that way ever since. But he won't think of that now, won't let it play the way it plays at night, like a perpetually repeating movie on the back of his eyelids.

She can't be more than nineteen. Their average age back then. An age that seems impossible now, and another war raging. Her jaw is sharp, an educated jaw, he'd say. She's probably in college, second year, not even thinking about what to major in, just having a ball sampling the options at her disposal. Her upper lip is full and soft. No lipstick, but shiny. Lip gloss, must be. He can see her rooting around for it in her bag, uncapping the tube, applying the gloss in quick, little up and down motions, starting at that delicious bow in front, moving out to a corner, back to center again, quick, up and down strokes, over to the other corner, then rounding the bottom lip and traveling the circle of them both, completing the circuit two or three times over so as not to leave a single centimeter untouched, unshined. How he'd like to be that tube of gloss going round and round those knock-out lips.

He thinks it would've been nice to serve his country with the support of his country. Those guys over there have that today. Support for them, not the war. 'Course they volunteered, while his batch was drafted, and that makes a difference. Later on, in his time, the demonstrators tried to fix that, saying, hold on, that's not what we meant, sure, we support the troops, just not what they were sent to do, but the atmosphere had already been poisoned. Not that he'd go along with that slogan they were chanting in '68: "If your heart's not in the USA, get your ass out now." He'd never go that far, but what exactly were they thinking back then, that's what he'd like to know. His kid sister, for instance, writing to tell him she'd laid down on the sidewalk that day in front of some bank pretending to be a dead Vietnamese child. Now what the fuck do you make of that, girl? Her writing to tell me that? She saying we killed kids?

Could he even be looking her in the face if that were true? But there he is, looking at her, though she's not looking back, and breathing now like normal, taking in air and letting it out. Full, round, complete revolutions. No constriction like there'd been since that time. No pulling of some thread caught on a nail, dragging the breath back, making him start over. He wasn't much older then than the girl is now, and he'd had trouble breathing all those years

Girl… There Was A Time

since. But today she boards his bus—Ortiz's Number 5—and he can
breathe easy again. He thinks he'd better not count on it, maybe after
she gets off it'll revert to the way it was and he'll feel the panic again,
like something tearing inside, with pain so sharp he thinks he's having
a heart attack and waits for it to radiate down his left arm like they
say it does when that's what you're having. But it doesn't radiate. It
stays right there, in the center of his heart, seeming to cauterize for
all time all memory of that other time. When it's through, it eases
up, but never entirely leaves him, coming back each time he takes a
conscious breath—that little pull, that catch—and he has to gasp for
breath and start again.

So he takes his eyes off the girl a moment to check to see if
this new ease is genuine. Ever since he returned to the States he's had
to breathe with his mouth open, due, the docs say, to some kind of
permanent obstruction in his nose or throat, an allergy, maybe, that
he'd picked up to something over there, something in the mud or
could be the napalm. He thinks of it like a ghost in his throat, a thing
that's been struggling all that time to break through and get from one
side of the swinging door to the other in peace and with ease, without that sudden, awful loss of breath, that instant's panic and image
of looming death. Could it be over now for real? Might something
in his heart have actually opened as he looked at the girl and something else shut, and might he breathe easy like this right up until the
moment he breathed his last?

He can't be sure. So he sits and watches the air come in
through his mouth and drop down into his lungs and circle around
and come back out his throat and mouth again. Still easy, still without
a catch, making a nice, smooth, unobstructed loop through mouth,
throat, lungs, and out again. A loop like the loop his bus makes,
traveling from 178th and Amsterdam over to Broadway and down to
135th, cutting from there across Dr. Martin Luther King Boulevard,
then following Riverside Drive past Grant's Tomb (where the girl
got on), past the Soldiers' and Sailors' Monument to 72nd Street,
swinging east, picking up Broadway again, and eventually making its
way across Central Park South, over to Fifth and all the way down to
8th Street, passing as it goes the luxury shops, the tourist attractions,
Rockefeller Center, the Empire State, then east on 8th back to Broadway, and south from there to West Houston, and a sharp right to its

final destination. A pit stop for the driver, a time check and chat with his dispatcher (for Ortiz, a smoke), then back uptown again, the same route in reverse. One complete revolution, like his breath is making now.

Sometimes he rides the bus all the way down to West Houston, then gets off and goes to the embarkation point and waits for the same Number 5 to pull up from where it's been resting down the block, and rides that one all the way back uptown again, completing the loop. Depending on the time of day and traffic, the full revolution can take anywhere from an hour and a half to three hours. On the last ride of the night, with the streets practically empty and only a few tired-looking nurses and short-order cooks and other rumpled laborers working the four-to-midnight shift to pick up along the way, and nobody getting off for stretches at a time, a driver can book it all the way up from West Houston to 135th in under half an hour. Carlos made it once in a record twenty-two minutes. But most times when he's made the trip down and is going back up again, he doesn't even get off, the drivers—Ortiz, for one, and Carlos, for sure, who are almost now like friends—let him stay on, maybe to save themselves the trouble of unlocking his chair and raising and lowering the platform to let him out, only to have to lower and raise it again not five minutes later, to let him back on. But there are other drivers, sticklers for the rules, who insist each time on a full disembarkation and new embarkation from the designated spot under the bus shelter a few feet further down the street, which marks the true beginning of the route.

So now, this morning, here he is, on his way downtown, the beauty of the girl filling his eyes and lungs. The door in his heart on well-oiled hinges swinging open, swinging shut, no bump, no catch, no panic, just easy in and out, like it was meant to do and hasn't done in nearly forty years.

Girl… There was a time.

He has a good view of her from where he sits. Up the aisle when it clears, then over to the right and that third sideways seat, facing in. Tall, slim body, fine, long, bare legs. He'd lay a twenty she could dance up a storm. It's been a lifetime since he danced. 1967. Last year of George Washington High. Dyonne Elliott in his arms. Back in the day, he could have taught this girl a move or two. Only she wouldn't have been born yet, not in his day, not in the days he still could dance.

Maybe she's an actress. He can definitely see her on stage, singing and dancing her heart out, iridescent black hair glistening in the lights. Dyonne Elliott was a beauty, too (probably a grandmother now). He carried her picture in his wallet. They broke up before he got sent. A good thing for her, sparing her the awkwardness of having to do it later.

Hope, they called it. Harlem's Tree of Hope. It stood in his dad's day in front of the old Lafayette Theatre at 7th Avenue and 131st. He could tell this girl about it, if she didn't already know. Actors and dancers, performance artists of various types, musicians and drummers like his dad standing beneath that elm, wishing on it to find them work. And sometimes the tree obliged. It was good to his dad, locating an ongoing gig for him with King Curtis' band right there on that stretch of 7th known as the Boulevard of Dreams. But in the summer of '34, the Park Department cut it down, needing the space to widen the avenue. So the Tree of Hope was felled, its mammoth stump left on the street, eventually to be slathered with preservatives and become something little kids with big dreams, like his dad was once, rubbed for luck. Sometime later, a piece of that tree was installed in the lobby of The Apollo Theatre. She must know about that. Maybe had even seen it, tried out for Amateur Night, and rubbed her hand across it, like everybody did before going onstage.

He remembered rice paddies and green fog and steady, soft rain. He remembered villages with sweet names and wells dug deep into their centers like hearts. He remembered dogs and chickens and wide, muddy rivers. He remembered crossing rivers at dawn and marching into mountains and wondering if he'd ever come out. He remembered his dad telling him in 1949 he could get a haircut and shave up in his neighborhood for 30 cents, and that was the year he was born, so on that day in April his dad went out and got himself a 30-cent celebratory trim. He remembered digging foxholes and shooting dogs and chickens. He remembered the names of the men, although he would not say the names of the dead, even to himself, here on this bus in this public place. Only later, at night, most nights, alone in bed, would he recite them, one by one and in the order in which they had died...right up to Pete, the last of the deaths of which he had any personal knowledge…and every time he would feel the weight in his stomach like a stone he carried for the terrible, secret shame of having survived. He remembered the fear that squeezed his gut and only loosened up a little when they were in some space they'd just cleared of the enemy and were sitting around smoking dope and telling jokes, but that never entirely let go. He remembered that fear and what it cost each of them not to show it. A lot of it he chose not to remember. But he remembered them saying it wasn't his fault about Pete, saying over and over there was nothing he could have done. Just the breaks, man. No one to blame.

Girl… There was a time.

It's a good hour still before the morning rush begins in earnest, and the aisle clears quickly. People climb aboard, pay their fare, move on. Seats for everyone. He watches how the people on the aisle on the right (right from his perspective, left as you're coming in) watch that row of singles on the left. Glancing over quickly, covetous-ly, then glancing away, as if they're afraid to be caught looking, like it might hand the idea to somebody else, and returning their eyes to whatever they'd been looking at before—the books in their laps, their watches, the view out the window, the passing city—then glancing back a moment later to reassess the situation, see if a chance might be opening up for them to make their move. Funny how when they'd first put in that row of singles nobody wanted to go near them. Too new. Too strange. Too lonely. Normal thing on a bus was two seats to a row. You had a partner, a seatmate, somebody when you were on the inside with your stop coming up you had to crawl over with your backpacks and shopping bags and briefcases and cell phones and wet umbrellas and whatever other junk you had with you that day. Somebody to shake your head about and maybe get up in the person's face over when that person was in the aisle seat and wouldn't slide in to the empty inside one, making you crawl over her or him with your bags and briefcases and wet shit dripping. Or maybe you'd think twice about getting up in the person's face—he'd seen that, too, watching from his vantage point in the back, that second thought, that reconsideration flickering across the face of the person having to do the climbing and crawling over the other one—'cause maybe the reason she…if it was a she…wouldn't slide in and just sat there, ignoring you, dead eyes dead ahead, and not even turned as far out as she might into the aisle to let you by, was that her stop was coming up, and if she did slide over, she'd just have to climb over you at the next stop with all her shopping bags and wet umbrellas and whatever else she had with her banging into your knees. Or maybe, if it was a guy, he was just plain crazy and would pull a knife and stick you with it if you asked him to move, for this was still New York, you know, lower crime stats or not.

But that's the way buses used to be on both sides of the aisle: two seats to a row. Then they put in this string of singles on the one side, and for a while, people steered clear. He watched them back then, eying those singles as they got on, keeping their distance, like maybe they were some kind of vicious new breed of animal that would jump out and bite them if they got too close. And then they caught on. Hottest seat in town. Exclusivity was in. Even guys getting on with wives wanted one. He'd seen that, too, the husband glancing over longingly at an empty single, the wife walking ahead, chatting away down the aisle, carrying on this conversation meant for him that he doesn't give two hoots about that passengers to her right and left can pick up pieces of as she passes by. "I don't know why you wore that shirt, Simon. What kind of a color is beige? And it doesn't fit either. Never did. I told you that first time you wore it. Let me give it to GoodWill. How often have I said that? But do you listen?" And the guy thinking—he can tell from the look of total boredom in his eyes—let her go ahead, find a seat in the back, I'll just take this empty single here. Then the boredom turns to regret as the husband passes by and knows he's lost his chance, knows, if he's honest, he never had a chance, for what would his fellow passengers think— even the ones, and there are a couple, who, having heard snatches of his wife's chatter, throw him looks of sympathy as he passes—if he should actually make that audacious move and plunk himself down into that empty single?

He watches them watching. He's good at watching. A skill acquired during his time on guard at night. Back then he mostly saw that green fog moving through the blackness like something alive. He watched it like he was ordered to do, watched and waited for it to come alive.

Now he watches how those on the right watch those single seats on the left and wait for them to open up. Sometimes a guy is so

anxious he makes a premature leap, moving out into the aisle before
the present occupant has fully risen from the seat. Then he has to ex-
ecute a quick retreat, hoping no one has noticed, but knowing that's
hardly likely, with him now exposed in the aisle and bent over in that
awkward, half-crouched position, his newspaper clutched up against
his genitals like with a sudden need for privacy. Others—women
were especially good at this—would spot the signs of imminent
evacuation—a passenger glancing up from her paperback, turning
toward the window to catch the number on the street sign going by,
closing the book, raising a hand to press the bell—and would time
it so exactly she'd have left her seat and arrived at the coveted single
at the precise moment its current occupant was rising from it. Then
the exchange went smoothly as a dance. One body rising, the other
descending. But sometimes two guys with their eye on the same prize
would make a move for it at once. The faster or more aggressive one
moving panther-like through open territory down the aisle and positioning himself in such a way as to lay definitive claim to his objec-
tive, forcing his opponent to back off before even getting close. The
law of the jungle in play.

Moving through that other jungle long ago, Pete ahead,
him behind, he watches how Pete proceeds with caution, taking
almost dainty steps through the foul green fog. And he thinks how
funny that is, for a guy so big to be taking such mincing steps. Funny
or not, he follows in line, stepping where Pete stepped. Then Pete
shoots up an arm and freezes. He half turns toward him. His face
in moonlight looks sick, whites of eyeballs greenish, mouth slack,
expression sheepish, like he's caught in the act of something and
wants to apologize. Pete can't correct. Whichever way he steps, he's
wrong. From where he stands behind, he stares at Pete and silently
acknowledges the situation. Not more than three feet separate them.
He knows he should go for it, grab him, pull him back, try at least.
But he can't move. He stays where he is, feeling nothing in his legs,
no connection or possibility of movement, and he thinks now it was
like his body had a premonition, his legs saying what you feel now,
this disconnection, this impossibility of movement, is what you're
going to feel forever. And then the explosion. The blast of light. The
sound. It's over in a second. Pete is dead. His legs are gone. The war's
over for them both. And later, his friends' faces, close to his, insanely

Girl... There Was A Time

large and blurry. Mayo and Toby and Delroy, their earnest voices in his ear—"Couldn't have done nothing, man." "Wasn't your fault." "Hang in, you'll be okay"—as they're loading him and Pete on the same chopper out of there.

Watching now from where he watches in the back of the bus opposite the exit door, he sees the dance of the single seat actually performed. He glances at the girl, sees she sees it, too. A woman in a black and red striped turban, seated in one of the single seats, pulls her compact from her bag, opens it, and glances at her face. (The operation itself he cannot actually see, the woman having her back to him, but he takes note of the small turnings of her head and the slight circular motions of her arm and shoulder, like she's going for her best side.) She powders her nose, drops the compact back in her bag. That's all it takes. Heads turn, eyes zero in. Then the turbaned woman lifts an arm, applies her fingers to the yellow strip of tape above her head, and even before the bell has sounded and the red notice lighted up, alerting Ortiz to the fact that a passenger wants off, a man across from and one row behind the disembarking woman juts his knees out into the aisle and angles his torso forward. At the same moment, a woman in jeans, who's been standing in front of the fine young woman with the dusky skin and lovely long legs, turns, sees the hand lifted to the yellow tape, and makes her move, stealthy and quick, across the aisle and down. The woman in the turban rises from her seat, the man swoops in from behind, but the woman in jeans, loping in from the front, has the clear advantage. She grabs the bar above her head, giving the rising woman just enough room to duck beneath her arm and turn toward the exit, coming, as she does so, face to face with the man, now preparing to swing himself forward and into her seat. No contest. The exiting woman turns into the man, allowing the woman in jeans to slide into her seat from behind her, and forcing the man, now blocking her path, to step aside, thereby forfeiting any chance he might have at the seat in contention.

He watches from where he sits in the back as the man, disgruntled to be so publicly out-played, dumps himself back into his former seat, which he's lucky to find still vacant. The fine young woman watches from where she sits in the front. She smiles, but not at him. It's a private, sweet smile, acknowledging an amusing human interaction. The corners of her shiny lips turn up, move into the slopes of her cheeks. Had that smile been directed at him, no telling what he might have done.

Girl… There was a time.

For sure he would have taken her dancing. And to concerts. He liked the Mills Brothers and the Ink Spots. He worshiped Jimi Hendrix. She'd probably be more into Mariah Carey and The Who, though he'd lay odds she would've worshiped Hendrix too.

Then the bus made its left at 72nd, turning away from the river and the Henry Hudson Parkway, and he caught a glimpse of Eleanor Roosevelt, bronzed by the slivers of light breaking through the leaves of her three protective oaks, and leaning in thought against her great granite rock. Wife of another president who took the nation into war. A war with cause, a president with brains. A man who also lacked the use of his legs.

Across to Broadway, a right there, and down the block to its stop in front of the glassed-in Indian restaurant on the corner. The doors open and now the girl is standing up, just as he'd known she would, as a white-haired woman, back so hunched her eyes can only follow the floor of the bus as she moves, climbs aboard. Quickly, gracefully, the girl extends one long arm to grasp the woman, who can't even raise her head high enough to look her in the face, by an elbow and help her into her seat.

Now the girl is coming his way. Approaching like something out of his imagination. With each step she takes down the aisle, she grows larger, more distinct, more desirable. Her eyes, he sees now, are not almond-shaped as they had appeared in the distance, but larger and nearly round, their dark, shining centers bright against their clear, white backgrounds, the thick brows neatly plucked into carefully rising and falling arcs. The swells of her breasts, issuing from the scoop of her sleeveless green T-shirt, look slightly damp. Her shoulders and upper arms are well-toned and muscular. The girl works out.

She is three rows away from him, then two. She ignores the empty seats on either side of her, so she must be moving toward the back to exit properly, through the rear door. Yes, she's still walking toward him, knees dipping slightly as she moves, and he sees she is taller than he had thought. Five seven, he estimates, or five eight. A goodly height for a girl. She holds herself erect. Like a dancer would.

She places her hand on the chrome rim of the seat before her for balance, he can see her at the practice bar, bending and straightening those shapely knees, gracefully moving an arm out and up to arch above her head.

Girl… There was a time.

Maybe back in high school. After Dyonne Elliott, before he got sent. That would've been his only time. He would have carried her picture in his wallet. Of course she wouldn't have been born yet, but he can dream, can't he? They would have gone to movies. Old, romantic ones with music. (Not so old for him, back then.) She would have liked *Singin' in the Rain* and *Porgy and Bess*. They would've had a 4th of July picnic in Riverside Park, his old orange blanket spread beneath them, fried chicken and deviled eggs, potato salad and pickles laid out to celebrate the country's birthday. "Your country thanks you for your sacrifice." They'd said that to him in the hospital, pinning the Purple Heart on his gown. *Girl,* he thinks. *Girl.* He sees they're coming up on Lincoln Center…of course, Juilliard, she is a dancer, she's on her way to class…and three people have stood up, crowding in from behind him. So when the girl gets closer to the exit, there's only room for her to stand facing him, her back to the door. She doesn't look him in the eye. People don't. They keep their eyes trained over his head, up at the ads, out the window, on anything but him. She's waiting for the bus to pull into its stop. It's a long wait. There's some sort of traffic jam ahead. She's so close he could swallow her.

Girl…There was… No, he's got to admit, there never was a time. His time for that has passed. Over at nineteen. He's eye-level to her midriff. Her skirt is short, her legs bare. He breathes her in. It's not the blood of the battlefield he smells, but a different blood. He remembers it, musky, viscous, a slightly sweet yet pungent scent. Dyonne Elliott wouldn't let him do it then. He draws it down into his lungs and thanks the girl for the second chance. Would this lovely young woman with the perfect white smile perform one day at the Apollo Theater? Would she rub the stump of the Tree of Hope before going on stage? Would she reach out now and rub his stumps and thank him, as she passes by, for his sacrifice?

The traffic jam clears. Ortiz maneuvers his vehicle into its stop. The rear door swings open, becoming two doors, or one split down the middle, both halves swinging freely, easily, like the valve on its hinges in his heart. A shaft of light floods the back of the bus. The passengers in front of her disembark, leaving room for the girl to turn from him toward the door, and as she swings around, a gust of air sends all the perfumes of her body into his face. The physical aroma of her being wraps around him like layers of mist. Layer after layer of pungent, musky scents, each giving way to the next as she takes a step and then another, moving past him and closer to the door. And in the light that pours now through the parting in that wide-open door, dance particles of life, molecules of living organisms, sloughing off from her body and settling onto his.

He surveys her long, straight back as she descends into the stairwell. Stepping down onto the curb, the girl turns and holds the door, as he knew she would, for the person behind. He sees her face one last time, then her back again, and she merges with the city.

He sits and waits for the bus to start up again. He thinks today he'll ride it all the way down to West Houston, then get off there and wait awhile before taking another Number 5 back uptown. He knows Ortiz wouldn't make him get off. Ortiz would let him stay where he was, would even come back and chat with him a while… telling him stories about his village and making the sign of the cross as he does in remembrance of his grandmother…before getting off himself for a smoke and a chat with his dispatcher, then getting back on, switching the routing sign overhead, revving up his engine, and moving his bus to its official embarkation point a few feet further down the block. But today he decides it would be good to actually get off and take in the air, still breathing easy as he was, and wheel himself down to the bus stop under the shelter those few feet further on, and wait there—surprising Ortiz by signaling him to pass him by—no matter how long it took (and with this particular bus it's bound to take a while) for another Number 5 to come along, then board that one and ride it all the way back uptown, completing the loop in reverse.

The Piano Room

The piano room, caretaker of her husband's spirit, had attached itself to his body like a carapace, running from the back of his neck down his spine and continuing along his arms and legs, making it impossible for her ever to think of the two of them, man and room, apart.

"Come in, Jenny," he'd say. "You're welcome."

Happily, she'd accept his invitation, enter the room, take her seat. The small armchair with the peach satin back positioned just off to his right and slightly behind so as to be out of his direct line of vision.

"Your pleasure, my dear?"

"Some Brahms, I think. No, Chopin."

Today silence, not her husband, welcomes her. As she takes her seat in the peach satin armchair to the right of his Chickering baby grand, silence runs up her back and arranges itself like a hat on her head. Silence scampers across the hardwood floor and nestles between her toes. Silence hovers over the picture frames above her head and casts its shadow down from the Venetian chandelier.

The bench where her husband had sat and in which he had kept his music—the music still there piled high beneath the lid—is pulled away from the keyboard as he had pulled it away, just far enough to give a tall man's knees the room they require.

Your pleasure, my dear?

The hard straight lines of the bench are at odds with the gentle sweep of the piano, that generous curve that draws in near the center as if taking in breath and bellows out again, round and full, at its extremity.

Some Brahms, I think. No, Chopin.

Silence clutches at her stomach and hollows her heart. Silence sweeps through her hair and creates an ache behind her teeth. Silence, like a suicide from a bridge, sails from an arm of the chandelier, grabbing at dangling crystal pendants along the way as if, reconsidering, to break its fall.

All the music that has been played in this room over the years laps against the wainscoting like a muted tide. All the Beethoven and Brahms, all the Mozart and Chopin, all the Rachmaninoff and Tchaikovsky, the Debussy and Ravel, all the Romantics who spoke to his soul. Music is interred in the walls as he is now interred. To all the rest, their twenty-five-year marriage, their days of reaching out and drawing back, their nighttime bouts of passion, their sleeping and waking in each other's arms, their dreams of tomorrow, silence speaks. Like something floating in a dream, her life has slipped away. Only in sleep, half-sleep, memory, fantasy does she have it back.

A French bistro on third avenue. A table in the corner. Empty water glasses long forgotten by their server. Her secret wish for the server to go on forgetting the glasses, forgetting them. Clutching her husband's hand across that table, or in a movie theatre in the dark. A whiff of whiskey on his breath. *My Jenny. My sweet.* The feel of his corduroy trousers, that musky smell near the crotch. In dreams, in reveries, she has it back. A ride in the Alpha Romeo down the eastern coast of Italy. The ferry at Brindisi. Swimming in the Aegean. White beach, golden sun, nighttime stars. The earth, his face.

I have known that. I have lived.

Her husband, her son, the three of them together. It was her life. It cohered. Her husband and herself alone, the boy now a man on his own, still it cohered. Then that first day of silence, then the next and the next, and the weeks and months that followed. All that she took to be herself, her life, slipping off to one side like a train onto a siding. Not far, just far enough so as to no longer cohere.

Wisp of a girl. My girl. My wisp.

Hardly that after twenty-five years, though she still has the small and shapely body. Still herself yet without him, not. Existing in a universe not fully hers but one that runs for miles, never inter-secting with her own but contiguous to it and in most aspects related. A parallel universe. A person both herself and not, living side by side in her apartment, wandering through rooms she recognizes but whose exact purposes, if asked, she could only guess at. A breakfast room for having breakfast in? Had they actually done that? Bacon

and eggs on that glass table? A piano room for absorbing silence?
Was that even sensible? She goes about, or someone very like herself
goes about carrying out small domestic tasks whose precise meanings
escape her. Watering plants, pulling sheets taut at the corners, dusting
shelves, going round and round the sink with a sponge. Who could
say why? Herself, yet not herself doing that. A double always by her
side and, like the peach satin armchair positioned just to her husband's right and slightly behind, out of his direct line of vision.

Left! She'd been left?

Clearly, a mistake has been made. A mistake so ruinous as
now to be beyond rectification.

But it is the morning of another day. Ten months have passed since
the day of silence. Or is it a year? She must dress, shower, do her
hair, her face. A year already? Ten months? A thin black stroke
on the upper eyelid, another on the lower. Leaning in close to the
mirror, angling her head to get closer still. Raising the pencil, making
the marks. Stretching the skin taut at the corners to keep the lines
straight. Her eyes in the glass peer at themselves. Her eyes? Hers? So
heavy lidded and with that startled, uneasy look?

She goes to the closet, opens the door, stands and stares.
Flashes of her husband, already his features are fading, staring, stymied, befuddled, before a hastily opened refrigerator. Snatched open,
she'd always thought, recalling his attack on the handle, his way of
flinging open the refrigerator as if to catch its contents by surprise.
Instead he'd been the one surprised, affronted, actually, finding nothing among all the foodstuffs within to satisfy cravings only seconds
earlier intense, now strangely diminished. There he was, left to stand
at the door, a befuddled, stymied look on his face.

Left! As she was left?

She surveys the clothes hanging in the closet. Something
casual would be her preference. Slacks and a T-shirt, even jeans. She
still has the figure for them. *Wisp of a girl. My girl. My wisp.* But a suit
is more suitable, and a silk blouse.

She is meeting another man for lunch. He will take her some
place upscale, and she must dress accordingly. They are meeting at
his office. Offices are not her natural habitat. Law clerks, partners,

third-year associates scurrying about. People confined to stations, desks, cubicles, working at the behest of some abstraction. A corporation, a company, or, as in Leland's case, a firm. Voices buzz in a language she doesn't recognize, go silent mid-sentence, mouths continuing to move. No sounds emerging. She doesn't know where to put her arms, what to do with her hands. For twenty-five years her hands were a wife's hands, a mother's hands, working of their own accord, competently managing everything that came their way. But in an office they hang limply by her sides.

Never had she craved a career. *You could if you wanted to, Jenny. You could do anything you set your mind to.* But she had her husband, her son, her home. Why would she want anything else?

She'd met Leland by chance in the confusion of his office several months ago, several months after her husband had left her. *Left her? Had he?* Her husband? No, that was the mistake. She could do anything she set her mind to, he'd said so himself. Why would a man leave a woman like that? "As his widow you are the beneficiary." Widow? Beneficiary? Was that the role she was now to play, this the suit her character was to wear? She didn't belong in that category or in this place. She must get home. She'd find him there, seated before his piano. Eyes brown. No, hazel. Chin a little rounded. No, pointed. Yes, pointed, she was sure. Long legs, she knew for a fact. His features blurred. She put her hand to her mouth. She would not scream. She'd act her part.

She'd gone to the firm those months ago—they called it that, the firm—about some trivial but essential, they'd insisted, detail requiring her presence and having to do with probate. *Probate?* What did that have to do with her? And in the confusion of the glass and the glare from the windows along the corridor, she'd lost track of the young woman in the pale gray woolen suit who had been sent to fetch her from reception and whom she was meant to follow without detouring or dawdling. And she really didn't think she had dawdled or detoured, although the young woman in the gray suit kept up a brisk pace. But perhaps she had, thrown off as she was by the glare. Perhaps she'd taken a wrong turn, gone left when she should have gone right, for suddenly she'd looked up and the woman she'd been following was nowhere to be seen, and she was in a part of the firm that seemed to

have veered off from the corridor and become suddenly more popu-
lous.

"Lost?" he'd asked.

Later, she would learn his name was Leland.

At the time she was aware only of a large frame, crinkly blue
eyes, an affable smile.

"Stupid of me."

"Not at all."

He'd directed her to the office she required and, after her
business there was concluded, had appeared coincidentally, for surely
it must have been a coincidence, at her side as she was waiting for the
elevator doors to open.

"Hello again."

Again, the crinkly blue eyes, the affable smile. And the large
frame, certainly she was aware of that, though not so much of the
space he filled as of a space he didn't fill but seemed to yearn to,
reaching out with his very pores and breath, his body almost physically expanding, but stopping short of touching her.

Ten months, or is it a year? The Venetian chandelier overhead, the
Chickering baby grand beneath. The peach satin armchair out of
his direct line of vision. She takes her seat, closes her eyes. Images of
Paris, the city of their son's conception, flicker as in a silent film on the
backs of her eyelids. Narrow cobblestone streets. Red shoes. Ridiculously high heels. His arm in hers. *Steady, Jenny.* Nineteen, a little tipsy,
and insanely in love.

Now, today. Leland taking her to lunch.

"My office. At one."

Hence the suitable suit. The silk blouse. She will not embar-
rass him in front of his colleagues.

Come in, Jenny. You're welcome.

She enters the room, takes a seat opposite him on the other side of the
imposing mahogany desk. From the window at his back, light streams
in, impairing her vision. She might be in a physician's office, awaiting
a diagnosis. Life or death? She holds her breath, prepared to bargain.

"You're looking lovely."

Life. She smiles, releases her breath.

"I'm just finishing up." Leland reaches for a pen.

He has told her about the case. A fifty-eight-year-old man, having spent twenty years in prison for a murder he almost certainly did not commit, has made a bargain for his freedom. The man on the other side of the imposing desk—the man with whom she is going to lunch—has picked up this other man's file and entered his life. For seven years now, he has stood by the man behind bars, pursuing *pro bono* every angle, following every lead, and in the end he has almost but not quite proved—"How could I, beyond all doubt?", evidence having gone missing over the years, witnesses having died—that the man has in fact not committed the crime. Plead guilty and walk free, he advises his client. The man takes the deal. The gates open. The man walks out.

"One more signature, and I'm done."

Into the air, a free man. Twenty years of his life gone, but free.

Leland turns the pen in his fingers, affixes his signature.

How could anything ever be proved beyond all doubt?

What she knows of Leland's life, can attest to with her own eyes—not the knowledge he has unhesitantly supplied of the wife and three children and golden retriever in Westchester—is this: the mahogany desk at which he sits, the window behind, the light streaming in. She raises her hand to shield her eyes. He puts down his pen, arranges his papers in a pile to his left. As he rises from his chair, his large body comes up before the window like a blind that lifts from below. The light is momentarily obliterated. He moves around his desk, takes her arm.

Her heels had wobbled on the cobblestones. The street was narrow and short. *Rue d'Hiver.* It didn't lead anywhere. Curving past the café and ending in a cul-de-sac. They'd circled back, followed a street with an altogether different name. A name she couldn't now remember. Red shoes. Ridiculously high heels. Nineteen, a little tipsy, and insanely in love. He'd taken her arm. *Steady, Jenny.* Slipping his hand high up between her breast and bicep. He gave a little squeeze. She answered with the pressure of her breast. That night their son was conceived.

"We're off," Leland says. "Where to?"

"You tell me."

She knows he has already chosen the place, made reservations, or his assistant has. Some place close.

Your pleasure, my dear?

She'd like to linger over lunch, have another glass of wine, but she understands that won't be possible if they're to make time for the hideaway.

"I'm a working man, you know."

They have been dating for nine months. Not dating exactly. Lunches, dinners. Regular retreats to the *pied-á-terre* his firm leases for the use of its out-of-town clients and those suburb-residing partners who must spend an occasional night in town. "Our hideaway," he calls it. No movies or museums. Just eating and hiding away. As if one led organically to the other: the intake of food for energy, the release of that energy. It happened almost without her knowledge, that slide into the parallel life, not hers exactly, but one running directly alongside. A glittering surface underfoot slick as ice, and there she was. Cardboard shapes sprang up around her. Life-sized replicas of the places they frequented—firm, restaurant, *pied-á-terre*. Stage sets to be demolished the moment they left, reconstructed instants before they returned.

Nine months of this, was it, with the working man?

"I've worked," she says, out of the blue. Her voice high-pitched and trembly. Not a voice that is her own. "You think raising a child, staying with a man for twenty-five years, isn't work?"

Surprise spreads over his face like a rash.

"Jenny, I didn't mean----,"

"No, of course not." She knows he didn't. No more than did she. The statement was altogether without meaning. She's embarrassed, doesn't know why she made it. The only explanation is she didn't. Not her. The person who walks by her side, sits in chairs alongside hers, uses a high-pitched, trembly voice, is the person who made that statement.

"Come," he says, and places his large hand over hers. Immediately she rises from the table. Always, he can bring her back to herself with a touch, or close to what she imagines is herself.

The *pied-à-terre* comprises a floor-through on the second floor of a brownstone on East 53rd Street, not far from Leland's office. The windows open to the humming sounds of traffic. By day the sounds are insistent, urgent, a barrage of blaring horns, occasionally accompanied by shouts from an irate driver. *Come on, move it will you? What's the hold up?* At night—those rare nights when Leland, having made the excuse of a work session that was certain to go late or an early-morning court date, can get away and spend the night—the sounds are softer, more mysterious. Though sometimes loud enough to jolt her awake as when the quiet is punctured by the wail of a police or ambulance siren. They never meet anyone on the stairs, going up or coming down. Nine months now and no encounter on the stairs? But of course there wouldn't be. It is a stage set, a cardboard façade, not an actual brownstone with actual people living in it.

I'll never leave you. She and her husband had promised that to one another. The promise had been broken, and allowances had to be made for her adjustment to the breaking. But the more time went on and the more she thought about it, the more she came to realize that it could not have been the man who sat at his piano and daily welcomed her who had left her, but some other man entirely. Some man whose features had all but faded now.

The attraction she feels for Leland is powerful enough to make her dress in a suit that is not entirely to her taste and to buy two others like it, so as to present the proper picture when she meets him at his office. The money she was left in the will and from the life insurance—*Left? Life insurance? Will?* Herself a *widow?*—provided her with sufficient funds to have any life she might desire and to buy whatever clothes would best complement that life.

With Leland, lovemaking is conducted almost entirely in silence. It is raw. Pure appetite, performed in a fever of desire. A fever, yes. She must be ill, out of her mind. Possibly hallucinating. Certainly, she isn't herself. Some other woman is reaching her arms across this man's broad, sweating back, opening her legs wide, so wide, sliding her hands down his buttocks to force him in. She herself, her real self, could never, would never behave in such a fashion. But how can she know for sure? Even now, this instant, in the midst of it, there is no way to prove beyond all doubt that she in not the woman doing this.

My girl. My wisp.

She stiffens in his arms and lifts her head as if at a sound in the next room.

"What's wrong?"

"Nothing," she replies, and there is nothing. Something seemed off, that's all. She lets her body relax and returns her head to the curve of his arm.

"That man," she said one evening, as they sat on the edge of the bed taking off their clothes in the *pied-á-terre*. "The one you represented *pro bono*."

"I've done more than one." Leland placed his ankle across his knee and untied the laces of one shoe.

"The one given life for murder. You got him out after twenty years. You told him to plead guilty and you'd get him out."

"Ah, that one." Leland let his shoe drop onto the floor and then, his sock.

"Either way, in prison or out," she went on. "His life didn't fit him. Twenty years in prison, living the life of a convict, knowing he was innocent. Released from prison, living as though innocent with the whole world, or most of it, anyway, thinking him guilty." She removed her shoes and stood up to take off her jacket. "His life could never fit him again." She took off her jacket and after it, her blouse and bra, skirt and half-slip. "People who remember the crime, the brutality of it…the young girl, fifteen at the time----,"

"Sixteen." Leland had removed his other shoe and sock, his shirt and trousers.

'Sixteen. Raped repeatedly, stabbed forty times…that made it personal. The police said so, you told me. Forty stab wounds made it personal. Probably someone who knew the girl or knew her family, had a grudge, and your client didn't----,"

"That pointed to his innocence. He had no motive."

She hung her suit and blouse in the closet and sat back down on the bed to take off her pantyhose.

"Presumed innocent. Still, people think he's guilty. The girl's sixty-nine-year-old mother, she thinks he's guilty. Not thinks. *Knows*. Knows in her heart he's the violent sex offender who raped and mutilated her sixteen-year-old daughter. A guilty man walking free. Wherever he goes, even though he's out and to all appearances innocent, the guilty man, the murderer, walks beside him. He'll never be free of him."

"Jenny----?"

She was naked now. They both were, sitting side by side on the bed. "For his whole life, for as long as he lives, his life won't fit him." She didn't know what she was trying to say. That other woman, speaking in that high-pitched, trembly voice, was taking her over. "It's like he's been cleaved in two. The two halves walk side by side down the street, but they'll never cohere. For the rest of his life he'll try to make them cohere but won't be able to." She felt dazed, disoriented. She thought she must be incoherent. "His life won't ever fit him again. You told him to do it. 'Plead guilty,' you told him. 'Plead guilty and walk free.'"

"Because I believed and still believe----,"

She leaned over and covered his mouth with her hand. She didn't want to enter into any discussion of what he believed, what his personal ideology might be. The man's life would never fit him again, that's all she knew for certain. She passed the hand that was not covering Leland's mouth over his chest. His broad, sweaty chest opened like a landscape before her. Little tufts of black hair swirled like bushes in that landscape that went on opening and opening before her as she moved her hand across it. After a moment, she brought her other hand down from his mouth, freeing him then to speak if he chose, to tell her what he believed and still believes, what rules or code he lived by. But Leland didn't speak. He simply drew her down onto the bed and held her against him and allowed her to pass her hands back and forth across his chest and over his shoulders and up and down his arms that felt like tree trunks to her, and around his back as far as she could reach, which, because of his size, wasn't very far, but she tried, she reached her arms as far as they would go and moved her hands over as much of his back as she could, kneading and caressing his flesh with her fingers, clawing her fingertips along his skin to move them an inch, a fraction of an inch further onto his back, to take in as much of him as she could, for she loved him, yes, she loved him, and he loved her, of that she felt certain, for he had told her so and she believed him. Why shouldn't she believe him, even though she couldn't prove what he said? For how was anything ever to be proved? Certainly not beyond all doubt, and she understood, despite the wife and three children and golden retriever in Westchester, there were vast places on her lover's large frame that had never been and never could be touched.

As usually happened after lovemaking, she returned a little to herself.

"It's like with that blond actress who plays that woman with cancer on TV," she said. "You ever watch that? Millions of people across America want her to die." She turned on her side and pressed her cheek to Leland's chest. She had to raise her head a little so she could speak, but she kept one arm stretched across his chest. "The viewers with cancer. They're the ones who want her to die They go on week by week, episode by episode, hoping to see her sink closer and closer to death. They want her to have her pain because it's their pain. They want her to have her tortuous treatments because those are the treatments they endure." She kept reaching out her fingertips, kneading his flesh, taking in as much of him as she could. "They want her to teach them how to die. They watch, hoping to find some comfort, some peace in dying through her death. And then, last week, she goes into remission. You see that one? It seems she will re-cover. Not be cured, but live. And they would kill her now with their own hands, for she has betrayed them. They have loved her, wished for her death, but she went into remission and left them behind. *Left them!* They hate her now."

But who is she to Leland? He to her? A petite, slender wom-an, nearly forty-six years old, but with a figure that still looks good in jeans and tight sweaters. And he, a large man, six-one or –two, one hundred ninety pounds, she estimates, with vast reaches of needy flesh, flesh she loves to gather in her fingers, knead and tend, a man several years her senior, five or ten, she'd never asked, not wanting to seem nosy, intrusive. *Intrusive?* But was he not her lover? Did they not come here to this *pied-à-terre*, their hideaway, he called it, several times a month, sometimes as many as eight in one month, and had they not been doing that for nine months now, long enough to fall in love, and did they not take off their clothes, each of them wearing business suits, as was required, and hang them, careful to leave nothing of themselves behind, neatly in the closet where no other clothes hung and none would remain after they had gone?

When he left her, as he would, to return his full attention to the wife and three children and golden retriever in Westchester—"Yes, I knew," she would say when he protested that he had never implied anything differently, that she knew it would come to an end, "I knew," she would say, for of course that was true, she knew like any story in any book, any play on any stage, it would come to an end—she would have her memories of all that had transpired between them to do with what she liked. The façade of the brownstone on East 53rd Street, the staircase on which they never encountered a single other living human being, the upscale restaurants, the suits not to her liking worn like costumes, the mahogany desk, the light streaming in. The memories would be hers. But even now, before they had become memories, even while she and Leland were eating in restaurants and undressing in the *pied-á-terre*, hanging their clothes in the closet and making raw and mostly silent love, their actions, even while being performed, were fading from her eyes. More and more she felt she was not an actor in the play on the stage before her, but a member of the audience seated beyond the stage lights, holding her breath, rapt with curiosity as to what might happen next, and even as she sat there watching and breathless, awaiting the resolution, the lights began to dim and went on dimming until the stage fell into blackness and nothing of the action could be seen.

She takes her seat beneath the Venetian chandelier in the peach satin armchair positioned just to his right and slightly behind, so as to be out of his direct line of vision. Silence surges from the floorboards and up through the soles of her feet. She seems to remember having been happy in this room, that this was a room in which she had always been welcome. Silence cuts across her flesh and mixes with the marrow of her bones. She lifts her fingers from the arm of the chair, and someone grips them hard in his, someone who never in all his life would walk out of a room and leave her behind.

                                                      The Piano Room

Nina's Man

"No," she said. "There isn't anyone."

He wanted to believe her but, then, why?

There must be someone. Why else would she be doing this? Yet she said no, there wasn't. It made no sense to him. They were happy, he thought they were. Not often, but occasionally he would ask—*We're happy, aren't we?* And always she would answer: *Yes, of course we are.* Knowing that she never lied, still he wondered. Why then, would she be leaving?

"I'll straighten up before I go," she said.

"No," he protested. "I don't want that."

"Please," she said. "Let me."

He watched her do it. Empty wine glasses swept off the table, dirty dishes cleared and washed. Crumbs collected in a napkin, napkin thrown into the trash. Potted plants lifted from the bookshelves, watered and put back again. Like a stage set of their lives being struck and set once more. She ran the vacuum, put the garbage out. She changed the sheets. Clive especially didn't want that. He wanted the sheets to remain as they were, captors of their bodies' aroma, given back to him at night.

Before she came to live with him, he'd made a special trip (*an excursion*, he called it) to show her his brownstone on Manhattan's Upper West Side. An introduction, pending her approval, to their future life.

"I'd like it to be a villa for you," he said. "A palace. A mansion."

Nina smiled and thanked him. She had a lovely, gentle smile. She never forgot to thank him.

"It will be a wonderful place to live," she declared. Her voice youthful, excited.

They were together for two years. The first time he touched her, he told her he loved her. It was too soon to say it, but he realized the minute the words flew out of his mouth it was already true. And too late to hold them back. He'd embarrassed her and was sorry for that. She flushed and looked away. She was young, vulnerable, she was shy. He tried to think of something else to say. Something that wouldn't add to her embarrassment. "How about a walk?" was all he could come up with. "The air will do us good." As if there were something wrong with them, something the air could heal.

Every now and then on that walk he glanced down at his shoes, shooting out shiny and bright beneath him. He took pride in their shine. Pride in himself for taking a cloth to them, polishing and buffing every morning, as was his custom. Pride that they accompanied the woman (*girl*, really) he loved.

He remembered how she hooked her arm through his. How the heat of her flesh radiated through his body. He remembered her beauty, how astonishing it was (*mesmerizing.*) He remembered her youth, the twinkle in her eyes (which were hazel), the curve of her mouth (which was gentle). Never did her youth or her beauty fail to astonish him. Never in all the two years they were together. *The best of his life.*

She was a slight thing, slender, standing no more than five-foot-two. Blond hair, curly, falling to her shoulders. Hazel eyes. Intelligent eyes. Intelligent face. With her on his arm he doubled in size. His hands grown large would part the world for her. His arms like tree trunks would hold back its terrors. He would love and protect her for the rest of his life. But then she said she had to leave.

"But why?" he asked, his voice cracking. "Why if there's no one?"

"There isn't," she said again.

"Then tell me why."

"Don't worry," she answered. "I'll be all right."

"Where will you go?"

She didn't say.

Again, he told her he loved her.

"I know," she whispered, and caressed his cheek with the back of her hand.

Already she had packed a bag.

He told her he had never loved anyone else.

"I know," she said again, her voice now almost inaudible.

　　　　　　　　　　　　　　　　　　　　　　　　　　Nina's Man

She smiled her gentle smile.

She told him she loved him back, and he took her at her word. A quiver went through him like sparks flying, hearing her say it. She hadn't said it often in two years. Shyness or youth, or both, holding her back. But each time she said it, he was humbled by her youth, shamed by her shyness. Her reticence was like the lightest of coverings—a silk shawl or featherweight scarf—thrown over her thoughts and feelings, which every now and then she would let drop, allowing him the awesome privilege of seeing what lay beneath.

It had been early November (an unusually cold month), just over two years ago (two years and two months) when she first wandered into his bookshop. He looked up and saw her there by the door. She clapped her mittens, white and woolly, before her face to banish the cold. Like a child, he thought. A precocious child, come in to examine the books. He watched her stuff her mittens into the pockets of her big down jacket. Watched her pull off her woolen cap and let the torrent of curly blond hair fall loose. It was so bright that hair, it might have been sunlight itself streaming through the window. He watched her leaning over the table where the featured art books were laid out. Watched how she paused over some, how carefully she turned the pages. A child with an interest in art. A precocious child, mesmerizingly beautiful. At once he wanted to guide and protect her. To teach and shape, as he taught and shaped the students at the night school he met with three evenings a week. Then not a child at all, he realized, nor even an adolescent. But a young woman, astonishingly young, no more than twenty, who had dropped in off the street to capsize his world. He waved his best salesclerk aside (he had three, all young), tightened the knot in his blue and white striped tie, and hurried to attend to her himself. Clumsily, he pointed out what was on display.

"Barbara Kruger," he said, as if she couldn't see for herself. "She has an exhibit at the Hirschhorn in Washington," he volunteered, as if she'd asked. He stopped himself short of offering to take her there at once, which was his immediate impulse, no matter they were in New York City and the exhibit in D.C.

He stepped forward, pulled back. "I'll let you browse on your own," he said, sensing that was what she preferred. She looked up and smiled her gentle smile, and again came his longing to guide and protect, to teach and shape.

He moved away from her then, tended to other customers. But always she was in his line of sight, as if that was already where she belonged—within the confines of his vision, the contours of his heart.

A few days later she came through the door again and he didn't hesitate. Seeing her examine the Lee Krasner book with such respect, he went up to her and impulsively offered it as a gift.

"Oh, no, I couldn't….," she began.

"My pleasure," he said. "I insist."

Her name was Nina. Clive told her his. Two days later she came into his shop again. This time just before closing. They talked. She stole his heart. She was an art student. Of course. A graduate student at NYU. How wonderful was that. He locked up early (a thing he never did) and took her to MOMA. A few days later, to the Whitney. Subsequently, to a prodigious number of uptown and downtown galleries. He took her to dinner and to the movies. They went skating in Central Park. He led her on the excursion to view his brownstone on the Upper West Side, and when at last she agreed to come and live with him, he knew he would never ask for anything more in his life.

Her parents, naturally, disapproved. He was too old, too set in his ways. They didn't say it to his face, but his age turned them against him. How could it not? He was forty; she was twenty-one. He was stodgy. She had never even had a serious boyfriend, so far as her mother or father knew.

"I love her with all my heart," he freely admitted. "She'll never want for anything."

They appreciated that, they said, but still the age difference was there.

It stood between him and his love like a separate person. A younger person. Looser, less encumbered. A man just starting out. A cooler, less stodgy, more suitable man her parents might approve. A man the right age to ask for her hand. Nina's man was how he came to think of him, that younger, cooler, less stodgy, more suitable man.

Every day of the two years they were together Nina's man was there between them. He was there when they spoke about art and music, Clive naming his favorites in each field, his twenty-one-year-old lover naming artists she admired, and he had never heard of. He was there, Nina's man, between them when they stood on line before movie theaters, she excited to see some new abstract French film, he fearing he wouldn't understand it. Not the language of course, that was a given, but the esoteric references. He was there, that man, while they waited in restaurants to be seated; and when finally shown to a table, he was there, causing Clive to feel the younger man's insecurity about the menu and the wine list. He was there, that man—*Nina's man*—wedged between them when they walked down the street, each with a hand in the other's back pocket (a thing Clive himself would never do). He was there, that man, with them in bed at night, enjoying Nina's loveliness and abandon.

When she left he was bereft. His world depleted, the sun extinguished, the birds gone silent. He grieved for her. He grieved for himself and for that younger, cooler, more suitable man he longed to be.

She left her keys on the hall table. The key to the outside door, the key to their apartment. He couldn't bear to see them lying there alone, exposed, the light glinting off them as it streamed through the window. He shoved them into a table drawer and tried to forget she had ever left them. Had ever left him. He got up in the mornings, shined his shoes, went to work. He took to unfairly criticizing his salesclerks, accusing them of sloppiness and inattention to detail.

"The edges don't line up," he snapped. "The Arbus needs more light."

He couldn't stop watching the door. He knew she wouldn't come through, but still he watched.

Eventually, he went to her friends, the ones she had mentioned and whose names and addresses he knew.

"Have any idea where she might be?"

They told him they did not.

"When did you see her last?"

They told him it was a day or two days or a week before.

"Did she talk about me? Did she tell you about us?"

They were the wrong questions. He took the wrong tone. He sounded like a homicide detective investigating a case. No one would give him information when he came on like that. He tried to ask easier questions, take a different tone. He tried to be a different man, that cooler, younger, more suitable man her parents might approve.

Her friends looked at him as if he were from another planet. Some of them, taking pity, asked him in. He sat in their chairs, drank their coffee, had a beer with the few who offered. Soon he ran out of her friends to ask for help.

Preposterously then, and in sheer desperation, he went to his ex-wife Meg whom he hadn't seen in ten years. Although he'd meant to, he had never told Nina about his marriage. Somehow in all the two years they were together he had never found a time that seemed right. The marriage had been loveless and brief—less by half the time he and Nina were together. Meg was now married to someone else. *Happily,* she said pointedly. A man named Marty.

"We get along great," she informed him.

"Nina was my life," he told her.

Meg rolled her eyes and lit a cigarette.

"Marty got a promotion. We're taking a cruise."

He nodded.

"To Norway, next December. To see the Northern Lights."

"That's nice."

"It's the best time to go. Driest in December. The aurora borealis likes it best when it's dry."

How like her to know that. The best time to go, what the aurora borealis likes. He had never been to Norway, yet he pictured the cold and the snow and the dark, impenetrable sky, the sudden illumination of stars. Standing at the edge of the world. A good place for Meg, he thought. And for himself, too, now that he was alone.

"Sorry to disturb you," he said.

She looked at his shoes. "Still polishing, I see."

Late one evening, he took the train to Queens, where Nina's parents lived. He knew she wouldn't be there.

"I'm sorry," her mother said. "She's not here."

They knew where she was, although they wouldn't say. For Nina would have been sure to tell them, not wanting them to worry.

"I'm sorry," her father said.

"We never fought," Clive replied.

"So she said," her mother answered.

"I know you didn't approve… the age difference and all."

"There was that," her father said.

"You were good to her," her mother added kindly. "She said that."

"I've been to her friends. They say they don't know."

"Don't worry," her father advised, also kindly. "She'll be all right."

It was a kindness on his part to offer the advice, and in the rise and fall of his voice Clive heard the echo of Nina's own, assuring him she'd be all right.

Seated on the Number 7 riding back to Manhattan, he thought again about the possibility of there being someone else in Nina's life. Given her youth, her beauty, her keen intelligence, it would make sense for there to be. Knowing Nina never lied, he thought she might have lied about that. A kindness to him, she would have deemed it, wanting to spare his feelings. An inherited trait, no doubt, for kindness seemed a family feature.

In the rocking of the train, Clive shut his eyes and fell asleep. The person he wasn't but longed to be—that younger, cooler, more suitable man—came and sat next to him. He turned in his sleep to confront the man, then opened his eyes and found the man physically there. Shaved head, piercings in his nose and along the rim of one ear. Black leather jacket, pushed-up sleeves, masses of tattoos boldly visible on his arms.

"Nice tats," Clive said. A thing he himself would never say.

"Thanks, man," the fellow replied.

Man. He'd never think to use that form of address.

The person next to him opened his mouth and yawned.

In the cavern of his yawn, colored lights played and eons fell away. Clive nodded off again and in his sleep reached out to grasp that elusive man. Almost he had him by the shoulders and was holding him in the way one holds a friend one hasn't seen in ages and fears may never see again. The train took a lurch, his body jerked from side to side, and he opened his eyes. The seat next to him was empty, and the train now was elevated, soaring along beneath a cloudless night sky. City lights played around him as the Northern Lights might play, were he in Norway to see them. And for a moment he thought he might be in Norway or Tokyo or Buenos Aires or any place else on earth where he might be that person he longed to be.

The sky vanished altogether then, and the train plunged into darkness. It would take him through the tunnel first to Grand Central, then circling round, back to Times Square. It was at Times Square where he had that evening, in what seemed now a lifetime ago, boarded a train to question parents in Queens about the whereabouts of the only woman he would ever love.

He walked uptown from 42nd Street. It was after midnight, almost one. Despite the hour, the streets around Times Square were bustling. Young people, boisterous, some drunk, were coming and going to and from restaurants and bars. A laughing young couple, oblivious to others on the street, burst from a corner bar and nearly bumped into him.

"Watch where you're going," Clive snapped.

"Whatever," the young man replied, and the woman gave him the finger.

It was startling, that finger, but especially that word: *Whatever.* He'd never think to reply to a comment with a word like that.

At 72nd Street, clusters of people, blindly hurrying, entering and exiting the subway station, crossing and crisscrossing, came near to colliding (but never quite). Further north, the streets progressively quieted and emptied block by block, and the people all but disappeared. He came upon a giant pile of leaves the sanitation men had yet to haul away. Instead of drawing back his foot and kicking it to make the leaves fly up and scatter, as a younger man might—as Nina's man might—he was careful to walk around the pile as a man of his age would do. An established man, a stodgy man, set in his ways. A man who religiously polished and buffed his shoes. A man who owned a bookstore specializing in art. A man who taught night school and longed to teach a certain young (very young) woman as he taught his students about the art in those books and the people who had made it. A man who had never found the right time to reveal a marriage, but who would willingly now, even eagerly, shout it from the rooftops if it would bring that young woman back to him. Give him another chance. He cried out at night for another chance. He would never ask anything more of her as long as he lived if only she'd return. He'd express boundless, joyful gratitude, offer marriage. Why hadn't he done so before? He should have, he knew, and often thought of doing so, but had never found a time that was right. Was that the reason she had left? *Come back, Nina! Please. Come back.* He would fall on one knee, beg her to accept his proposal, swear to be loyal and faithful forever, swear never to leave her. For that's the kind of man he was, constant and faithful, loyal and trustworthy. He swore it to her on his life. *I'll never leave you, Nina. Never.*

By the time he got home he was crying. He went into their bedroom (always he would think of it as theirs) and shut the door. He slid down the wall and sat on the floor with his knees pulled up to his chest and his head on his knees. Somewhere above him a window opened in the brownstone then almost immediately slammed shut. The silence of the night was pierced once by the shriek of a police siren, moments later by the wail of an ambulance.

That he had never loved his wife, that it was loneliness that brought them together was why his life with Nina would be different. The difference lay in love. In the single, unhappy year of his marriage he had learned how gaps open up when love isn't present, how inadequate are the attempts to bring civility and simple common decency to fill those gaps. With Nina there would never be such gaps, never a need to make attempts to fill them. With Nina there would be love. *Always, Nina. Now and forever.* Tears streamed down his face and collected in the fabric of his trousers. He told her all but love was meaningless. He told her when love is lacking the gaps that open can't be filled. Civility won't fill them; simple common decency won't fill them. *Only love, Nina. Only love will do.* And they had that already. It wasn't something they'd have to struggle to attain. She knew that, she did. So why had she done this? *Why had she left?*

He lifted his head from his knees and looked out into the room. He remembered her voice when she'd said there was no one else. Steady, gentle. He believed her. He'd had no reason not to believe her. She never lied. Why then had she left? *Why?* He slapped his head with both his hands. He jammed the heels of his hands into his eyes. He felt tears on his face and didn't bother to brush them away. Looking up, he saw the room through the blur of his tears. He saw her standing there, slender, delicate as a shadow, weaving back and forth. He remembered the first time he took her in his arms. Here, in this very room. Her body so thin, so fragile, he feared the pressure of his arms would snap her spine. He held her away from him, then pulled her close and gently led her to the bed. He remembered telling her how much he loved her, vowing never to leave. He suspected even then it was too soon to speak of love, too soon to make such a vow. Not for him too soon, but for her. Embarrassed, she had flushed and turned away. He remembered her flush, how sweetly she had turned her head away.

Nina, he murmured. *My Nina.*

He remembered taking her dancing. A feather in his arms. He remembered leading her out onto the floor. His hand on the small of her back, her curly blond hair swaying from side to side. He remembered his mood. Ecstatic. Jubilant. He remembered stopping dead in his tracks in the middle of the dance floor, suddenly, horribly aware of who he was and that he didn't know the steps.

It didn't matter, he told himself, not knowing the steps. It didn't matter being stodgy and set in his ways. The difference in age didn't matter. All that mattered was love. And they had that already. *We had it already, Nina! We did!*

He only meant to guide and instruct, to teach her about art, about the dedication and passion of artists. For that's who he was. It was his nature to teach.

And she was grateful to be taught. Grateful he made the effort. Within a year of their first meeting she graduated with honors from NYU, set her sights on Columbia's prestigious graduate Art History and Archeology Program, where, by chance, he'd done his own graduate work. He walked her around the campus on registration day, orienting her to the place as a teacher might. He named the buildings for her: Low library, Miller Theatre, Hamilton Hall. He drew special attention to Schermerhorn Hall. "That's where you'll be taking most of your classes." He pointed out Buell Hall. "See that gabled, brick building there with white trim? That's the oldest building on the campus. Last standing remnant of The Bloomingdale Insane Asylum," he told her. "Built in 1885," he added academically.

They strolled leisurely, walking hand in hand, but he felt the pull on her of students walking by. Once, she stepped aside to let a group of what were likely freshmen pass between them, and he was forced to drop her hand. She walked on, seeming not to notice.

Sitting here now on the bedroom floor, memories flooding back, he recalls the dance floor and not knowing the steps. He recalls walking her around the Columbia campus, pointing out the buildings, naming them for her. Was that the problem? Naming the buildings, pointing them out? Was that why she had left him? But that's who he was. He taught, he instructed. He guided and shaped. He loved. And now, bereft, he wept.

After she left, Clive continued getting up in the mornings, shining his shoes, straightening his tie, opening his store, locking it up, teaching night school three evenings a week. For that, too, was who he was. Soon after she left, as if in tribute to her memory, he stopped criticizing his salesclerks so unfairly. He still insisted that the edges of the books be aligned, that the lights be precisely focused, but he did so more gently, for suddenly and as if for the first time, he was aware of their youth, their vulnerability. He stopped saying her name, stopped hearing her voice, stopped watching the door. For days, even weeks, he forgot to glance up when it opened.

It had been November when they met. Another November when she left. A new November had now come again. Winter dragged on. Snow fell lightly. The nights were cold and long. Then a young woman walked into his shop; his eyes flew to the door. He saw white, woolly mittens clapping before her face to banish the cold. He saw a woolen cap removed, curly bright hair falling loose. His knees went weak. His heart leapt in his chest. It was, of course, not her. He turned away, withdrawing into the recesses of the shop, letting one of his salesclerks attend to her.

Late one night, as he walked through the darkened rooms of his apartment, touching the places she had touched, the corners of tables, the rims of chairs, trailing his fingers where hers had trailed, the latches of cupboards, the handle of the stove, he saw her there. Across the kitchen in a shadowed part of the room, standing at the fridge, the door pulled open, her head cocked to one side, peering in. He stepped closer. She turned and looked at him, hazel eyes twinkling, the question of what he'd like for dinner on her lips.

It was December and he was frying a pork chop when he heard the knock. Lightly, tentatively, it came. He knew at once. But the downstairs door was always locked (the tenants were good about that), so how did she get in? Pressed all the buttons on the intercom? Waited for someone to press back? Usually, someone did. It was a thing of concern in the building and contentiously discussed at tenant meetings. The knock came a second time, and in the smoke rising from his pan he saw their life together restored, his world righted, old dreams rejuvenated. The future beckoned. Birds sang.

He turned off the stove and went to the door.

"I'm sorry," she said. "I made a mistake. Can you ever forgive me?"

He motioned toward the couch, poured her a glass of wine. Malbec, her favorite. The bottle untouched since she'd left this house.

"It was a mistake," she said again. "A stupid mistake."

He sat at one end of the couch, facing her, not close.

She told him she had missed him. Said how lonely she'd been. Again, she said she was sorry.

"You were so good to me. More than I deserved."

She shook her head, bright curls went flying. She said she didn't know why she had done what she'd done.

"It was stupid," she told him. "The biggest mistake of my life."

After a moment he replied, "No. Not stupid." He said it with conviction, in that instant realizing its truth. "Not any mistake."

She put down her glass, reached for his hand. He took her wrist. It was so thin his fingers overlapped. He held her away.

Then he told her what he knew. "It wasn't a mistake," he said again. "You didn't do anything stupid," he told her, and told her why.

He told her the obvious things—her youth, his age, her life being all before her, his already much behind. He told her he would always love her. He told her she would never have cause to doubt his love. It was hers forever as surely, he said, as her hazel eyes and gentle smile were hers.

She began to cry.

She had been right to leave, he told her.

She turned her face away.

It was courageous of her to have left, he wanted her to know. Maybe she'd lost her courage now, he suggested quietly, but only temporarily. It was reasonable for her to return to the place where she'd been loved. He took her chin and turned her face toward him. Not stupid, he said. There'd been no mistake, she would come to understand. Leaving was the right thing to do, she'd see that in time. Leaving was the only thing to do, he knew that now. Knew it suddenly, unequivocally. And he knew why although he didn't say. He knew but

Nina's Man

didn't say it was because he hadn't kicked the pile of leaves to make the leaves fly up and scatter. He knew but didn't say it was because he had named the buildings for her on the campus. He knew but didn't say it was because he could never bring himself to address anyone as *Man* or think to reply to a random remark with the word *Whatever.* He knew but didn't say it was because of his need to guide and instruct, to teach and shape. It wasn't any mistake. He knew but didn't say it was because his shoes were always polished and buffed, his tie securely knotted. He knew but didn't say it was because he needed the edges of the books aligned, the lights precisely focused, because he was made that way, because that's the man he was, not some other man, not some younger, cooler, less stodgy, more suitable man, not hers, never hers. Never, it broke his heart to say it, Nina's man.

A Moment's Peace

Florence had gone that day to the park for a little peace. She'd taken her book, a novel she'd started the day before and had put down and taken up again today, which she might or might not read. She might just sit in the sun and enjoy the park. Finding her favorite bench empty, she took a seat and looked out across the low iron fence facing her to the grassy incline leading down to the path that led to the playground below. Beyond the path was the promenade with its central flowering garden; beyond the promenade was the Hudson River sparkling in the sun, and beyond the river was New Jersey. High-rises in Guttenberg, she believed it was, returned her gaze. Years ago, living with her parents and younger brother in Riverdale, further north, it had been Palisades Amusement Park that looked back at her from across the river. She had watched it then, perched high and precariously close to the edge of its cliff, fearing it might fall.

Today, just past noon, the sun is high overhead and comes to her filtered through the leaves of an overhanging Ginkgo tree. Down on the promenade, she sees it peopled now as on most sunny days by joggers and walkers, by home attendants guiding wheelchairs and mothers pushing strollers, by little kids on tricycles and older ones on skateboards or scooters. She marvels at the speed the older kids attain, one foot on their means of locomotion, the other furiously pushing the ground away to propel them forward. She marvels at the apparent ease some show in those mind-boggling maneuvers they perform with their skateboards, the wheelies and toetappings, the dips and turns and spins and swerves, the 108s and 360s (she's heard them called), as if they're dancing on water.

At a distance off to her left are three massive Civil War cannons, preserved in bronze for reflection by post-war (Civil and ensuing) generations. Each cannon weighs, she'd read somewhere, more than eight thousand pounds. Peripherally, she sees a blur of children, no more than a fuzzy outline, atop one of the cannons. Turning her gaze to a bench not far from hers but closer to the cannons, she sees a woman sitting alone contemplating something—knitting? a book?—in her lap. A mother evidently, Florence concludes, noting children's discarded jackets and toys left in a heap on the bench beside her.

Returning to stare at the sun-dappled river and the city on its opposite side, she judges the approximate distance and determines the end to be closer than she would like. Until recently she had never given it a thought. Who does until a diagnosis is delivered and one's hand is forced?

The humidity is low today, the wind barely noticeable. Sparrows eye-level to her hop onto and off the iron fence before her. Pigeons gather at her feet, nervous for food; finding none, they disperse in a huff. Now a small boy, just under two, she estimates, makes his way up the grassy incline from the path below where his mother stands holding his stroller, patiently awaiting his return. Reaching the iron fence just opposite her, the child grabs a spoke in each hand and stares through with dark, unsmiling eyes. The sparrows scatter. Florence asks the boy his name, receives no reply. A helicopter sputters overhead. Birds chirp in the trees; people pass to and fro behind her bench; traffic hums distantly in the street. Florence closes her eyes and lifts her chin to feel her face warmed by the sun. Opening her eyes, she finds the child gone from the fence, the mother and stroller vanished from the path below. She reaches for her book.

A few pages into the story—lovers in Paris clearly destined for an unhappy end—a child's cry sounds off to her left in the direction of the Civil War cannons. There's something wrong with that cry, it crosses her mind, but Florence blocks it out and returns to her book. The lovers enter an upscale restaurant, find a table. Cloth menus are produced, maroon in color. The man holds his menu before his face. The woman studies the back of it, presumably deciphering the gold-lettered mirror image of the restaurant's name embedded in the fabric.

The child's cry sounds again. Yes, there's something off about it. Too loud, too harsh. A single sound, flattened out like the bleat of a goat or the bark of a sea lion. In either case, not a normal cry.

Distracted from her book, Florence looks once more across the river. Whatever time is left is hers. To feel the sun on her skin, to watch the ripples of the water and the sailboats on the Hudson, to marvel at the kids showboating their skateboard skills, to do with as she pleases.

Again, the cry. Demanding and blunt. She turns and sees it is a boy on the cannon. She has an impulse to silence him with her look—that hard, disapproving look she throws over her shoulder in movie theaters at people talking too loudly in the row behind. Or perhaps not especially loudly, but merely conversing in whispers through the trailers as if it didn't matter that she enjoys the trailers, that they help her determine which films to see next. Occasionally, she'll be obliged to turn and throw her look a second time, for people who whisper through trailers are not above whispering through the film itself. And she had come to that theatre, as she'd come to the park today, to let her mind go and watch or not watch the film or the river as she chose, to read or not read her book, to consider or not the implications of the diagnosis she'd been given.

In regard to the boy on the cannon, she understands her look will have no effect. He will be impervious to it, show no reaction, no chagrin or apology. The flatness of the sound he utters tells her a diminished intelligence is at work in the child. She is sorry for him, truly she is, but it is not her business. So she will sit where she is on her bench, book in hand, ignoring the boy and his sound, letting her eyes linger on the river before her.

And what, after all, could the implications of that diagnosis be but that, sooner or later, we all must go? Sooner, in her case, than later, but no sense quibbling. It is simply the nature of things. Friendly, unfriendly. Nice, not nice.

Can't you help a little? Can't you try to be nice?

Could she try, she wondered? Could *nice* be produced with a conscious effort?

Picking up her book again, Florence finds the lovers where she left them: in their expensive Parisian restaurant, the man's face still masked by his menu, the woman still attempting to make sense of the lettering inscribed on the menu's back. Florence has never been to Paris, but she has sat in restaurants like the one depicted in the novel, staring, as the woman in its pages stares, at the back of a menu while a man—her long ago lover and almost husband—contemplates his choices printed on its front. Starters to desserts, entrées, salads, sides, they're all before him. A cornucopia of gastronomic possibilities. Less than an hour earlier he had been seated on her couch, legs spread, and she on her knees—her *knees!*—on the rug before him. How much nicer could you be than that? If only he would look up from his menu, tilt his head to one side in that way she finds so touching and say, *Florence…Flo…what looks good to you?*

The child's cry comes again—rough, flattened out, desperate. Florence turns away from the terrible sound and looks toward the mother sitting on her bench. For she is the one who should acknowledge that cry. But resolutely the mother keeps her head down, eyes focused on the knitting or the book in her lap. A mother ignoring her child's desperate cry? Is that what is considered nice?

The cry again. This time Florence whips her head around and sees it all in a flash: the bleating boy, seven or eight years of age, sprawled on his belly at the back of the Civil War cannon, attempting to sit. She notes the boy's ungainly movements, his wide lips and too large mouth. She notes the enormously thickened eye-glasses, the shiny black helmet, made shinier still by the sun glinting off it. She sees the sister, it must be, eleven, maybe, or twelve, facing the boy from the front of the cannon, talking to him, chatting pleasantly. Florence registers the helmet on the boy, none on the girl. No bicycle or skateboard or scooter nearby, temporarily abandoned in favor of the cannon, and no obvious need, therefore, for the helmet. She notes the boy's unnaturally skinny limbs, the thickened lenses, the flattened sound, barking for his mother. Still, the mother, focused on whatever it is she has in her lap, denies him that attention.

After all, she knows her boy is safe. She buckled his helmet beneath his chin herself before sending him off to climb on the cannon. An object that stands no more than two-and-a-half feet off the ground and presents no danger to children like his sister who don't need to have their heads protected from a fall of so small a height. But her son, with his impaired vision and poor muscle control, might easily slide from the cannon's slippery surface and land on his head on the unforgiving hexagonal-shaped paving stones below. That cannon is but one of countless objects in life that present a threat to the boy but none to children like his sister. Normal children. Likable children. A raft of otherwise innocuous objects turns pernicious when the boy approaches, and his mother must be prepared to outwit them all. Bedposts, doorknobs, tables, walls, the height of curbs because he has no depth of vision, pillows, even, for their smothering properties—any one or all of these might render grievous harm to this mother's stricken son. And in the heavy helmet, the skinny arms and legs, the bulging eyes, the wide lips and barking cry, Florence sees that he is stricken. A web of mysterious symptoms attaches to that boy slithering now on his belly along the cannon's surface, skin to skin like a sea lion on a rock, his cries so like the barks that creature makes when agitated or distressed.

Accident of birth, Florence speculates. Pressure on the um-bilical cord. Placenta deprived of blood. Insufficient supply of oxy-gen to the baby's brain. Or prior to birth, some disaster in the womb. A hereditary disease or mutant gene passed on. Either way, not the mother's fault. Even so, guilt accrues and she succumbs. Always she succumbs. Always she lets him have his way.

Don't be like that, dear. He's only little.

Her every waking moment spent looking out for him, calcu-lating risks, adjusting the world to make it safe for him. For *him*! Her youngest and most special child. Preferring him, favoring him, how could she not? So cute. So little. So likable! A perfect angel when he wasn't screaming his head off.

What's so special about him?

Florence herself never carried on like that, screamed like that. So why did her mother never succumb to her?

Not all children are likable.

Momentum halts and sense goes dead. Her own mother saying that!

A presence like a massive iceberg pushes up inside her at the sound of those words. Straight up through her heart and into her skull. Since earliest childhood she had felt that presence there, a great block of ice, inhibiting breath and sometimes speech.

Not all children are likable.

Her mother at the sink, her back to her. The words coming from a stranger's mouth, it has to be, on the other side of her moth-er's face. The presence pushes straight up through her heart, crashing through bone and tissue on its way. Breaking the surface of her skin, sealing her in ice.

                                                    A Moment's Peace

She's old now. Older than her mother had been when she spoke those words. Older even than her mother was when she died. She's been coming to this bench to stare out across the river for three months now, since summer began, and they didn't give her more than four.

The boy's cry comes again. It tugs at her. Raw and guttural, it calls her out. What could account for his condition? Cerebral palsy? Brain damage? Or something deeper within the child, something immune to medical intervention and resistant to human understanding? It was too late now, Florence recognizes, to determine causes, decipher meanings. Too late, her mother dead all these years, for reconciliation. She stares at the river, yet the cry tugs at her. She follows the route of a lone sailboat southward toward the 79th Street Boat Basin, sees two others emerging, yet the cry draws her back.

Her mother had made a pet of her baby boy, coddled and pampered him like a pedigreed pup. Wetting her fingertips with her own saliva to slick down the hair at the crown of his head. Even doing him up in lacy dresses when he was an infant.

The boy on the cannon continues barking for his mother, though his sister is right there, laughing and chattering and giving him her full attention—something she has done, Florence knows all too well, for most of her young life. Every day, in one way or another, that older sister had to attend to her younger brother's needs, ministering to him as though she were his mother and not just a kid herself.

Why is it always me watching him?

A little help is all I'm asking. He's your baby brother, after all.

The sister does her best, climbing onto the cannon, attempting to distract her brother with her easy laugh and pleasant chatter. But it is not enough. It will never be enough.

Still the boy barks for his mother!

Lacy dresses! Florence had looked over the rim of the cradle, gripped its edge, been appalled. *Don't rock it like that! You'll wake him!* Masses of tulle, just like those tutus some people attach to the hindquarters of dogs. And like a dog her mother carries him about the house, covering his face with kisses, whispering little nothings in his ear. *My precious. My darling. My baby boy.* And when he was bigger and running about on his own, always reaching out to scoop him off the floor or squeeze the flesh of his fat thigh when he passed near.

Once Florence had jabbed him in the belly to make him cry. *Why can't you be nice, Florence? What's wrong with you?*

That she asked the question meant it was what she thought: for five years before her brother came along, she had lived with a damaged child. Five years, day in, day out, thinking that.

Florence returns to her book. But now she looks through the cloth menu raised before the man's face to his face itself. Strained lips, tightly drawn. Steel-gray eyes all but closed. Not reading the menu as she'd thought, but looking inward, contemplating, he must have been, how best to break it to her. He is a lovely man, she had thought even then, seconds before he spoke, and it became the last she would see of him. The inward look directed outward, kind and caring. The angle of his head tilted just so to take her in. It had touched her then. Touches her still.

I'm so sorry, Flo. I never meant to hurt you.

She visualized the woman it would be. Had to be. Tall, taller than she. For he is six-foot-three and would prefer a woman on his arm who approached him more closely in height as they meandered through the crowds at those charity dinners he was obliged to attend and she detested. Slender, too, the woman would be, though she herself was slender. And with straight hair, not frizzy like her own. Shiny and auburn, she pictured it, cut to frame her face. She sees her sitting at a dinner table opposite him, casually tucking a strand of auburn hair behind one ear. A gesture he would find endearing. And of course, a woman who could cook.

"It doesn't matter," he had protested earlier when she'd burned the beans. "We'll go out." She'd been on her knees before him, the beans happily burning in the kitchen, him sitting on the couch, pants down, legs spread. *Nice? Was that nice?* They were to be married, so it was all right. The date not set and no one told, but weeks before he'd asked and she'd accepted, and then she burned the beans and they had to go out.

She never guessed. Why would she? Her life was as she dreamed. A man of her own. A lovely man. A wedding to be planned. Now she's there in the restaurant, yet not there, not anywhere. Now again the words are spoken, and the blood freezes in her veins.

I'm so sorry, Flo. I just can't.

The icy presence makes its move. It rises and rises, pushing up through her heart and into her skull, breaking skin and sliding down her arms and legs, entombing her in ice.

He can't? He's sorry? At first she thought he meant the restaurant. Thai, on Grove Street. They'd chosen wrong, the cuisine wasn't to his liking, he couldn't stay.

I never meant to hurt you. It just happened.

Someone at work. Not his own, the woman's, a partnering firm. She doesn't know her, as if that makes it all right. Again the words come dimly from within her tomb of ice.

I'm so sorry, Flo.

Now high above her bench a plane passes on its way and through the roar the boy's bark comes again. The sun was high that day, too. Remembrance, vague at first, emerges through the roaring jets and barking cry. She hasn't thought of it in years. Bruce, the pampered pet, the baby brother, is a baby no more. He's six, she's eleven. It's summer vacation. A rented house in Cape May near the water. She's in the back yard, trying to read. Bruce is running circles around her lawn chair—vinyl, she recalls, with green and white stripes—poking at her through the slats as he passes, shouting for her attention. Inside the house their mother is making lunches, packing up things for the beach. Their father is stacking things to put in the car. She doesn't want to go. She wants to stay where she is and read. *Why are you like that, Florence?* They'll be out in a few minutes, both of them insisting she get in the car, her mother exhorting her to pretend at least to have a good time. *It's the beach, for heaven's sake!* Fifteen minutes, twenty maybe, to make the sandwiches, pack up the towels and sunscreen, the swim goggles and rubber tubes and all the rest of the paraphernalia. If Bruce quit bothering her, she could finish her chapter by then. Maybe discover the source of the laughter Jane Eyre keeps hearing at Thornfield Hall.

But Bruce won't stop. He keeps running around her chair, poking at her through the slats. She reaches out, grabs him, pinches his cheek as her parents' friends, those people purporting to be aunts and uncles, are always pinching hers. But she pinches hard. So hard her nails scrape his cheek and cause a red blotch to bloom like a rapidly opening rose. Bruce slaps his hand to his cheek; his eyes go wide in astonishment; he opens his mouth to scream; she covers it with her hand.

The blotch has faded, and she makes him swear never to tell. *I'll kill your precious rabbit if you tell. I will, Bruce. I swear. I'll slit its throat!* She threw him her look, and he saw by the look she meant what she'd said. That disgusting white beast with the horrible twitching nose. She'd kill the thing…what was its name? *Sam!* That was it. It comes back to her now. Its name was Sam. Lifeless-looking beady eyes and horrible twitching nose, gnawing its way along the base of the hedge. Bruce had begged and begged to be allowed to bring the thing along with them on vacation, and finally—inevitably—their mother had succumbed. Always she succumbed; always Bruce got his way. *I'll slit its throat if you tell! Swear it, Bruce. Swear you won't!* Bruce must have envisioned red blood running from his beloved Sam's white throat, for his eyes went wide into horror and he swore.

He kept the secret for years. Kept it locked behind his eyes. He finished first grade, proceeded through second and the rest of elementary school, while Florence went on to middle school and junior high and high school. For all that time they led their lives, went to college, moved out of their parents' house, moved to different cities, Bruce kept the secret. He married, had children. Florence saw him periodically. Thanksgivings, Christmases, the illness of one parent or the other, finally the death of both, drawing them back to Riverdale. Through it all, Bruce kept the secret. Then one day not long ago, he heard she'd been sick and came to visit her in the hospital—kidney stones, not the life-threatening thing he didn't know about—and she looked into his eyes and saw that the secret had slipped its lock there behind them and dissolved into nothing.

Once more, the bleating comes from the damaged boy. It butts the air like a goat. There's a hopelessness in the sound Florence cannot bear and she turns to silence it with her look. Through his thickened lenses the boy meets her gaze, but hers is not the gaze he seeks, so he turns toward his mother and cries out again. Still his mother seems not to hear. She keeps her eyes fastened on the thing in her lap. Now

Florence makes it out. It's a book she has in her lap and all she wants is a moment's peace with its pages. That's all Florence had wanted that day in Cape May sitting with her book in the green and white vinyl lawn chair in the sun. "Shut up, why can't you!" she'd screamed at Bruce. But Bruce had gone on circling her chair, poking at her, shouting for her to get up and attend to him. "Shut up and let me read!" She'd reached out, grabbed him, pinched his cheek. Pinched it hard enough to leave a mark. She hadn't faulted herself then or since. It was no more than he deserved, the nice one, the likable one, the one to whom their mother always succumbed.

The boy on the cannon emits another cry. A joyful one this time, for his mother has at last risen from her bench and is making her way toward him. No longer needed, his sister slides off her end of the cannon and walks back toward the bench her mother has just vacated. Mid-way on the pavement, mother and daughter pass one another without a word. The boy struggles to his knees, angles himself backward, opens his legs to accommodate the cannon's girth, and with a triumphant cry, manages to sit. Reaching him, the mother wraps her arms around her now exultant son, holding his head, enormous in its shining helmet, to her breast like a trophy.

Florence stares again at the sun skipping along the river. Her last allotted summer for such staring. When it comes it will be too soon, and already too late. Too late to be nice, to make amends, to capture love, to be other than what she was.

It was a small gesture, that way he had of tilting his head to one side to take her in. Maybe no one else in all his life would be touched by it. She hoped that was the case, leaving for her alone the remarkable sensation that small gesture instilled in her. She never understood how things between them had reached the point they had. Even today, so very many years later, ice runs in her veins upon the echo: *I'm so sorry, Flo. I just can't.* It numbed and shocked but remained. She read of their marriage—his and the auburn-haired woman—in the newspaper. Quite the social event it was. A marriage that was to have been hers. She'd never come close to another, something in her having failed to thaw.

Linda: Seeking A Sign

Linda filled the salt and pepper shakers. Twenty sets in all. Eight
for the counter, twelve for the tables. It was a repetitive act. Repetitive as in performing the same act over and over; also as in having
performed the identical act in some previous time. She pulled the
twenty-five-pound box of sugar down from the shelf in the place
they called a pantry (actually an alcove) where it was kept, away from
the boiling pots in the kitchen and the grease that splattered from
the skillets. She filled the sugar cannisters. Twenty of them. (Again.)
Eight for the counter, twelve for the tables. Some of the cannisters
required only a cup or two of sugar to bring them to a level; some
required a half pound or more.

It was odd being alone with her husband now that the children had
left. Strangely unnerving. At times she knew him so little he might
have been a stranger. The two of them, strangers to one another. Or
was she being foolish? *Too sensitive? Overreacting,* as he called it.

Linda unscrewed the tops of the ketchup bottles (also twenty and for
the same distribution), noted which bottles required refilling, which
did not. She filled those running low from the big gallon jar, also kept
in the pantry (alcove). She did the same with the bottles of mustard.
Although she didn't need to unscrew all the tops of the mustard bottles because people tended to use less mustard than they did ketchup,
and she could tell merely by picking up the bottles and weighing
them in one hand which required refilling, which did not. Of course
some people liked both ketchup and mustard on their burgers, but
they were in the minority.

    Twelve tables were all the place could hold; that felt like
enough to Linda, more than enough on those days Cassie (the other
waitress) called in sick (now with a cold, now a sprained ankle, a sore

throat, an unspecified stomach complaint), and she was left to serve the entire luncheon crowd on her own. Breakfast was no problem even if Cassie didn't show, for most people sat at the counter for breakfast, which she and Juan (the counterman) could cover easily. Only one or two couples took tables at breakfast.

I don't need you. I've never needed you. Brave words. Fallacious words. For of course she did, of course she had. Why else would she have married him?

Married right after college. Loving him, needing him before even knowing him. The first man she had ever loved. Would ever love—that she knew even then. Children appeared almost at once, and in a series. Her husband in graduate school (then post-graduate, then post-post), studying his little bugs, as she liked to call them. She at home tending to the children. Three of them. Ducklings in a row. Grown now, waddled off, leaving her behind, her husband adrift from them, from her as well. Chiseled out as from a storybook scene, cast ashore.

Hiring. The sign, looking outward toward the street, had filled one entire pane of the four four-paned glass windows on the front of the coffee shop. Immediately it caught her eye. She went inside at once and applied for the job. Interviewed skillfully. Hired on the spot. A coffee shop on the corner of Main and Bond Streets, one town over from their own (hers and her husband's). A redbrick building with a slanted roof and three steps leading up to the entrance.

Rita was the name of the person who conducted the interview. She was also the manager of the place and the cashier. "You'll fit right in," Rita told her. "You're way overqualified, but I never question a person's motive for seeking a job."

Her husband is new to her in his solitary state. His sexual need, ravenous yet unpredictable. Strange, sometimes frightening. The way he can abstain for weeks, his pleasure greatly intensified when he resumes. The way he opens his mouth, baring his teeth (wide and sharp) as if to devour her. The way he furrows his brow, curls his lip. Contemplating some cutting remark? Some joke? Since the children left, her husband has been uncharacteristically drawn to jokes. That smirk on his face, the lifted eyebrows. Has she said something to cause him to smirk? Something foolish? Something stupid?

It was a temporary job. Certainly it couldn't be anything other than temporary, although she'd already had it longer than she'd intended. Meant to show her husband something (what?). That she didn't need him (had never needed him?). But of course that wasn't true. Her big, broad-shouldered, brilliant husband, gifted scientist, of course she needed him. Meant to show him she could manage on her own? Of course she couldn't. Certainly not on a coffee shop waitress' salary. Even with tips she came up short every month.

"Stretch it out," Cassie advised. "Make it like taffy."

Linda was older than Cassie, older than them all: Juan on the counter, José and Ed in the kitchen, even Rita (cashier and manager), who made a ritual of bringing in digital photos of her first grandson's milestones (three since Linda had been on the payroll: first smile not attributable to gas; first sleep through the night; first tooth), passing her cell phone around so everyone could see. Linda didn't mind being the eldest in the crew. It made her feel maternal (again). Protective. Useful. Feelings she hadn't known since her children left home. Nor did she mind taking advice from Cassie about the job, about how to handle her finances, or anything else she might care to offer. This was the first job she'd held in a long time. A very long time. Since college in fact (she'd waited tables then, too) and was a bit out of practice.

Thirty years out of practice. But it's like riding a bike. You don't forget. And on this day toward the end of August, some thirty years later, the mechanics of the job, the routine of it, come back to her tenacious as a muscle memory.

Of course any remark she might make would be foolish or stupid compared to any the gifted scientist might make. But never has he held that against her, never touted his superior mind. Until now. Until the children have gone. With his jokes and cutting remarks. With his lifted eyebrows. His smirk. It occurs to her she has never truly known her husband. Not as an individual, a separate being. Never actually seen him. As if the children clouded her view. But without the presence of the three of them now, he stands revealed. One hand

                                                    Linda: Seeking A Sign

on his hip, a little apart from her (is he loathe to touch her?). Joking, laughing. *Laughing at her?*

"Was that a shower or have you been out in the sun too long?" he'd quipped one morning shortly after the last of the children had left. She'd just come out of the bathroom wrapped in a towel, her face puffy and red. She knew how she looked. She bristled, and quickly walked past him. "That's a joke, darling," he called after her. *Darling…* he said it like in the old days (or almost), warmly, without insinuation…and then the remark. Cutting. Mean-spirited. *Can't you take a joke?* No, she can't. "If that's a joke, it isn't funny." It galls her, scorches her skin. She hadn't known her husband, usually so immersed in his little bugs, to be a man who makes jokes. Normally (like a scientist), he's an orderly man. Fastidious. Scholarly. An esteemed microbiologist, he might very well have considered jokes beneath him. Who was this man now making comical (to him) remarks? She doesn't know what to do with jokes coming from his mouth. It throws her. "Can't you take a joke?" Should she take it? Laugh it off? Defend against it? *Darling…*, and then the sucker punch. She teeters as if off balance. Like walking on flat slippery rocks. "Really, sweetheart. You're overreacting." *Sweetheart. Darling.* That was the man of her dreams. The only man she would ever love. This was a different man. One she hardly knew. A man who came to life after the children had grown and gone their separate ways. After she and he were left alone.

But surely she knows him. Of course she does. Tall. (So tall.) Handsome. Brown eyes. Shock of gray (almost white) hair, triangular in shape, above his left ear. Powerful arms. Sometimes they squeeze her so tight she fears her ribs will crack. She has known him for thirty years. He's hardly a stranger. Not a thief, not an intruder in her house, as she'd imagined once in the middle of the night, awakened from a nightmare about her youngest, Julie, walking down the road, being hit by a motorcycle. She'd heard footsteps in the hall and nearly dialed 911. Heavy footsteps. Ominous. "Who is it? Who's there?" she'd called out, on the verge of hysteria. "Me," he'd answered. "Who'd you think it was? Santa Claus?"

Another joke. Also not funny. But it was his house as well and how could he be an intruder in his own house? Those heavy (ominous) footsteps anybody's but his own? Their house, his and hers. Two stories, four bedrooms on Maple Avenue, a twenty-minute drive to the university and his precious research lab. A house now much too large for them. Their children were born here. *Their* children. His and hers. He loves them, loves her. She knows that. Knows what he loves: looking out the window watching the birds; opening the front door to the morning sun, even a thin, steely winter's sun. He loves bringing in the mail on Saturday mornings, sorting through it with her, his fingers grazing hers as they reach for the envelopes. She knows how it brings him joy. He has always loved touching her, even just slightly grazing her flesh. Yet lately he lifts his eyebrows, furrows his brow, smirks and makes bad jokes.

"You're too sensitive, darling. You're overreacting."

Too sensitive! Overreacting! Was she? Was it an overreaction not to know her big-boned, brainy husband? Brown eyes, black when angry. Shock of gray (almost white) hair, triangular in shape, above his left ear. Handsome. Tall. (Very tall.) Six-foot-three to her five-foot-two. Bending over her like a tree when they embrace.

The routine comes back to her, thirty-some years later. Filling the salt and pepper shakers, the sugar cannisters, the mustard and ketchup bottles, placing the cutlery on the table. Knife and fork and spoon at each place, water glass, coffee cup and saucer. Twenty places in all (again). Eight for the counter, twelve for the tables. She could do it blindfolded. She could do it in her sleep.

I don't need you. I've never needed you. And to prove her point, which wasn't really a point, more a lashing out, a wild expression of anger (or fear), she leaves the house, their house, gets a job, finds another place to live. Not far away, only one town over, a small apartment on Main Street just down from the coffee shop. Second floor. Above the deli. It's only temporary, of course. Until she can get him in focus. See him again.

She might still be that college girl waiting tables, long blond ponytail swinging from side to side as she makes her way around the room. Sawdust on the floor. Big round wooden tables. Stained with beer. Blue and white striped apron tied with a bow at her back. White socks, white high-tops. Keeping an eye out for the one she will love, the one she will marry. Already she knows, though they haven't yet broached that awesome subject. Certainly, they will marry. She knows it in her bones. Knows it as if it has already happened. She, walking down the aisle on her (adored) father's arm, her mother in the front row. Her good, kind, respectable father who'd never once suggested she was making a mistake. Did he harbor such a thought? Was the thought keeping him awake at night? *Why, no, Dad,* she would have told him had she known to put his mind at ease. *Never been more sure of anything in my life.* White lace trailing after her; her handsome young bridegroom, nervous in his rented tux, waiting at the altar. There it is before her, months, years before it happens. The children they will have. Four boys, he wagers; three, she counters, hoping one will be a girl. The pains they'll take to raise them. Their fears of failure, their (overwhelming) pride when the first, then the second, then the third (her wish for three having been granted, the last a girl, her Julie) shows the burgeoning of a truthful nature, inherited from her father, she believes, that will serve them well in life. All had shown it at an early age—Alex, Jamie, Julie—accepting the consequences of their actions, not blaming others (except for that brief period when Jamie blamed first his baby sister, then his imaginary dog for eating his homework).

And then the children are gone. Their house depleted (disembodied, it seemed). Her husband a stranger to her, an alien in the house. Furrowing his brow, making bad jokes, a man she does not recognize. And who is she, a middle-aged woman (fifty-four years old to be exact), a server in a coffee shop? It is another life. Hers but not hers. One she had inhabited in some former time.

Stop, you're hurting me! Was that her voice? Were those his fingers grasping her upper arm? Unlikely from a man, an esteemed scientist, so absorbed in the peaceful study of his little bugs. But there they were the following morning, faint, yet unmistakable: red marks—fingermarks—on her upper arm. And over what? One of his lectures she hadn't wanted to attend. *Please, darling,* he begged. She resisted. He grabbed her arm. *You're my wife. I want you there!* She pulled away. *Darling, please.* And then the force of his grip, the fingermarks on her arm. Never once in all the years she'd known him had he laid a hand on her.

Now the three men—joint owners of the local hardware store—come through the door. The first of the lunchtime crowd. She's used to seeing them in a pack. They take their usual table in the middle of the room. Linda fills their water glasses, distributes menus. They greet her affably, as is their custom. "Howdy," one says. "Nice day," another. "How you doing?" the third. She answers in kind, then walks away to give them time to peruse the menu. Not that they need time. They will have what they have every day—cheeseburgers for two of them, no cheese for the third, all cooked medium. Only once in all the time she's been working here—six, seven weeks (or is it eight already?)—has she known them to deviate from this order. Then it was roast beef on rye for one, the usual cheeseburgers for the other two. The one who ordered roast beef never did so again, settling for a burger, plain, no cheese.

She tries to remember if something had happened between her and her husband that might account for the feeling (fear, is it? Alarm?) she has come to have when alone with him. Other than the footsteps in the hall she heard (or thought she heard) in the middle of that night. Other than the jokes he's prone to make, the lecture she had scorned at first but, coerced (*Please, darling*), had ultimately attended. She can think of nothing.

Understanding that longtime marriages can devolve into routine, become stultifying, that couples can (suddenly) feel trapped, begin to long for new horizons, she tries to remember feeling trapped, longing for new horizons, becoming stultified. She can't recall any of that. Doubts her husband can either.

Linda returns to the hardware men, having in the interim seated two other couples (one toward the front, the other in the very back of the room). She gathers the menus from the men, secures them beneath one arm, takes their order (no changes today), switches her pad and pencil to her left hand, pours their coffee with her right.

"Thanks, Doll," one man says. The others nod.

Doll. She could take him up on it, seeing the glint in his eye, knowing what he's offering, knowing it better than he does himself. She could welcome him after work to her small apartment on the second floor above the deli (his place, she assumes, would be littered

　　　　　　　　　　　　　　　　　Linda: Seeking A Sign

with wife and kids). She could feel his body pressed against hers, feel his tongue probing her mouth (its pink tip already familiar to her as he chases a trickle of ketchup down his chin). She could feel again that stab of pleasure intense as pain that makes her cry out in her husband's arms. How badly she misses it. How long it's been.

Or she could let it go.

I'm not your doll, she might say, but refrains. *I'm a happily married woman,* she might tell him, flashing the gold on her ring finger.

She is not the sort of woman who cheats. Never would she step out on her husband. Betray him, deceive him. Even though she has come to think now that the children are gone she means no more to him than those microorganisms he's so obsessed with. Less. For those little bugs are his life. Peering through a microscope, monitoring their every move, experimenting, tracing their interactions with human beings: his life. Giving lectures, publishing his findings for other scientists of equal renown to dissect: his life. Besides, the man addressing her as doll is a friendly man, harmless. But is any man truly harmless? Is her husband with his fingers squeezing her upper arm, leaving marks? With his jokes? "Was that a shower or have you been out in the sun too long?" *Overreacting,* he calls it when she objects. *Too sensitive.*

She tries to remember the last time they had an argument. A significant one, not over money and the way she spends it, or the times— innumerable, exasperating—she kept him waiting while she dressed, or at a restaurant or some other public place they'd agreed to meet. She can't remember a time. Oh, yes, there was one. Just after Julie left. In front of the movie theatre. *You know how I hate to wait! You do.* Remembering how he had slammed the flat of his hand against the framed poster of the movie stars with such force she'd thought the glass would surely shatter. Remembering how shaken she'd been.

And the look in his eye when he did it—hateful, murderous. All she'd been able to see at the time were his eyes for they were still wearing COVID-era masks. His eyes exuded murder. His hand slamming the glass. And in front of people who had gathered to admire the poster. The fear she'd felt. (Was there fear as well as love in what she felt for him?) Flat, frozen eyes. Narrowed to slits. Black as coal. *Obsidian.* Staring at her, *into her,* above his mask. Devoid of moisture, dry as desert stones. A killer's eyes. *He could kill me now. He's capable of that.* How could she have forgotten that?

And she hadn't been very late. No more than five or ten minutes. They'd made the movie, hadn't missed even a word of the beginning. One of his favorites, hers also. A revival of *The Third Man* with Orson Welles and Joseph Cotten. They hadn't disturbed the audience by walking in late, hadn't made them pull in their legs, shift in their seats. Hadn't shocked them by walking in naked. How he would hate that, appearing without clothes, being exposed, on view. None of that had happened, and still his killer eyes bore into her. She'd wanted to scream, to run, but her jaws wouldn't move, her body was paralyzed. And she'd nearly forgotten that! Erased it from her memory over time. He's overworked, she must have told herself. Distressed about Julie's leaving. More so than he'd admit. Would ever admit.

Now she's refilling water glasses, coffee cups, offering or retracting menus, retrieving cutlery accidentally dropped on the floor. *Dessert?* she prompts. Not many people in for lunch have time for or interest in dessert. The hardware men are already signaling for their check. So, too, the couple in the very back of the room. The place empties out, fills up again. Empties out, fills up.

She and Cassie give each other wide berths as they work, trays held aloft, stomachs sucked in, concentration etched in their faces. Seating people, taking orders, food, drinks, shouting commands into the kitchen: *Burger, hold the cheese! Coke! Diet Coke. Hot tea! Lemon!*

Had she made him feel small (inconsequential) at some time? Certainly not intentionally. She wasn't that sort of woman. Had she bested him in some way, given him reason to hold a grudge? Again, nothing comes to mind.

And then it does. Swims into her consciousness like an eel.

Chess! Of course. That one match. That one night, a week before she left. Of the two, he was by far the better player, foreseeing future moves well in advance of her, cleverly designing, redesigning his strategy, waiting for the moment he would inevitably pounce. But that one night (and never before) she'd had the advantage. *Guard your queen,* she'd cautioned, seeing her chance. A thing he hated, instruction in the middle of a game. Or at any time. And from a woman!

Linda: Seeking A Sign

Anathema to the male ego. There was no one in the house but themselves to hear her say it. Julie had been gone for a month, the boys for longer.

Check! No one to hear or see. *Checkmate!* No witness. No whistleblower. This was worse than keeping him waiting while she dressed or in front of a movie theatre. This was beating him at his own game. A game in which he excelled. *Triumphing over him!* He'd shot up from the table, arms swinging wildly, knocked the board over, scattered chess pieces across the floor, sent knickknacks flying off the shelves. He'd gone to bed without speaking to her. Had barely acknowledged her in the morning.

And the vehemence he'd shown. The look in his eyes. Glowering like a cat's. The wild swinging of his arms, not caring where they landed, sweeping her collection (which he hated) of tiny glass animals to the floor, scattering chess pieces, toppling the board. Eyes not brown but purely black. *Obsidian.* Sunk deep into their sockets. Caved in. Punched. As by a fist.

Four o 'clock. Quitting time. She unties her apron, hangs it on the hook inside her locker, bids good day to her co-workers, heads out the door. The sun, still bright, is low in the sky. It is windy and quite cool. She is glad she has brought a sweater with her. She pulls it from the handbag (oversized) she carries with her every day to work. She threads her arms through the sweater's sleeves as she walks across the park. Leisurely, she makes her way to the bench beside the lake. *Her bench,* she thinks of it, for she has formed a habit of sitting here for a while—often an hour or two at a time—when the weather permits. No boats bespeckle the lake, it is too small for that, only a few ducks. It is the wind calmly brushing the surface of the water, creating long slow ripples (undulations) moving toward her, moving away, moving toward her again, that draws her to this spot. Again and again.

Now she sees a pile of trash (unsightly) tossed at the edge of the lake. Half-eaten sandwich, broken beer bottle, crumpled napkin, used plastic forks and spoons. *Outrageous!* To think that someone was so inconsiderate (*thoughtless!*) as to leave the remnants of their meal beside this lovely lake to mar its beauty. She gets up, gathers the trash, throws it in the receptacle beneath a tree, sits down again.

Then from the corner of her eye she sees him. Or thinks she

does (the sun is in her eyes). Her big-boned, broad-chested, brainy husband, sitting at the far end of her bench. Face averted. Eyes cast down. He doesn't see her (at least not yet). What is he doing here? Has he left work early? (Doubtful.) Put his microscope aside? (Hardly likely.) Canceled a lab assistant's evaluation? Or has the evaluation been canceled by the assistant himself? (Her husband has three, all of them Asian men.)

Her heart skips a beat; she suppresses a gasp. Yes, she sees clearly now, it is he. That shock of gray (almost white) hair, triangular in shape, those powerful arms. She would know him anywhere. Or thinks she would. Is it joy she feels or trepidation?

But now she sees the man is not sitting on her bench, but on one passed hers. The distance between them seems immense. Her husband (possibly her husband) appears very small. Diminished, shrunken. Is it really he? She can't be certain. Has he come at last, as she so often hoped he would, to find her? Why then is he sitting on that distant bench? Why hadn't he looked for her? He wouldn't have had far to come. One town over, a coffee shop on the corner of Main and Bond. He might have glanced in the window, seen her there, walking up and down, tending to people in her blue and white striped apron. His wife, a server in a coffee shop! Would he have been overjoyed to see her or repelled? And why hadn't he sought her out before now, reclaimed her? He's had enough time (more than enough). Seven or eight weeks (nearly two months!) since she left. They'd communicated only once by phone during those weeks, he inquiring as to her health, her plans for return; she assuring him she was all right, giving no hint of location or mention of return. *Or did he not want to reclaim her?*

She feels a sudden surge of rage. All this time—nearly two months—and no attempt to find her! Was it truly that he felt more for his pathogens than he felt for her? Those horrible fungi and parasites, most invisible to the naked eye, to whom he has devoted thirty years (the span of their marriage) of his life. How obsessed he was. *Obscenely obsessed.* Testing and analyzing, studying characteristics, epidemiology, routes of transmission, control and prevention, while barely speaking to her. *Detached. Preoccupied.* His mind elsewhere. On his little bugs. Always on them. Had he been happy (relieved) to see her go? And how had he harnessed his need (his ravenous, unpredict-

   Linda: Seeking A Sign

able sexual need) over those two months? Possibly he hadn't harnessed it. Possibly he'd unleashed it on other women. Invited them to their house, *their bed?*

Leaning forward, she peers at him, attempts to get him in focus. Now she sees he is full-sized. Long legs, long back. Face averted. She feels a pang of longing, remembers his fingers grazing hers, running up and down her spine. *Hello!* she almost calls out. *I'm here. Over here!* But she can't be absolutely certain it is he. The sun occludes her eyes. *Who'd you think it was? Santa Claus?* He has a paper sack beside him. She sees that clearly now. His fingers are busy taking something out of the sack (pieces of something), scattering them on the ground. Bread it must be. Yes, bread. Her husband is feeding the birds!

She is sure now (almost sure). His thighs are spread; his arms hang between them, fingers busy scattering breadcrumbs on the ground. The rage inside her builds, then subsides. She sees him on his distant bench, a full-grown male, powerful, volatile. Pitched forward, staring at the ground. He doesn't see her. (Or pretends not to.) How easily could she rise from her bench, approach him from behind, hit him over the head with something sharp, the broken beer bottle, for instance, she'd tossed into the receptacle beneath the tree? *A joke, darling. Can't you take a joke?* Yet her husband is feeding the birds. A gentle, nurturing act. She knows him. Of course she does. A killer's eyes? The man she loves (and fears)? Surely, she is being foolish. *Overreacting.* She will get up and go to him, go home with him. Of course she will. He will open his arms to her, and she will run into them. He will fold over her like a tree. They will sell their two-storey, four-bedroom house on Maple Avenue that is too large (by far) for them now that the children have left. They will buy another house. Smaller, more compact. In the same general area, of course, close to his sacred laboratory. One bedroom or maybe two, anticipating a visiting child, a grandchild (eventually).

His paper sack is empty now. He is crumbling it, preparing to throw it in the trash. He rises from his bench. (So tall. Remarkably tall.) A great clatter of wings accompany him. Battling, beating wings. The birds hover in the air a moment, ascend into the sky, disappear. The man turns toward her, waves his hand as in a greeting, turns and walks away. Is it a game, that wave? Is it a joke, walking away? She will go after him. Certainly she will. He is her husband after all. She knows him. Knows what he loves: looking out the window, watching the birds, bringing in the mail on Saturday mornings, sorting through it with her, his fingers grazing hers as they reach for the envelopes.

Surely there is nothing to be afraid of.

By the Pond

In her opinion, sails keep secrets. Tucked in the tops of their billowing white canvas and to be released or not as they see fit on some prevailing wind. Today, the wind is not high, only exuding small, sporadic gusts as if mildly impatient. From where she sits on her bench, Emma watches the model boats coursing serenely around the pond. Sloops and schooners, yachts and ordinary, everyday sailboats. The smallest of which is her favorite. All are built precisely to scale. Wind-powered, most of them. A few, the more ostentatious and expensive of the lot, radio-powered. And all of those, without exception, have men at the controls. Fathers, Emma takes them to be. The women—mothers and nannies, the nannies far outnumbering the mothers, as befits this upscale East Side park—are less concerned with the boats. Now and again they toss them approving glances, internally remarking, perhaps, on their beauty or pace, but for the most part they keep their eyes on their charges as they amble leisurely around the pond, some pushing strollers, others with older children in tow.

Shielding her eyes from the sun, Emma surveys the flotilla before her. She is pleased to see her favorite sailboat nicely holding its own among the bigger boats. The sun is hot, and it costs her something of an effort to keep her arm raised, her fingers stiffened as in a salute to shield her eyes. Age, she would have to ascribe it to, as she ascribes so many other minor aches and pains these days. But the pain in her left arm as she brings it down is new. So, too, is the sudden wash of cold sweat breaking on her face and neck as the arm descends. Frightened, she leans back against her bench, pulls a handkerchief from her bag, and runs it across her brow. White linen, lace-trimmed. Almost antique. Like herself, she reflects. David had given her the kerchief years ago. David, her darling David.

A sudden swell of children's voices returns her to the moment. Looking up, she sees a gaggle of young boys in flip-flops and summer shorts gesticulating wildly while running around the rim of the pond. Each is calling to the boat he had brought with him from home that day or had rented from the boathouse for the afternoon. Exhorting it onward, willing it courage. Some of the boys brandish long poles and kneel at intervals along the pond's hard, stone edge. Oh, their poor, young, naked knees, Emma commiserates, seeing that. But the boys, having no thought for their knees, but only for the safety of their boats, lean far out over the water and use their poles to poke at their precious vessels as they come in close to prevent them from ramming into other boats or hitting up against the edge of the pond. The boys who are lucky enough to have radio-powered boats jump up and down at their fathers' legs, vociferously begging for the controls. More often than not, they are refused, and the fathers, seemingly oblivious to the begging boys, go on vigorously pressing buttons on the controls in their hands to direct the course of their boats.

Yes, thinks Emma. *Secrets surely accrue to those billowing sails.*

For more years than seem possible, she has been coming here to sit beside this pond. Two decades, could it be? Three? She comes every Saturday when the weather is fine, beginning in April as the pink and white cherry blossoms usher in the boating season and continuing, week after week, year after year, until the end of October when the season closes.

Yes, three decades it would be. She sat here on this very bench long before the place grew so grand. Even the bench was not so grand then, its green paint peeling, its wooden slats splintering. She sat here before that fancy café opened with its white-jacketed servers and glass-topped outdoor tables, when the only available refreshments were hot dogs and sodas offered by a single elderly man beneath a patched and striped umbrella at the pond's south end. She sat here when there was no swanky boathouse renting out pricey model boats and offering lessons on how to sail them, but only a dilapidated clapboard shack where for a pittance boats could be stored. She sat here when those fathers now jealously guarding the remote controls from their sons were the same age as those sons and when the mothers were girls and the nannies, most of them, not even born. She sat here when the practice of sailing model boats drew only a few enthusiasts from the immediate neighborhood. But as the years passed, more and more people came from further and further distances to place their boats on that pond and watch them sail across, and here she sat, watching still. She is now as much a fixture of the place, Emma supposes, as the Alice in Wonderland statue at the north of the pond or, to its west, the glorious Hans Christian Andersen reading from *The Ugly Duckling*, stovepipe hat behind his outstretched right arm, small bronzed duck (a climbing place irresistible to the youngest children) by his feet.

Three decades. How quickly they pass. They tumble about in her head like great soft hollow tubes filled with events that once meant everything to her, and with the faces and figures of people she knew but, other than a few, David among them, could not now even name. How quickly it goes. In a moment, no more, it has all but evaporated. Yet this she has. This bench. This pond. These children's voices. These boats.

David never sat with her on this bench. He wasn't much good at sitting anywhere. Movement was his thing. Being off and away and out a door. Down a road, disappearing even as she called to him. Slipping from her as these boats slip from the hands of the boys and men as soon as they are placed on the surface of the water.

I'll call from the road.

The sound of his promise sweeps toward her on a gust of wind. Even after all these years, it takes the breath right out of her. She leans forward, presses her handkerchief to her face.

"You all right, lady?"

From the far end of the bench comes the question. She drops her hand, inspects the man. She must look a fright if such a person—not related to any of the children by the pond, nor even a resident of the area, but a stranger to the neighborhood, unmistakably out of place, possibly even homeless, by the looks of him—should make such an inquiry. Still, it is a public park, its benches open to anyone seeking a moment's peace.

She nods her head in response to his question, and the man doesn't say anything more, just stares out across the pond. Emma stares, too, but with a lack of concentration now that allows her to sneak quick, surreptitious glances at the man. Not homeless, she ultimately decides. Just rumpled and weary. A laborer, most likely, his soiled shirt and khaki pants suggesting recent engagement in some type of physical work. A window washer, perhaps. A painter or electrician, though not accompanied by any bucket or brush or other identifying tool of his trade. On lunch-break, it would make sense, from a job at one of the Fifth Avenue apartment buildings across the way. Let him enjoy his break, Emma tells herself, glancing away and returning her full attention to the boats.

It is the inverted reflections of the sails she particularly loves. Those upside down triangular images caught in the glass-like water of the pond. Same width as the sails above, same angles, same heights. Completely intact, those reflections, when you'd expect them to bend or be foreshortened by the contact with the water. Only the wrinkling differentiating them from their counterparts. Where the sails above are smooth, the ones below are slightly crumpled. Nevertheless, they travel as a piece close beneath their boats. It is that that amazes her—how they travel beneath, not alongside or behind, but directly beneath as if attached by invisible wires, their pointed tips and taut sides slicing the water's surface like knives.

Now in a sudden gust, the wind picks up, and the smallest of the sailboats keels to one side. It goes over fast, the tip of its sail skimming the water's surface. Emma sits forward. It is a tense moment, but not a catastrophic one. She knows the boat won't capsize. Small as it is, its deck is securely sealed and its hull self-righting, preventing it from even taking on water, let alone actually tipping over. After a moment, the boat rights itself, as she knew it would, and continues on its way around the pond.

Emma sits back, relieved. As a child, David was a loner. It was one of the few things about himself he'd ever voluntarily revealed. That, and that he'd always been happiest going someplace else. As soon as he was old enough to be out on his own, he'd leave the Washington Heights apartment he shared with his mother (his father having left them both a month before David's birth) and walk through Riverside Park, exploring it first on foot, later by skateboard or scooter, traveling its tiered narrow strip from 72nd Street to 125th. Later still, riding the cobalt-blue, two-wheeled, sixteen-inch Schwinn bike his mother had bought him in honor, she said, of his love for exploration, he'd continue on across 72nd Street, proceed down to 59th and from there all the way to Hudson River Park and Manhat-

By the Pond

tan's southern tip before turning back. Only when in his senior year at Bronx High School of Science did he find the courage to venture up to the park's northern end at 158th Street before circling back. Coming and going, staying out later and later over the years, he explored the pathways and hills, the narrow, winding trails and broad, sweeping promenades. Always alone. Always, he told Emma, without regret for being alone. He told her about the feral cats he saw and the river rats, some bigger even than the cats. He told her about the flowers and plants, about the wild turkeys and red-tailed hawks. He told her about the green and red berries he came upon but couldn't identify, about picking them off their stems and rolling them about in the palm of his hand, but always stopping short of eating them. He told her about the angry-looking fungi deep in the undergrowth, and about what crawled on the ground and grew on the bushes and flew in the air. He discovered nature, he told her. A city kid's nature. And his own as well. That it was his way to go, and go alone, Emma understood from the start. Perhaps marriage for him had been a mistake.

But it wasn't that, he insisted. It was his job. A salesman is required to travel. And how else was he to provide for her?

Still, she thought it was more than that. She thought it was that he didn't want to stay.

"Is there someone else?" she asked well into their second decade of life together.

"You know me better than that," he replied.

She knew him well enough to know it was a lie.

Though not technically a lie, for it was probably not someone else, but a series of someone elses, a scattering of them like pebbles along the road.

She must stop thinking about him. Where he had gone, who he would be with now. He would take it wrong if he knew, for he had a tendency to take things wrong, ascribing intention where none existed. She was curious, that's all. Even today, she is curious. Still, she knows she has to stop. He's not her concern anymore. And yet, she feels he is.

"Give it here! Give it!"

A man's sharp cries are borne her way on the wind. Glancing up in alarm, she sees one of the fathers, a foot braced for support against the pond's rim, hastily grabbing back the boat controls he had only just reluctantly relinquished to his son. A collision is imminent. The father's boat, a sloop, is headed directly for an oncoming schooner. There seems little way to avoid the inevitable. Panicked cries erupt from those close to the man and boy. Figures with waving arms rush toward the scene. The father is determined to save his boat. Pressing hard on the buttons with both hands, he feverishly thumps his fingers into the remote. Extending his arms, fingers still thumping, he turns his body to the right, attempting to steer the sloop in that direction and out of the schooner's path.

"More, Dad, more!" the boy shouts encouragingly, while the man goes on drumming the controls and swerving his body to the right.

A brief but intense struggle ensues, the man battling with the remote, the boat seeming not to respond, and then suddenly it does. Abruptly dipping its sails as if in capitulation, it swerves to the right and gracefully takes itself away from the rapidly approaching schooner. Narrowly, the two prows miss; disaster is averted. Cheers go up.

A job that kept him moving was a saving grace for David, and Emma was glad he had it. It answered his need to be on his own, but more than that, in her opinion, it spoke to something deep within him. An aversion, she would have to call it, to being pinned down or explained. Never could he stand any probing of his state of mind. Always the quick smile, the raised, dismissive hand, the ready retort. Brushing things off before they could adhere. When he was at home, seeming constantly, almost purposefully, preoccupied. On the phone, engrossed in the mail, submerged in the news. Even during sex, avoiding her eyes, looking away.

She knew he'd done things as a boy to guarantee rejection. Lying, stealing. He told her stories of items going missing from his mother's bureau drawer, his high school science lab. He admitted to concocting fabrications to explain the disappearances. Somebody had broken into the house or the lab. *A mysterious intruder, a wily thief.* His ingenuity had amused her, his use of the word *wily*. But it was early in their marriage. They were just beginning to admit things to each other, and she had no way of knowing these childhood habits

                                                            By the Pond

of his wouldn't altogether die out as he grew older. Then a ring that had belonged to her grandmother vanished from her jewelry box and was later found in his coat pocket. Some months afterward, her own topaz broach was discovered in his sample case. *Now how did that get there?* Caught out, his first instinct was to laugh. She remembered the sound—startled, caged—the shrugged shoulders, the upturned palms. She adored him, even so. Playing at being bad, not being it. No matter what, she loved him. He knew that, and she was glad to have given him the knowledge of her love for all those years before he moved on.

Pharmaceuticals were what he peddled. Drugs of all sorts. Legal, she presumed.

"There's always a market," he told her, satisfaction in his voice as he said it.

The entire northeast corridor was his territory. Sometimes he'd be away for weeks at a time, returning only for a day or two before taking off again. Dozens of people to see, he explained. Doctors, pharmacists, supply managers at hospitals, directors at clinics. A certain amount of socializing was necessary.

"To keep the customers happy," he explained.

It made him a handsome living. More than adequately providing for the two-bedroom condominium on the 14th floor of the Fifth Avenue building in which, for longer and longer periods, she lived alone and from whose tall front windows overlooking the park she could see the pond. Two bedrooms they'd wanted, each with a bath, anticipating children.

"You do want children, don't you?" she'd asked.

"Of course," he'd replied. "But I think one will be enough."

To make him happy, she'd agreed.

David stayed at home with her for two years after it happened. Guilt, she'd assumed, for having been out of town when it occurred. It was his phone call from the road, in fact, that had precipitated the tragedy, drawing her away from the baby, securely tethered, so she swore to him and to the police and to anyone afterward who ever asked, in his bath-chair.

She could not very clearly remember the years that David stayed at home. Initially, she was barely aware of his presence, being barely aware of anything that went on around her then. And when she did come to notice him, he seemed not so much there as moving around somewhere inside a fog. The grieving years, she named them later, hoping in the naming to relegate them to the past, yet today, some thirty years on, the grieving hasn't ceased.

David's employer, in deference to what he termed their "difficult circumstances," of which no one ever spoke more directly than that, redrew David's territory, temporarily assigning him to local hospitals and clinics and nearby private medical practices to keep him close to home. Considerate of the man, Emma thought, though she never quite grew comfortable with having David so much about. As for David, as the weeks extended into months and the months into the first year and then the second, it seemed less an employer's consideration than a husband's obligation. He performed it dutifully, but Emma almost palpably felt his yearning to be elsewhere. Out on the open road, under the stars at night. But she hadn't trapped him. There'd been love on both their parts. Yet something in him did seem trapped. An animal thing. A part that could not be tamed or domesticated. It simply didn't fit him—she couldn't ignore what was right in front of her eyes—staying at home with a wife, grieving or not.

When the fog of those years began to clear and she began again more or less to function, she did wifely things. Making him breakfast before he packed up his case and went off to work, cooking him dinner when he returned. In between, she took her meds, cleaned the house, careful to avoid certain rooms, mostly she slept. They must have talked, broached the subject, ventured into the world, gone out now and then for a meal, or to see a film. She had vague memories of them doing such things in those two years when David was so much at home, memories that would flicker before her brightly like flames a moment, then be extinguished. But for the most part those years passed before her eyes as though someone else were watching them—a total stranger, perhaps, or even her baby boy, lying just below the water's surface and watching with open eyes as one by one, the weeks and months and years floated by above.

Those were the years in which she felt herself dragged into oblivion by the drugs her doctor prescribed, and kept there—had that been his intention?—by the samples David possessed and liberally added to her dosage. She was in a stupor most of the time, and that was hard on David and terribly unfair. For he was grieving, too, though silently and from afar.

Then at the end of the second year, he picked up his case and walked out the door.

I'll call from the road.

For years afterward it went on. The long absences. The calls from the road. Him coming and going, making a living, providing for her needs. Her shutting doors behind him, opening them upon his return, recognizing him less and less each time he crossed the threshold. Stooped, gray-headed he became, listing ever more to his right as if tugged in that direction by the weight of the case in his hand. At the end, pulling open the door to welcome him home, she wouldn't guess it was him.

Now Emma glances again at the man at the far end of her bench and finds him sleeping. He looks like a nice man. She thinks it might be all right to speak to him when he wakes up. About her marriage. About the event that transformed it. About the beginning and the end of marriage, though not the end of love. About her feeling that love is always with her, this love she has for a man that seems attached to her by something invisible yet altogether indestructible as the reflections of the sails in the water are attached to their boats.

She thinks of the time when that love began. When it burst from her and flew toward him, that tall, lanky young man in corduroys and a hunter's-green shirt, standing at the door of the foreign language class. Love. She hadn't known it by name then. Now it was all she would ever know of it. That one man, that one face. Those dark eyes. *Beginning Italian.* The two of them had registered for the same course. The serendipity of that. For them both to have an interest in the language of a country that neither of them had ever visited, or would. All she knew at that moment was that she would be his until the day she died. The knowledge made her simultaneously shy and brave. She turned her head away from him in shyness, bravely turned it back. She said something stupid, asked if this was beginning Italian, when the course name was clearly posted, along with that of the teacher, right there on the door. He looked at her, and his dark eyes smiled. She thought he must know what she knew. She told him her name. He told her his. She would have told anyone walking by right then that she had met the man she would marry. Except it was her secret and she didn't want anyone to know. Two years later, walking down the aisle of the Universalist Church on East 74th Street, she felt she would never be happier. Her parents were there. David's weren't. His mother had died the year before, and his father had never returned from wherever it was he had gone. Only a few friends from David's work were in attendance. Neither of them had many friends; they had that in common. She held his hand all through the vows. She thought she would never let it go.

She imagines telling the sleeping man at the far end of the bench about the wife she had become. She'd learned to cook, as women more or less had to in those days. She never did it particularly well, but David seemed not to notice, and that, perhaps, ought to have been a warning. She never fully comprehended her husband's need always to be someplace else. She thinks if she told that to the man on the bench he would understand. For how much does one person ever truly know about another? She had learned not to take it personally and to accept that it wasn't about her, but him, about the need he'd always had to keep moving away from wherever he was that had only intensified after the event.

The man on the bench awoke then, jolted into consciousness by the arrival of a small blond boy. About three years of age, Emma estimated, and wearing bright blue sneakers. For whatever reason puts such an action into the mind of a three-year-old, the boy had jumped onto the bench, grabbed the man's hand, and lifted it into the air like a trophy. Awakening to find a child peering over him, his hand held triumphantly aloft, the man looks at Emma and smiles. She smiles back, and the three of them remain that way a moment, man and boy with hands clasped, arms raised high, smiling woman looking on. And in that moment Emma thinks absurdly of herself and this rumpled man as that child's parents, committed to loving him for the rest of his life. Then the boy's actual mother appears, out of nowhere, it seems, the look of panic on her face giving way to relief as she spots her child, safe on the bench.

"I'm so sorry," she says, sweeping the boy into her arms. "Forgive me. I only looked away for an instant. An instant, that's all, and he was gone."

Emma and the rumpled man insist there is no need for apologies, yet Emma knows there is. She feels a little faint as she watches the woman strap her child into his stroller and walk away down the path.

She thought of David on the open road all those years, under the stars at night. She thought of him driving down highways and turnpikes. Music playing, it would have been. She thought of him climbing ramps and passing through underpasses, great stretches of anonymous asphalt rolling on before him and behind. She thought of him pulling up to toll booths, pulling off at rest stops to fill his tank, relieve himself, get a bite to eat. She thought of him getting back on the road to cover a few more miles before turning in at some drab motel for the night. She thought of him behind the wheel early next morning, radio playing, case on the seat by his side, samples inside. The road for him was all, the distance, the space. More than the sales, more than the socializing. She thought of him returning to her, crossing the threshold, becoming less and less recognizable as the years went by. Or maybe it was that one trip bled into another in her mind, making of all the time he was away one long, undifferentiated time composed of days and weeks and months and finally years of comings and goings, looping out and winding back upon themselves like intersecting smoke rings in the sky.

And then he was gone for good.

Everybody leaves, someone said. Perhaps it was the man on the bench.

I know that, someone answered. Perhaps it was herself.

She closed her eyes and lifted her chin. It had been a long, cold winter. She did not think she would survive another.

Over and over came the voice. *I'm sorry. I'm so sorry.* Over and over, the plea for forgiveness. *I only looked away for an instant. An instant, that's all.* Over and over, the sight of the tub, the bar of soap, the rubber duck floating in the water, the baby securely tethered in his chair. Over and over, the phone ringing in the next room. Over and over, the image of herself going to answer it.

I'll call from the road.

Distinctly, she heard it, that promise he made and never failed to keep.

Yes, surely sails keep secrets, tucked in the tops of their billowing white canvas. Secrets of a marriage, of a man on the road, of one or more women who may or may not have been his lovers. Secrets of a wife at home, emerging from a fog, carrying a love for a wandering man through the years, carrying that love even today, as unseemly as that might now seem, given her age. She thinks of their child, the one he had said would be enough, and she knows that none of the secrets in those sails should be visited except in memory where, as if frozen just beneath the water's surface, everything exists forever and nothing can be changed.

"You all right, lady?" comes the question from the far end of the bench.

"Yes," she replies, crushing the handkerchief in her hand. "Thank you for asking."

She lets out a breath and the sails of all the model ships take it in. Upon their inhalation, the sails billow in unison and merge into a single sail of towering size, and that one gigantic sail smartly comes about and bounces the fiery orb of the sun off its boom and straight into her eye.

City Legacy

"Can he hear me?"

"We can't be sure."

Breathing fills the room. Big heavy breathing like some pervert on the phone.

"Norm? Norm, dear?"

Can't be his. He doesn't breathe like that.

"Does he know I'm here?"

"It's hard to say."

"When will he wake up?"

"There's no way to tell."

Big, slow, heavy breathing. Rhythmical. Like something emitted through the pipes of an organ.

"I'll come back later. Stay as long as you like."

Something's wrong with his key. It won't turn in the lock. It slides right in but won't turn. Not once in all the years he lived in that hotel had that key given him the slightest bit of trouble.

"Can you hear me, Norm?"

Slid right in, turned soft as butter. Now this.

"I'm here, dear. Right here."

Before he loved her, he loved that room. And before the room, the city.

"The doctor said I could stay as long as I like."

He remembers everything in that room on the second floor. Old oak bureau, its middle drawer coming out left end first, and always with a squeak. Iron bed with the sagging mattress. Wooden table and chair, small as a child's, that Max the manager sent up when he saw him bringing work home from the office night after night. The window looking out onto Sixth.

"At first I didn't think he was a doctor. Looks too young to be a doctor."

He loved every single thing in that room. The window most of all. Loved looking out it. Loved sitting by it reading his papers, feet propped on the radiator. Loved its thin, gauzy curtain blowing soft and cool as a woman's stocking across his face.

"They all look like babies these days, don't they, Norm? Doctors, firefighters, police officers. Your life in the hands of babies."

When he finished with one paper, he'd toss it on the floor, pick up another. When he finished with them all, he'd go to the window, rest his arms on the sill, lean way out for a look, not caring that his sleeves came away black with grime. Manhattan grime. Unique to the borough. He knew if he watched the street long enough, he would see everything worth seeing anywhere in the city.

"Some sight, you are, Norm. Surrounded by machines, tubes going in and out. They're for your own good, you know that, don't you, dear?"

Now something like a beating of wings takes place in his heart.

"Never mind. We'll have those tubes out soon enough, and you home where you belong."

Then all at once, his key slides in and turns in the lock.

"Shall I read you the paper, Norm?"

The door flies open, and he sees the room. Exactly the way it was. Every piece of furniture, few as they were, every bit of dust, the same.

"You always loved your paper, didn't you, dear?"

God, how he loved that room!

"Here's something might interest you."

Look at it, sweetheart. Look at the room. Nothing's changed. Not one single thing.

"A proposal allowing that old hotel on 72nd to build commercial space and rent out rooms to transients."

The room was a tight fit, snug as a narrow-hipped woman, but suiting him just fine.

"I suppose you'd be in favor of that. You lived in a hotel once, didn't you? The Warwick, wasn't it? Though you were hardly a transient."

His room was on the second floor of what even then was an

old hotel.

"Lived in it for seven years before I came and got you out."

Still standing, glorious as ever, northeast corner of fifty-fourth and Sixth.

"Here, Norm. Let me fix that pillow for you."

Years ago some moron changed the name to Avenue of the Americas, but no New Yorker worth his salt ever called it anything but Sixth.

"That better, dear?"

Every night, seven years running, he came home to that hotel loyal as a lover. And if he ever brought a woman up, it was a passing thing and one to which the room gave tacit consent.

"Shall I go on about this hotel?"

The grime on the windowsill dirtied his hands and left thick black streaks on his white shirt sleeves. But that was okay by him. Those streaks being proof of his own personal connection to the city.

"Do you want to hear more about it, Norm?"

No kidding, Mabel, that's how I thought of it. My own personal connection. As if all the streets and buildings, all the bridges and tunnels in this town had been subjected to mortar and pestle, granulated into ash and sprinkled on my windowsill so I could carry them around on my clothes and under my fingernails wherever I went.

"They're thinking of converting that old hotel to condos, plus affordables for transients."

It was part of me, Mabel, see? That soot, that oil and ash. A tangible part.

"Some tenants oppose it, of course, liking the place the way it is."

A gift from the city to me. Now I'm thinking it's time to return the favor.

"You didn't mind, did you, dear? Me coming along and taking you away from your hotel?"

A gift to you, Mabel, my love, of the city I love.

"Sometimes I think you minded. But seven years alone in one little room, it broke my heart."

To make you see it, dear. So clear you'll never forget.

"Can you say something, Norm? Can you speak?"

For all the years I lived in that hotel I was close enough to the ground to poke my head out the window and read the headlines on the papers piled in front of Pete's. Stacks came flying off the truck, each tied with a thick brown rope. Pete whipping out his knife, sheathed like a secret at the small of his back, and cutting fast, straight through those ropes. *Whoosh* went the ropes as they tore. *Whoosh* went *The New York Times, The New York Daily Mirror, The New York World-Telegram and The Sun, The New York Journal American, The New York Herald Tribune, The New York Post, The New York Daily News.* Hear it, Mabel? Hear them tearing?

"Can you hear me, Norm? Can you give me a sign?"

I want you to hear it, dear. I want you to see and remember.

"Cause there's something I gotta tell you, Norm. Something hard. And I need to know you're hearing me."

It'll be my gift to you, my dear. A gift of things as they were before your time with me, to survive my time with you. A gift like a new coat.

"Hardest thing I ever had to say."

No, not a coat exactly.

"You might think it's silly after all these years."

More like a lining to a coat than the coat itself. Yes, that's it. I'll bring the sights and sounds of the old days back to life and offer them to you to wear like a lining beneath your present life.

"But it's not silly, Norm. Not to me."

I'll make you see it, Mabel. I'll make you hear and smell and taste and touch the sights and sounds as they were.

"I'll need your full attention while I'm saying it."

The aroma of hot dogs and sauerkraut, of roasted chestnuts and pretzels, slightly charred and loaded with salt the way he likes, comes up from the street and wafts in through his window which he never, even on the coldest days, closes all the way in winter and flings wide in summer.

"Are you listening, Norm?"

Seven years alone in that hotel, and he can't honestly say he was ever lonely. There was always a guy to talk to at the front desk or on the door. Alan, first thing when he leaves for work. Sid, when he comes back at night. And Phil, till four o'clock every morning in the bar downstairs. They never let him by without a wager on a game or a weather forecast.

"I know it's gonna hurt you, dear, and I'd cut out my tongue before doing that, but I gotta tell it to you, face to face."

The stench of garbage at the curb, one summer for sixteen days running during a strike, and of hot tar being laid rises clear and unequivocal, but even that he doesn't mind. It's his city and he'll take it any way it comes.

"I don't know if I can get it out, but you'll never have any respect for me if I don't."

Night after night, the city comes up to him like company through that second-story window. Horns honking, sirens blaring, police cars and fire engines tearing down the Avenue. High-heeled women racing for cabs, truck doors slamming, and pipe hitting pipe with Con Edison forever somewhere working overtime.

"Some might say it's no fair springing it on you like this, you being captive to those tubes and all."

New York. His city. His streets. And every night like clockwork, three minutes past one, the clatter of hooves on concrete coming ghostlike out of the park at 59th Street.

"I gotta say it, Norm. It's now or never."

The sound of iron on asphalt reaches a peak and he gets up out of bed and leans way out the window for a look, and there he is, all sleek and shiny in the night.

"You listening, Norm?"

Hello, friend. Long time no see.

He tosses his head like after a bath and gives out with his lovely snort.

What a sight you are. Black as night. Streetlights shimmering on your quivering flanks. And carrying that cop on your back straight and stiff as pride itself.

"I gotta tell you this."

Then on you trot, and I return to bed and lie there listening to the clatter of your hooves diminishing and finally fading out entirely as you take your rider on down the Avenue and out of hearing.

"I'll never be able to look myself in the eye if I don't get it out."

Everything's different now, Mabel. Disney's taken over Times

Square. More than half my spots are long since gone. Friendly corner bars destroyed, classiest cigar stores taken out.

"You look trapped in that bed, Norm. Can't move, can't speak. Can't check your watch. Remember how you checked your watch night after night to see if it was time to head for that restaurant of yours."

They took the best of the old eateries, too.

"Your hangout, you called it."

My hangout, I called it, the menu permanently engraved on my mind. Roast baby chicken, liver and onions, and the specialty of the house, beef stew.

"I must've made my own beef stew for you a thousand times, and you always said it was good as the original."

Dug it right out, like that mastectomy thing they did to you last year and whatever the hell they did to me this morning.

"That right there, Norm, that's the closest you ever came to a lie."

Only it wasn't something growing that didn't belong. That place belonged. When they took out Dinty Moore's they cut the heart right out of the block.

"Two, three nights a week you'd go. Even when we were newlyweds."

Place to meet the gang, light up a cigar, lay a bet on a fight.

"All those years, it stood between us, a rival for your affections."

Open kitchen in the back and Anna Moore, bless her, sitting upright by the cash register kept, urbanely, in the rear. The soul of the neighborhood, it was.

"And how you loved your friends at Dinty Moore's. Sometimes I thought you loved them more than me."

I know you didn't think much of the gang I hung with, Mabel, and you're entitled to your opinion. They're mostly all gone now, leveled like the joint itself, but they were what I knew of family in the days before I knew you.

"Forgive me, Norm, I never was much good at saying things straight out. That's your specialty, not mine."

Wasn't a night of the week except Sundays, when Old Man Moore closed up and I'd head on over to Mamma Leone's, that two or three of the guys, including the ones with wives, didn't find their way to my table. Slaps on the back. *Hi ya, Norm. How's the wife?* Highballs all around.

"I wish I could say it straight out, Norm. I wish I could find the words."

It was a short walk from my hotel over to Dinty Moore's, and whichever way I went, down Sixth a few blocks, past Radio City Music Hall and the RCA Building, before cutting over to Broadway and across Duffy Square, I'd see someone I knew.

"It had a lot to do with that hangout of yours."

Or, my preferred route, because that's where the action was, straight across 54th to Broadway and down the eight blocks from there, I knew the men in the newsstands on the corners along the way and the women working the streets.

"All through our marriage, Norm, to the day they tore it down."

Hi ya, Norm. How ya doin'? they'd call out. And not in pursuit of their trade but just because they knew who I was and were used to seeing me around.

"Don't hate me for saying this, dear, but I wasn't sorry to see it go."

Put up a big, fancy hotel in its place. All Mickey Mouse and Donald Duck now where it used to be. Tell you the truth, Mabel, between the ducks and the hookers, I'll take the hookers any day.

"Oh, gosh, Norm. I don't think I can do this. Forget I even brought it up. How about I just hold your hand?"

I'd pick up a paper at Pete's and a couple of cigars in the shop on the corner and continue down Broadway past the Capitol Theater, past Ripley's and Lindy's—the real McCoy, not the cheap imitation they got today—I'd go on past Loews's and the Colony and the old Camel's sign across the street. I never could approach that sign without stopping to look up and wonder at that guy blowing out those gorgeous rings. One after another, each a perfect circle of smoke.

"Thing is, Norm, your life at Dinty Moore's was like your real life and the life you had with me just filling in until you could get back to it."

I read somewhere they paid him five bucks for that sign. Can you beat that, Mabel? Five bucks for feat like that!

"All those years taking a back seat to a bunch of men and a plate of stew. It wasn't easy, Norm, you gotta know."

I'd saunter on down Broadway, the lights of the Automat beckoning in the distance, neon flashing, tourists gaping, until I got to the south side of 46th. There I'd make a right, walk west a quarter of a block, and there it was—Dinty Moore's. Remember, dear?

"But that place isn't the thing, Norm. Not the real thing."

I took you there more times than maybe you'd have cared to go, and I went without you when you declined to come along, and I don't say that wasn't wrong, but it was a guy's place and it's easier with men. Nothing hidden. Nothing secret.

"It's the only thing I ever kept from you in forty-two years of marriage."

The place was a habit with me. Addictive as dope. And I don't claim I didn't overdo it, leaving you alone once or twice too often.

"It was only the one time, Norm, I swear."

Once for sure.

"You'd gone to your hangout again...,"

Just my hand on the knob gave me a thrill. My fingers tracing the Old Man's initials etched in glass.

"And this fellow from my hometown happened to call."

To the left as you come in, along the bottom of the great oak bar, that long shining brass rail. A sight to knock your eye out.

"I never gave him our number, Norm, I swear. He must've got it from my mother."

And behind the bar, Jimmy giving me the high-sign, letting me know: *Dewar's and water coming right up.*

"I'd loved him in high school, but it wasn't love any more. And maybe I was a little mad at you for leaving me alone again that night."

Black-coated waiters, chefs in white hats. Brass pots gleaming in the open kitchen beyond. Knives exposed, sharp as razors. White-tiled floor, mirrors everywhere. And Old Man Moore coming up the center aisle to escort me to my table.

"I felt like I wanted one last taste. Like with that piece of candy and the final cigarette, remember, when I was giving up sweets and smoking."

Starched white cloths, big round tables. Cold beets waiting, whether you wanted them or not. Table reserved for me till nine.

"Just a taste before relinquishing."

It was a second home to me and kinda hard to relinquish.

"I never saw him again, Norm. Never even hankered to. You're the one true love of my life."

Things were simpler with the guys. No mincing words or counting drinks or worrying about somebody holding something against you in the morning.

"But I never told you, and that always made me feel small."

I like things simple. Always have.

"It's haunted me all these years. Made me feel ashamed. Not about the boy, about not telling you."

The way I figure, simple things give you courage. The smell of hot tar. A slap on the back. A horse's hooves clattering on concrete. Pete's knife going *Whoosh!* through the ropes.

"It takes courage to be honest. You always had that, Norm. Not me."

Mabel. My Mabel. My old love.

"Fear is my greatest character fault. Forty-two years, and I never found a way of telling you."

No woman alive ever kept a secret like you.

"Forgive me, Norm."

I don't blame you for anything, dear. How could I ever? Though I gotta admit when you moved me across to the East Side of town and into an apartment you kept so clean we might as well been living in the country, I missed the grime. But you were a country girl to start, so I never held a grudge.

"The thing is, Norm, the boy's not the thing. Not the real thing. The real thing is this right here."

And I knew about the hometown boy.

"No way on earth I'm gonna live through this."

Did you forget my habit of stopping to chat with the men on the door? I waited forever to hear it from you. But after twenty, thirty years went by, it sorta lost its urgency.

"Well, I've said it now, and that's a load off."

Me and you, Mabel. You and me. That's all that counts. I

never loved a woman more.

"We've always had each other, Norm. You and me. Me and you. Never talked about an ending. Never made a plan."

That big heavy breathing's reaching out now like it wants to take over. What d'you say we let it have its way?

"We should've made a plan. You should've taught me how."

Here's what we'll do, sweetheart. You'll do the breathing for the both of us. Just take a breath and let it settle down inside your lungs, then let it out. And with each breath you take mine will descend and rise with yours.

"Oh, God, Norm. How am I ever gonna do this? You gotta tell me how."

If we do it right, my breath will go on filling your lungs and rising up, and all the things I've seen and heard and smelled and tasted and touched will go on rising and rising in you.

"Or did you think I'd just know? That it's some dumb woman thing?"

On each and every breath you take you'll know the sights and sounds and smells that got me through. The city I loved all my life will be lifted out of the rubble of the wrecker's ball and rise in you, my other great love.

"What is it, Norm?"

Birds in his chest soaring now, fluttering. His arm flying out. He finds her knee.

"Oh, Norm, you've touched my knee!"

Oh, what a lovely knee!

"That sent a thrill straight through me."

Look in the drawer, Mabel. Find the key. Open the door, see the room. Remember everything you see.

"You reaching for something, Norm? Something in that drawer? Something you want me to see?"

Remember it for me, Mabel. Remember it forever.

"Let me get it for you, dear. Is this it, Norm? This old key to your room in that hotel? You kept it all these years?"

Everything will be all right now. Everything will be just fine.

"You were happy in that room, weren't you, dear? I know you were."

Mabel knows. Everything's all right now. Mabel has the key.

"I like the feel of this key, Norm. It's kinda heavy. Its weight gives me courage. I'll keep it for you always. I'll remember everything the way you told it."

Mabel will see the room. She'll see the old oak bureau and the iron bed with the sagging mattress. She'll see the gauzy curtains at the window and hear the sounds of traffic in the street below. She'll smell the aroma of hot dogs and sauerkraut. She'll see the papers stacked at the curb in front of Pete's. She'll hear Pete's knife slicing through the ropes. And the horse! Don't forget the horse.

The key is in the palm of her hand. His hand covers hers. He's touched her knee. That lovely knee. The big heavy breathing rises and falls. Rises again and does not fall. Only rises and rises, taking their two hands and the key between them; taking this room with its machines and tubes and that other room on the second floor of that old hotel. Rising and rising, taking the bureau with the squeaking drawer; taking the iron bed with the sagging mattress; taking the gauzy curtain and the radiator and the newspapers scattered on the floor; taking the window looking onto Sixth; taking the horse; taking his lovely snort and his clattering hooves, lifting them all up, rising higher and higher, up to the ceiling and straight through to the city sky beyond.

Whoosh!

VOICES

ONE

ROBROY

     He's ranting. Letting loose. It feels good. Ugly language flying off the bench. Obscenities. Blasphemes. An old woman about his age, plastic shopping bags at her feet, sits next to him. After forty seconds of his ranting she gets up, gathers her shopping bags, walks away. Only a few feet. She won't go far for fear of missing her bus. The old man continues ranting. Loud, angry bursts erupting like cluster bombs from the bench. He's not aware the old woman has gotten up, walked away. Maybe he didn't even know she'd been sitting next to him on the bench. The bench is empty now, except for him. Other people are standing around, but no one will dare take the seat next to him. Actually, there are two free seats next to him, one on either side. No one will take either seat. He's shouting like a maniac. Streams of foul language rend the air.

     RobRoy leans forward, places both hands flat to his bony knees, continues shouting almost gleefully.

     A man walks toward him. A young, tall, slender man. Yankees baseball cap front to back.

     "Hush up," he says, bending low to see his face.

     That's all. Two words. Quiet, low. Definitive. He's less than half RobRoy's age, but seems to know him, to have been around him or others like him all his life.

     He says it only once. *Hush up.* Leaning down, peering into the ranting guy's face. Once is all it takes. The ranting guy goes silent. Instantly. Like he's been shocked. Nothing more comes out of him. No shouting. No ranting. He's emptied out. Two words from a stranger and he's done. The space where his hands lie on his bony knees seems to collapse. His trousers go loose on his legs. There's nothing left of him. He stares straight ahead into the street. The man wearing the Yankees baseball cap straightens up, walks away. He doesn't go far. He passes by the old woman, then walks back to where she stands, plastic shopping bags at her feet, waiting for the bus. He stands next to her. She looks at him. They do not speak.

The bus won't come for a while yet. Not the bus they are waiting for. Other buses pull into the stop, pick up passengers, pull away. But not the bus they want. The Number 5 is notoriously slow in coming. After a long while they will see it off to their left, appearing ghost-like out of the evening sky. Its number and destination in flashing red lights high above the windshield. It will lumber toward them, stop while they board, start up again, head west toward the river, make its turn north and continue on uptown, keeping the river on its left, the sunset a golden bullet in the driver's eye.

Other people arrive, wait for the bus. A man with a bushy white beard sits down on the bench next to the man who had been ranting but is quiet now. Sometime later an old woman, not as old as the first, nor as old as the man himself, sits down on his other side, depositing her plastic shopping bags at her feet. RobRoy is hemmed in now by people on either side but doesn't seem to notice. He stares into the street. Traffic goes by, east and west. The people on either side of him know nothing of his history, his previous ranting, the obscenities spewing from his mouth. To them he's a blank page. Unmarred. Fresh.

It's fresh for the ranter too. Made so by the words of a stranger. Uttered quietly but with authority. *Hush up.* Apparently, that's all he needed to muster a fresh perspective: someone to tell him how to behave. He's not a bad guy. Not a monster. Not someone with a savage heart. He didn't kill his father. Didn't kill anyone.

Not that he didn't think of it once or twice. Once for sure, when he and his father and mother lived in the apartment with many rooms in the city and his father raised his skinny hand and slapped his cheek hard enough to turn it red. Not after that, he didn't think. There'd be no reason to. For after his mother left and his father lost his job and the apartment and started drinking in earnest, he and his father moved to the boardinghouse where they lived essentially separate lives. Pretty much keeping out of the other's way. Like him, his father wasn't a bad guy. Not a monster. Never hit him but that once. Never once hit his mother.

He stares straight ahead into the street. Traffic goes by, east and west. His whole life could go by while he waits for the Number 5.

CHRISTINE

She wasn't his mother. He knew that for sure. First of all, she was too young to be his mother, no more than fifteen or sixteen when she came to live with them. But it made him feel good to pretend she was, like ranting obscenities on the bench made him feel good. Pretending things about her began long before the ranting, when he was just a boy. Or not much more than a boy. Maybe twelve or thirteen years of age. It probably didn't make her feel good or not good or any which way when he pretended she was his mother. She probably didn't even know he was doing it. "Did you know?" he asked her later. "What'd you think?" she replied. He thought that she knew. Even at twelve or thirteen years of age he thought the way she asked the question meant she knew.

Her brown eyes glistened. She had a ponytail. "Black like night," he once referred to it. *Ebony*, she preferred to call it. When she wanted to let it down she took the rubber band off, put her hands under her hair, fanned it out and shook her head, freeing the hair to hang loose, which it did, halfway down her back.

She was called Christine. He heard his father call her that. "Come over here, Christine. Lie next to me." He was watching from the doorway. That space where the door didn't close. Christine lying in his father's arms, trapped, it seemed. His father's skinny arm coming up over the rise of her breasts, his other hand pressing down on her mouth, not hard, it didn't look like, only enough to stifle her gasps. She had a way of making these gasping sounds, a whole series of them, quick and sharp, like in continuing surprise. Her back was to him as he watched, and to his father. His father was pumping into her, his right hand covering her mouth, pressing down to keep her gasping sounds from escaping. But they escaped anyway. The two of them not knowing he was watching from the doorway, him pretending she was his mother. His father never shut his door all the way the whole time they lived in the boardinghouse, like he forgot he wasn't the only one living there or didn't care. Watching, he wondered if that's how they made him, from the rear like that. Decided if that's how he got born, then she actually was his mother. Considered

                                    Voices—One

maybe another kid was being made as he watched. A baby brother
or sister implanted in her awkward like that, backwards. There'd be
something wrong with it, he was pretty sure, if it got born that way,
so he decided it was a good thing that baby brother or sister never
came out of her in all the time she lived with him and his father in
the boardinghouse.

"Eat," his father said, and he ate. "Sleep," his father said,
and he slept. "Come over here, Christine. Lie next to me." It was no
different.

HANK

His father was called Hank. RobRoy had no idea what his
father did with his days or nights, but he has a vague memory of
himself in a highchair, his father sitting in front of it, pulling his chair
up close in little jerks. The jerks made screeching sounds on the floor
and sent him back and forth in his seat. He remembers his father
making faces at him, crunching his eyes, jamming his tongue against
the inside of his cheek, dangling it from his mouth. Lifeless, gro-
tesque.

He remembers his father's cough. Loud, abrasive. A smoker's
cough, it was called. He remembers how his father's cough seemed to
line up with his mother's words, taking aim as she spoke them, firing,
shooting them down, one by one. Sometimes it went on all morning.

His father was like two men to him. One, the man before he
was seven; the other the boardinghouse man. The first man dressed
in a three-piece suit, shiny shoes, always a tie. He appeared now and
then in the apartment, riding in as on a wave through the rooms.
Remaining a moment, reading a paper, maybe eating something—an
apple, a slice of cheese—then riding away on his wave out the front
door. He pretty much forgot that first man early on. The second man,
the boardinghouse man, would stay with him until he died. That
man dressed in jeans which he never filled out, wore a succession
of black T-shirts and never a tie. He remembers him holding a beer
in his hand or some other alcoholic drink and saying to him when
he was eleven or twelve and his mother had been gone a few years,
"She's gone." That's all he had to say on the subject. "She left."

Mostly he remembers his father, both of them, alone and

living in a separate space. Behind a wave, was how he saw it. Far off, almost imperceptible. Every so often the wave would crest and break, and his father would appear, riding it into a room. Frequently grabbing the phone from his mother's hand, shouting into it. Once and only once, long ago, he had slapped his cheek hard enough to turn it red.

When he was two, he saw himself in the ocean, locating his father's distant wave, diving through and pulling him out. But he was only two; couldn't swim, couldn't dive, couldn't pull anyone out of anything.

CORINNE

His mother's name was Corinne. He remembers that, and that she said his hair was the color of sweet corn and called him RobRoy. A name of her own invention, combining his first and middle names. After she went out of his life, no one called him that any more. He remembers her laugh—a wild laugh like a bird of prey soaring through the apartment, seeking him out. It began low in the back of her throat and got louder and louder as it progressed, piercing his ears at its loudest. Then like a light bulb suddenly blowing out, it would unexpectedly quit. He remembers his mother had golden hair and was young and pretty (which most small boys will probably say about their mothers) and had that wild laugh and a voice that played like music through the rooms of the apartment. (Though maybe he was making that up about the music.)

He remembers her speaking on the phone a lot. Brisk. Businesslike. Ordering things. Furniture, tiny silk lampshades for electrical fixtures shaped like candles that protrude from the walls, ornate birdcages though they didn't have any birds. Every so often his father would ride his wave into a room, grab the phone out of his mother's hand, shout, and send everything back. This was before the boardinghouse, when his father had a real job (something in insurance, he thought) and the three of them lived in the apartment with many rooms in the city. He remembers how the rooms branched off to the right and left along a long white hall, although he doesn't exactly remember what they looked like, or in which order they lay.

He remembers certain things about the rooms. The blue silk sofa in the living room in particular. One day that sofa sprouted

big red spots like patches of roses. Turned out it was blood. Could
as easily have come from inside the sofa, bursting spontaneously up
through the fabric, as from the outside, like from a drone throwing
patches of roses down from above. He especially liked the idea of
the drone. He saw it circling round and round, having no strategy
or purpose other than to cause confusion. He remembers his mother laughing her wild laugh as she took a cloth and blotted those
red spots on the sofa then sprayed them with salt and cold water, a
concoction of her own invention. He remembers her zeroing in on a
spot, blotting it with her cloth, zeroing in on another, spraying it with
her concoction of salt and cold water, and letting loose with her wild
laugh. "Gotcha," she'd say, coming down on a spot. "Take that,"
she'd say, coming down on another, firing the spray bottle at random
from her hip like a machine gun. Turned out the blood was her own,
having come from an altercation she'd had with a wine glass. She'd
squeezed the glass until its stem broke, cutting her hand. All the
blotting and spraying with her machine gun never got the blood out
entirely. Eventually she got rid of the sofa, ordered a new one, and
this time his father didn't ride into the room on his wave, grab the
phone out of her hand, and send it back.

Being a child, RobRoy thought it was funny. The sponta-
neous sprouting of the big red spots, the drone he liked to pretend
was circling round and round above, the spray bottle clutched like
a machine gun in his mother's hands. Her shouts of "Gotcha," and
"Take that." Her wild laugh. How could a child hear his mother
laugh like that and not think it was funny? He heard her laughing
wild like that many times through the years before he turned seven.
Then, save in his imagination, never again. He heard that laugh
coming from somewhere deep in her throat, getting louder and louder as it progressed, then quitting suddenly before whatever had provoked it was finished. He tried to make his own laugh sound like that.
He remembers chasing his mother from room to room, laughing as
wild as he could. But his mother didn't think it was funny. "Hush up,
RobRoy!" she'd yell. "What the hell do you think you're doing?"

Later, when he was no longer a child and came to reflect on
it, it occurred to him that his mother's laugh had more times than not
been associated with some domestic event resulting in things flying
against a wall. An ashtray or dish. She'd laugh. Shattered glassware,

broken china. She'd laugh. Even a rending of flesh, always her own, as with the blood on the sofa. She'd laugh. Superficial knife wounds, lacerations. She'd laugh. To a child still under the age of seven, it was funny. Kids that age don't know much. He probably didn't even know that when he chased his mother through the rooms of the apartment and laughed wild like that, he was more often than not afraid.

There were periods in his young life, frequent periods, when his mother didn't laugh her wild laugh. Didn't laugh at all. Went silent for days on end. Stayed in her room with the door shut. During those periods RobRoy did his best to make his mother laugh. He'd go up to her (provided she opened her door, which oftentimes she wouldn't), press his nose against hers and give his best imitation of the wild way she used to laugh. "Hush up, RobRoy," she'd say. "I'm not laughing now." And those two words, *Hush up*, were enough to make him stop cold. He'd be forced then to endure her silence until at last she emerged from her room and her wild laugh burst from her throat once more, freeing him to mimic it again and to chase his mother through the apartment until she ordered him to stop. Once, as he was laughing wildly and chasing his mother through the rooms, his father rode in on his wave, rounded a corner, came up to him, and slapped him hard across the face. Only that once. But enough to make him think of killing him. "Quit your cackling," his father shouted. His cheek went hot and red and stayed that way for hours, days, decades, even though his father only hit him that once.

CHRISTINE

"You don't talk much, do you?" Christine said to him one day.

"I talk enough," he replied.

"I'm gonna be a costume designer," she told him another day.

"What's that?"

"Design clothes like for people in Hollywood."

"What's Hollywood?"

"You don't know anything, do you?"

"I know more than you."

"Yeah? I know you watch us from the doorway. I know your

eyes land like bugs on my skin."

She was just sitting there in the big middle room that divided his and his father's. Sitting on the edge of the rickety couch, legs tight together beneath her short leather skirt, his eyes traveling up her legs, starting at the ankles and ending at the place they came together and disappeared beneath her skirt. He liked what she said about his eyes landing like bugs on her skin. He didn't know she knew he was watching, but now that he knew, it made him feel good.

"Do you know every time I watch? And every time I don't?"

"How would I know when you don't?"

"You've been here a long time."

"Not so long."

"One day you weren't here, and then you were. Are you going to stay?"

"Do you care?"

He didn't answer.

"I think you do."

"Where did you come from? Where did he find you?"

"On the road."

"Were you lost?"

CORINNE

Out of her hands. It was a phrase Corinne despised above all others. "Utterly," she said. He liked that word, utterly. "I utterly despise it." It made her feel sick to her stomach. She'd hear it on TV or maybe read it in a book or magazine. It drove her crazy, she said. *Out of her hands.*

RobRoy came to associate that phrase with a certain look in his mother's eyes. A nervous look, like she didn't know where she was or why. Or who he was or why. He saw that look most often when she picked him up after school. He'd be standing at the top of the school's stone steps looking down, and he'd see her waiting there by the curb, apart from the other mothers, not talking to them, not forming herself into a group and chatting about this or that the way the other mothers did. Just standing there by the curb, alone, apart. And sometimes she'd look up and see him at the top of the steps and stare straight at him for the longest time, confused, bewildered, as if trying to remember who he was.

It happened once or twice when she picked him up from kindergarten. The confused, bewildered look. Then more and more often when he was in first grade. Bewildered. Blank. By the time he was in second grade it had become an established and shocking occurrence in his life. His mother staring at him from the curb, not knowing who he was. It happened so often in second grade it passed from being shocking to being something to be expected.

Not always. Not every single time she picked him up after school did he see that look, but maybe one out of six or seven times. Not so much a look of bewilderment, though certainly that, but more a look of panic. Like she was about to throw up. Seeing her son and not knowing who he was, she'd panic. And he'd understand the situation was *out of her hands.*

He thought it must be something he did or said, some way he behaved that made the memory of who he was go completely out of his mother's mind. He was no one she knew. No boy she had ever seen. Not himself at all, but some other boy. There were days in second grade (more and more) when being picked up by his mother after school made him wish she wouldn't. Seeing her scanning the children at the top of the school steps, coming at last to him, passing over him, coming back, looking him square in the eye and not knowing who he was. He wondered if other kids could see it too. But there were days when it didn't happen, when she knew him. And on those days, she'd rush from her spot by the curb, swoop to her knees on the pavement before him, spread her arms wide like some sort of religious figure to receive him, and cover his face with kisses. He adored her then.

But on the days she didn't know him, he wished she wouldn't ever come for him after school again. He wished a nanny would pick him up. Stephie wasn't a real nanny. She was a nice black lady who called him Sweetie Pie and helped his mother when she had dinner parties and was allowed to sleep in the bedroom at the far end of the long white hall when those parties lasted really late. He didn't remember his mother allowing anybody else ever to sleep in that room. *Remember, RobRoy, you can't be too careful who you let in your house.* Some of the kids in his class had real nannies, and he knew his father could afford one because he had a job back then (something in insurance,

he thought, but wasn't exactly sure), and he knew it was a good job
because his father could pay for all the things his mother ordered
for the apartment, except when he didn't want to and rode in on his
wave, grabbed the phone out of her hand, and sent everything back

CHRISTINE

He came to understand that Christine hadn't been lost exactly. Just wandering along the highway. She liked to wander, she told
him, and when his father pulled his truck over and stopped, she got
in.

"That was stupid."

"Who asked you?"

"He could have been a serial killer. An axe murderer."

They had conversations like that (half conversations actually,
for he was mostly silent) during the time she lived in the boardinghouse with him and his father and he pretended she was his mother.
A twelve or thirteen -year-old with a mother who was maybe sixteen. He saw them getting rid of his father, running away together,
getting married. Or maybe his father would conveniently die of
natural causes, or causes related to smoking and drinking, for he was
old already and drank and had a smoker's cough that could go on
all morning. He wouldn't be able to catch up with them if they got
a decent head start. They'd ride off on the plow horse one of their
neighbors kept in the yard behind the boardinghouse. The two of
them on that one horse. Himself in front with the reigns, of course,
her behind, his beautiful bride-to-be. The horse wouldn't go very
fast, but fast enough to outrun his father's truck if they left in the
middle of the night when he wouldn't even know they were gone.

Christine talked a lot about Hollywood, so he decided that's
where they'd go. Out west, past places he had never been, through
deserts, across mountains and fertile valleys and fields of corn.
They'd find a place to live, a neat little house with a white picket
fence. The fence was important to him. He'd always wanted one,
having seen them in movies and magazines and associating them
with wraparound togetherness and everlasting happiness. He'd grow
up fast and find a job and marry her. He'd become her supporter and
comforter, and they'd be happy ever after.

When he started thinking seriously about running away

with Christine and finding that house with the white picket fence, he stopped pretending she was his mother and began thinking of her as his wife. An almost thirteen-year-old kid could have a wife. They did in Guinea and Afghanistan and places like that, he'd read about it in school, although maybe it was illegal now. He let the notion grow in his mind—Christine becoming his wife, himself her husband. On the mornings his father was out doing odd jobs like plumbing and carpentry for people in the neighborhood, which he'd resorted to after he started drinking heavily and lost the insurance job (if that's what it was) and they moved to the boardinghouse, RobRoy would show Christine just how good a husband he could be. He'd wait in the kitchen by the stove (a red and white striped apron tied over his jeans) for her to emerge from his father's room. When she came in, sleep-staggering and hungry for food, he'd make fried eggs and bacon and toast the way she liked, easy over on the eggs, crispy bacon, toast just dark around the edges.

"You do eggs nice."

"I can do more than eggs."

With his father out doing his jobs, he'd take her back to his father's room and lay her on his father's bed, which was bigger and more comfortable than his own. Her skin was warm. The flesh up and down her arms and on the inside of her thighs where her legs disappeared beneath her leather skirt was soft. She didn't try to stop him. He saw the clothes on the floor she'd taken off for his father, socks and jeans, a T-shirt and panties. He knew he could be better than his father. He wouldn't trap her with his arm or try to stifle her gasps with his hand. He'd let her move free as she liked and gasp as loud as she wanted. He wouldn't do anything backwards or from the rear, but everything in a rightful and romantic manner, and all the time he'd be covering her with kisses and telling her how desperately he loved her.

He loved her for herself and everything about her. Loved watching her dress and undress (that especially). Could watch it over and over, like a scene from one of his favorite old movies. *Roman Holiday* or *Sabrina*, both starring Audrey Hepburn, who in her impish way looked a bit like Christine, but without the ponytail. He loved watching her take off her T-shirt; loved the way it snaked up over her skinny torso, exposing her ribs, and finally her long-awaited breasts.

She never wore a bra. He loved the way her arms tensed as she pulled the T-shirt over her head. Sometimes he would help her, but mostly not, maybe stepping forward as if to help, then stepping back, awaiting the appearance of her breasts. They were definitely little, but he loved that too. He loved that she was skinny, loved that her arms were strong for a girl, muscular shoulders and biceps that flexed as she pulled the shirt over her head. Loved her ponytail (*ebony* he remembered to call it). Loved the way she took off the rubber band, put her hands under her hair, fanned it out and shook her head, freeing the hair to hang loose half-way down her back. He never worried about his father coming back from one of his jobs and walking in on them. Never thought what would happen if he did. Maybe he should have, but he never did. He was just so happy, so goddamned happy being with Christine in that way. He loved watching her breath go up and down as she lay beside him in his father's bed. Loved that her breath smelled sometimes of toothpaste, at other times of coffee and lollipops. He loved feeling her bare feet touching his. Loved listening to the refrigerator humming down the hall, the wooden shutters banging outside his father's grimy window. Loved that they were warm and cozy inside.

ROBROY

When he was three, he waited by the door to his parents' room for his father to come out riding on his wave. His first father, the apartment one. Big as a tree. He waited by that door while day turned to night, night to day. He waited there for hours, days, years. And then he was four and forgot what he had been waiting for. He turned away from the door and went back to imitating his mother's wild laugh and chasing her through the rooms of the apartment. And then he was five and had completely abandoned his aspiration of locating his father on the far side of his wave and pulling him out.

He was in first grade, then second. His mother picked him up after school, oftentimes standing by the curb apart from the other mothers, waiting for him to come out. Seeing him, she'd sometimes stare at him for long uncomfortable moments as if she didn't know him. When he turned seven, she gave him a birthday party. Three boys, three girls. Ice cream and cake and balloons. His father was playing golf and couldn't attend. The next morning, his mother disappeared.

Gone, his father said. *Left.*

Then he was eight, nine, maybe ten. He dreamt about his mother coming back from wherever she'd gone. He saw her entering his room, sitting on the edge of his bed, running her fingers through his hair. Same dream every night year after year.

When he was eleven or twelve, the apartment disappeared, and the boardinghouse appeared. Peeling paint on a clapboard exterior. A plow horse in the neighbor's yard. A refrigerator humming down the hall. His house, his and his father's. He got used to it.

"Eat," his father said, and he ate. "Sleep," his father said, and he slept.

He went to a different school. Different women came to pick him up. Different women passed in and out of the boardinghouse before Christine. A parade of them. Some old, some fat. Some young and skinny. None as young or skinny as Christine. He watched from the doorway of his father's room, listening to the different sounds they made, noting the different ways they moved. His father never shut his door all the way, like he forgot his son was in the house or didn't care.

Then Christine arrived, and the others stopped coming. Not long after that, Christine moved in. He pretended she was his mother at first and wondered as he watched from the doorway if that was how they'd made him, backwards like that, with gasping sounds coming out of her mouth. After a while he dropped the part about her being his mother. That really wasn't what he wanted. He wanted something special between them, but not that. More like what his father had. He wondered what it would be like if his father disappeared and Christine was his and he was the one she loved.

Many years later, sitting on a bench, staring out into the street while waiting for the Number 5, he still wondered about that. Did she love him? If he had found her, would they be together now?

Up and down the street in front of him the traffic flows east and west. An old man with a bushy white beard sits on his right, an old woman on his left, plastic shopping bags at her feet. Two old people hemming him in. He sits in the middle, as old as them. Three old people sitting on a bench, waiting for the bus. He can't remember how it happened that he got so old. The man on his right issues a cough and instantly he hears his father's cough. Not like this man's—erupting in short, discrete bursts, each sounding apologetic for the interruption—but delivered in a long rheumy series of bursts that start and stop and pick up again and could go on all day. Nothing apologetic about his father's cough. It was more like a rattlesnake that just keeps climbing and climbing out of his throat. He remembers being in the boardinghouse and wanting to reach down into his father's throat, grab that rattlesnake and chop off its head. It wouldn't be long now until he and Christine made their escape and rode off on the plow horse in the middle of the night.

CHRISTINE

After a while she talked about leaving, said she'd been there long enough, time to move on. "Where to?" he asked, not wanting to know. "Los Angeles," she said. "I could be a star." Something burst in him then, hearing that. Something living in his belly and filled with screaming. A bodily organ of some kind, a sac. Bursting and letting a hundred thousand screams fly loose. He tried to stifle them with the Kleenex tissues she'd left out on the dresser, with the T-shirt she'd taken off for his father and dropped on the floor, but the screams wouldn't be stilled.

"Don't go."

"I thought you didn't care."

His mother's voice comes back to him. Sharp. Businesslike. She's on the phone, ordering stuff for the apartment. "Shut up!" she suddenly yells at the person on the other end. "I wasn't talking to you," she cries. "Why do you keep talking when I'm not talking to you?" The other person must have gone silent then. Or hung up. Waves of silence came off the phone while the screaming inside him filled the room.

"Don't go," he said again.

"You won't even remember me."

He did of course. Sitting here on the bench, staring out into the street, waiting for the bus, he remembers her to this day.

"I could make you stay," he told her.

"How could you do that?"

He showed her how. He took a needle and thread and punched it through the hem of her T-shirt and the patch of his jeans that rose up into a peak when he bent his knee. "Now you're mine."

She cut the thread with her teeth and pulled her T-shirt free.

Again, her told her not to go.

"Okay," she said. "For now."

HANK

His father was "devastated." Everyone said so. No one told him what it meant. People who came to the house, people he had seen at his mother's dinner parties said so. People he assumed were from his father's office said so; friends from his club said so. He heard them in the hall, whispering in twos and threes. *Devastated*. Stephie said so. *Mind your daddy now, Sweetie Pie. He's devastated.* Even people who said they never could see what he saw in her said so. Except her beauty, of course. They'd give him that. She was a stunner.

They would never understand. Hank knew that. People he had known all his life would never understand. He accepted that. For him, understanding didn't come into it. He laid it down to mystery. The mystery of her laugh. The mystery of her beauty and of her fury when glassware was smashed and plates hurled against the wall. The mystery of their union. Gone now. She had taken it all away. He stood in the hall and stared at the front door. He sat on the blue silk sofa, the boy at his side, stared out across the room. He couldn't move. He couldn't turn his head to look at the boy, just turned seven. She threw him a birthday party and was gone in the morning. "Your mother's gone," he said. "She went away." "Where'd she go?" the boy asked. "When's she coming back?" He turned and left the room.

Hank saw her everywhere, and when he looked again, she was gone. Little by little over the years he drank more and more; his strength evaporated, and his stamina, his ability to hold down a job. Then the ornate birdcage that had never housed a bird disappeared. Then the tiny lampshades that fit over electrical fixtures shaped like candles disappeared. Then the blue silk sofa and all the rest of the furniture. Eventually all the rooms in the apartment and finally the apartment itself disappeared.

He stopped going to his club, although his membership was paid in full until the end of the year. He stopped playing golf on weekends, stopped going to work. He lost his job and let his hair grow. He couldn't pay the rent, couldn't afford the city. He let Stephie

go. A guy in a bar told him about a boardinghouse out of town. He
and the boy moved in; the boy was eleven or twelve. He did odd jobs
for his neighbors: carpentry and plumbing and electricity. He wore
a tool belt. He drove a truck. His shiny shoes gave way to boots, his
three-piece suits to overalls. He drank to excess. He had a succession
of women in. Fancy women. Whores. He never asked their names,
didn't want to know, didn't care. Years passed. The boy was fifteen or
sixteen. They drew a line down the middle of the boardinghouse. He
and the boy each kept to his side.

TWO

ROBROY

The high-pitched shriek like that of an animal on its way
to slaughter came from the administration office. He was in second grade. It was around one o'clock in the afternoon. A Friday in
late November, as he recalls. After the shriek, came the principal's
announcement over the loudspeaker that school would be closing
early. All parents had been notified, Mr. Talbot told them somberly,
although he didn't say of what. Parents would be arriving shortly, or
sending someone in their place, to retrieve their children. RobRoy
remembers that his mother did not wait by the curb that day apart
from the other mothers and look up when he appeared at the top of
the school steps and stare at him as if she didn't know him. Instead
she ran with the other mothers and assembled nannies half-way up
the steps to meet him as he came down. It was like a stampede, a
herd of women (mostly) rushing up the steps, gathering children in
their arms, embracing them, taking them away. He remembers the
mixture of cries and wails, remembers that some of the mothers
(even some of nannies) were crying. The children exchanged frightened looks. None of them knew what had happened. He remembers
being half-way down the steps and his mother rushing up, tripping on
a step and falling down hard. He remembers her torn stocking and
blood trickling down her leg. He remembers her frantic embrace, the
cradling of his head in her arms.

Later, they watched the funeral on TV. Watched as it was
played over and over. He remembers his mother jumping up from
the blue silk sofa, standing stiff and tall, placing her hand over her
heart. He remembers her instruction to him to do the same. "Stand,
RobRoy. Now." He remembers the way she arranged his right hand
not over his heart, but in a smart salute at his temple. He remembers
her saying, "John-John did it. So can you," although he was a much
bigger boy than John-John at the time. He remembers her declaring
it was only right they pay homage, wondering what that meant. He

212

remembers his father riding into the room on his wave, clicking off the TV, and shouting: "What the hell's the matter with you, Corinne? Letting him watch that." He remembers his father riding out of the room and his mother repeating everything they'd done—the rising up, the standing tall, the placing of her hand over her heart, the arranging of his right hand in a smart salute at his temple. Remembers doing it over and over, day after day, as the funeral was played endlessly on TV. He saw it so often he came to see the heavy black veil the widow wore falling down over his mother's face and himself shrinking to the size of John-John.

CHRISTINE

Christine was good to her word. She didn't go. "For now." She nestled in beside him, and he grew adept at eliciting her astonishing gasps and hugging her naked skinny body tight and plundering it—he liked to think of it like that, *plundering* it—with his increasingly competent cock. She did too, she told him. She liked the idea of being plundered.

More and more his father became a looming figure in his mind. To be ignored at peril. Yet he ignored him. He saw him walking up the street, approaching the boardinghouse. He ignored him. He heard the heels of his workman boots hitting the pavement louder and louder as he approached. He blocked out the sound. He saw him entering the boardinghouse while he and Christine were otherwise engaged. He saw him standing menacingly above the bed. He put him out of his mind. However, in the back of his mind, he knew he should stop. Stop the plundering, stop the gasping sounds, stop the pure sweet joyful ecstasy of it all, but he couldn't. He wouldn't. And finally he didn't. This was the best time he had ever had in his life, the absolute best.

CORINNE

His seventh birthday, May 23, 1964. A Saturday. Almost six months to the day after the assassination of the handsome young president, the world still stunned. She made a plan. She threw her boy a party, invited three boys and three girls. Hank wouldn't be there, of course. Wouldn't even be in the city, Westchester taking precedence. His country club taking precedence, his golf game with his cronies. "But it's his birthday," she protested, on the verge of tears. "I'll be back Sunday night," he replied. "I'll see him then." Often she came to the verge of tears for no apparent reason. But today she has a reason. She lets the tears gather in her eyes, never quite falling, freezing at the rims. Frozen crystals through which to see. She wonders now if Hank will be back on Sunday night, wonders if he even went to his club in Westchester, boarded the train, played a single hole of golf with his friends. She wonders if he didn't have a friend closer to home, one right here in the city perhaps, under her nose. Foolish to be wondering such things. Hank isn't that sort of man. *My beauty*, he calls her. *My long-legged girl.*

She has Stephie in to help. She'll stay the night in the bedroom at the end of the long white hall. She'll be there in the morning. It is important to have someone there in the morning. She has put fresh flowers in her room, changed the sheets. Stephie is good with children. She herself is not. Or only rarely. A glaring failure. One of many. She stands at the threshold, looking in at the party. The girls are adorable in their festive dresses. The boys are wild. Bouncing up and down on the blue silk sofa. Popping balloons. Shrieking with laughter. Throwing globs of ice cream (picking it right up in their hands), pieces of birthday cake. Store-bought. She doesn't bake. Another failure. The list goes on.

Now a handful of chocolate ice cream lands on the red-haired girl's gorgeous dress. Ice-blue, ruffles at the neck, exquisite. A loving mother had bought that dress for her daughter. Picked it out, adjusted its hem. A real mother. She herself is not. Or only rarely. The ice cream sinks into the fabric of the dress, sinks into whatever the girl is wearing beneath. The girl—Millie is her name—looks down at her dress and screams. Frantically, she shakes her skirt up and down to throw the ice cream off. Her mother will be furious. Any real mother would be furious, returning to see what has happened to the lovely dress. And here is RobRoy, her precious boy, looking at the girl, then at her, in horror both times. He has seen the ice cream sail across the room and land on Millie's dress. Does he think she threw it? Does he imagine she's capable of that?

Millie is inconsolable. She jumps up and down and howls. Her arms shoot up in a position of surrender; her little hands flap crazily. Her screams draw the attention of the other girls. They go silent in solidarity. The boys look away. Except for RobRoy. He continues to stare in horror at Millie's dress, then at her. Millie is now desperately clawing at the dress as if to rip it from her body. Corinne rushes to her. She wraps her arms around the child. Not too tightly. Not with a force that would frighten her. Briefly, she feels her upper arm press against the girl's face. Quickly, she pulls it away. Had she meant to comfort her or to stifle her screams? Cut them off at any cost? She can't be sure. Millie stamps her feet and screams. She must pry her loose from where she stands. But gently. Ever so gently. She must carry her out of this room, through another room and another, take her into the bathroom. She must manage to undress her, bathe her. Carefully. So carefully. Can she do it or will this be another failure to add to the list?

She signals to Stephie, alerts her to the problem. She bends down, hushes Millie. "Good girl. Pretty girl," she croons. Aren't these the words a real mother would use? She lifts Millie up. The child screams and struggles in her arms. A muddy river of chocolate ice cream runs down the front of her dress. "We'll fix it, Millie," she promises. "We'll fix it." She carries her out of the room, down the long white hall, past the living room, the dining room, the cutoff to the kitchen, past her room, hers and Hank's, past RobRoy's room, past one bathroom and into another. Stephie follows.

She must get the child's clothes off, bathe her. "Easy," she says to the screaming girl. "Easy now." Millie struggles, waves her arms, kicks her feet. "Stop!" she says. "Stop it now!" Was she shouting? Was she pressing her hand over the girl's mouth to stifle her screams? Certainly, she didn't mean to do that. She manages to remove Millie's shoes. Mary Janes, of course. Any real mother would buy those for her daughter. She will never have a daughter. Through room after room, her son's look of horror trails her.

She takes off Miltie's socks, the exquisite ice-blue dress, the stained undershirt beneath, the panties. She hands them to Stephie to throw into the wash. Millie writhes and screams. She stands her in the tub, runs the bath, tests the water. Not too hot. Not too cold. Millie struggles to cover herself, as if embarrassed to be naked in front of a stranger. But she's not a stranger, or not completely. Millie must have seen her calling for her son after school. "You know me, Millie," she says to her. "You know you do."

Gently, she pries the child's arms away from her body. Gently, she washes her. She can be gentle; she can be tender. The child's body is as delicate as a flower. How much easier it would be, it crosses her mind, to care for a flower than a child. She could put her in a vase, water her, fill the room with fragrance, walk away, come back some other time. Now she lifts the child out of the tub, wraps her in a towel, an oversized bath towel big as a shroud. She dries her, hugs her. Not too hard. Not too forcibly. Again, she tells her she is pretty. Again, she tells her she is good. She fetches RobRoy's pajamas and socks, dresses her. RobRoy won't mind. He would be proud to see his mother behaving as any mother would.

"Okay now, Millie? Sure you are. You're okay now."

Now she must think of something to do with the child. Some game to play while they wait for the ice-blue dress, the undershirt, the panties, the socks to go through the washer and drier, wait for Stephie to bring them back to them. Some game she played with RobRoy. Surely, over the years, she had played games with her son.

"Would you like that, Millie? Would you like to play a game?"

Calmer now, the child nods. Her bottom lip trembles.

She must do this right. She cannot fail today. It is her son's birthday. Seven years today. She must return a happy, smiling, red-haired girl in a spotless ice-blue dress with ruffles at its neck to the party. The party must be a success. She knows it will be. She cannot fail today. She must successfully launch her son upon his seventh year of life. Then, when the day is done, she will carry out her plan.

"Pretty Millie," she whispers. "Sweet Millie." Carefully, tenderly, she wraps her arms around the girl, rocks her back and forth.

She holds her a little away, looks into her face. Millie smiles, actually smiles. Her bottom lip stops trembling. Corinne is overjoyed. She shouts out loud in joy and claps her hands. The girl is startled, jumps back. She hadn't meant to startle her. Gently, she takes her hand, leads her into the bedroom. Leads her, doesn't drag her. There in a corner of the room she finds a rubber ball RobRoy has left behind. Red and blue stripes, basketball size. RobRoy won't mind. He's always been good about sharing his toys.

She rolls the ball toward Millie. Millie catches it, rolls it back. Corinne applauds, praises her. "Good Millie. Smart Millie." They do it again, then again. The game is working. They roll the ball back and forth. Millie is laughing now. Each time she catches the ball and rolls it back she laughs.

"Oh, Millie! Sweet Millie," Corinne exclaims "Look how good you are at this."

She is right to praise the child. Right to make her laugh.

Stephie returns with the undershirt, the socks and panties, and the dress, washed and dried and pressed, ice-blue, virginal. Corinne dresses the child, pulls up her panties, her socks, fastens the straps on her Mary Janes.

She stands the child in front of her full-length bedroom mirror, turns her around and around. Not roughly. Not too fast. She wouldn't want to make her dizzy.

"See how beautiful you are. How beautiful is your dress."

Millie smiles. She is happy. Corinne has made her happy. The dress has been restored to its pristine state. No real mother could have done more.

There's one other thing she must do. She takes her hairbrush from the dresser top, repositions Millie in front of the full-length mirror, brushes her hair. Strand after strand of lustrous, long red hair flow like streaks of blood through the brush. Slowly, cautiously, she brings the brush down from the top of the child's head, draws it out to the very ends of her hair. Gently, ever so gently. Millie moves her head from side to side in concert with the motion of the brush. She smiles. She is happy. Corinne has made the child smile, has made her happy. She is a success. The party is a success. She lets the child prance before the mirror a moment, lets her turn this way and that admiring herself, admiring her beautiful blue dress, her lustrous shining red hair. Corinne will not look into the mirror herself. She will not confront that other person looking back, that scrawny aged double spirit passing back and forth just below the surface of the glass.

She returns to the room where the party is in full swing, the lovely red-headed girl in the exquisite ice-blue dress on her arm. She might be a fairy godmother or a wicked stepmother escorting an innocent debutante to her first ball. She might be anyone at all. Or no one.

She pauses in the doorway, steps back, watches herself lift Millie and throw her back into the party. She watches the smiling child fly through the air; she watches her soar across the room. She sees her land in the middle of the astonished boys and girls, taking her place among them, carrying on with those other seven-year-olds who have carried on without her while she was away, eating cake, eating ice cream, tossing balloons into the air; and she sees her own precious RobRoy, the child of her heart, carrying on without her when she will have carried out her plan.

HANK

He had his job, his golf club, his home life, his son, his wife. His golden-haired goddess. The love of his life. He gave her everything she ever wanted, conceded to every whim. It could have gone on like that for years, for decades even, until the end of his days. But his love for her made him blind. Things changed, and he didn't see them change. Sometimes he thought she seemed not quite herself but didn't make an issue of it. Sometimes her voice sounded not like her own. Too high, too loud. Shouting when she didn't need to shout, when he was right there in front of her and could hear her perfectly well. She hasn't slept well, he told himself. She's distracted, or possibly coming down with something. Sometimes she looked at him as if he were a stranger. He passed it off, tried not to mind. Small things, really. Because they were so small he hardly noticed them.

Some things she said didn't make sense.

"The junk mail arrived," she announced one evening as he walked in.

Why would she tell him that? Junk mail always arrived. Always, she threw it out. As he kissed her a whiff of bourbon came his way. It's not yet six o'clock. He won't mention it. He's no one to judge.

"There on the platter in the hall."

She pointed to the outer hall. He looked where she pointed.

"It's come to bury us."

He sees the platter, sees the mail. She's fanned it out, arranged the edges of the envelopes like petals of a flower.

"Do something, can't you?" she shouts. "Get rid of it!"

He takes the platter into the kitchen, throws its contents into the trash. The incident is forgotten, never mentioned again.

Oftentimes she can't meet his eyes. Or meeting them, looks

away, stares into space. Preoccupied, he thinks. Lost in thought.

"Hello, Hank," she says one evening. "How are you, darling?"

And everything's all right again.

They go to friends' houses for drinks. They have people over. They go out to dinner. Heads turn as she walks in. She casts her dazzling smile at people she knows, sometimes at people she doesn't.

"Who is that, Hank? That woman in the terrible hat. I know her, don't I?"

"No," he replies. "I don't think you do."

At times she flies into a rage over something he would deem inconsequential. The grandfather's clock has stopped. She stamps her foot. An expected package doesn't arrive. Cups and saucers fly past his head. Crockery hits the wall. Stephie is late. Shards of glass cut her arm. Blood stains appear on the blue silk sofa. Her blood, her lacerations. Always self-inflicted. Never would he lift a hand to her. *His long-legged girl. The love of his life.* He grabs his hat, walks out the door. Things will be better when he returns. Calmer, more manageable.

His golden-haired goddess. His angel. The only woman he will ever love. He never had another, never wanted one. Until she left and left him with a son.

A seven-year-old who stares into space as his mother often does. Who, unlike his mother, rarely speaks. And so he drank. Because of her, because of him. Because she went away and left a silent, staring son in her place. He drank because he doesn't know why she did what she did. Because he doesn't ever want to know.

The note was propped on his bedside table. *Take care of my son. Tell him I love him.* Propped there like proof. Proof she'd planned it all along. Proof he'd been too blind to notice. It enraged him, galled him. He lit a match to it. Had she been planning it while she lay in his arms? While things were going well? Or he thought they were. He watched the page burn. Had she done it because he went to his club, because he missed his son's birthday party? Because he let things go and tried not to mind? It was his fault then. His fault because he hadn't noticed, because he was blind. His fault she did what she did. He couldn't live with that. He couldn't live with himself.

And so he drank. He drank to save his life.

Years later, when the boy was eleven or twelve, he lost his job, couldn't pay the rent, couldn't keep Stephie on the payroll, couldn't afford the city. He lost the apartment and found a place in a boardinghouse on the sordid rim of a low-level suburb, a place where he'd never wanted to live, and became a man he'd never wanted to be. He picked up jobs here and there, handyman work, which he'd learned from his father—carpentry and plumbing, painting and electricity, fitting wires, aligning shelves, fixing pipes. He picked up women. He had them in. Lots of them. One after the other. They helped him forget, or nearly forget, and he was grateful to them for that. After Christine arrived, he told them to go. They left hairbrushes, twisted tubes of gel and soiled menstrual pads in their wake. They left food on the table, dirty dishes in the sink. He didn't care, for he had come across a woman in the road. A girl, really. Barely more than fifteen or sixteen. He stopped his truck; she got in. There were no other women after that. She helped him forget, or nearly forget, but it wasn't close to love.

What he'd had with Corinne was love. All he would ever know of it. He'd never expected to have a woman like that in his life. She was beyond him, way out of his league, unfathomable. She was a mystery, a gift. It went on like that for years, for his whole married life, and could have gone on like that forever except suddenly she was gone. Left him a note. *Take care of my son,* as if he would do anything else. *Tell him I love him,* as if he would tell him anything else.

ROBROY

The morning after his seventh birthday, his mother disappeared. He looked for her everywhere, searched every room in the apartment. He raced down the hall, burst into the bedroom at its far end. He woke up Stephie, made her look. She called the police. He never saw his mother again. Never understood why she had gone away. Was it something he had said or done? Was it because she didn't love him? His father told him she'd left a note saying she loved him, but not saying what she had done or why.

Some thirteen years later, when he was twenty, he picked up the phone on a whim one night, called his father and found out what she had done. But not why. Never why. It wasn't fair to him or to her. How could it be fair to a boy who had just turned seven? To a woman who was thirty-eight years old?

Take care of my son, her note instructed. *Tell him I love him.* His father told him over the phone that night, across country, thirteen years later, that the note was proof. Proof she'd intended it all along. He didn't care. Proof, his father claimed, she'd had it in mind for years. Proof didn't matter to him. It seemed to matter more than anything to his father. *Proof I was blind,* his father said. He didn't know about his father's blindness or care. What she'd done just made him mad. So mad he thought he'd never forgive her. The police called his father at his club in Westchester. He came back early, having missed a day of golf. *Tell him I love him,* she wrote in the note. How could that be true? How could she love him if he wasn't worth living for?

He never saw the note. His father had destroyed it all those years before in almost the same instant he'd found it propped on his bedside table. *Crumpled it,* he told him. *Lit a match to it.*

By the time he was told what the note contained, RobRoy was already a man living on his own in a rented room far across the country. From where he sat in that room that night, three time zones away, he could hear the ice cubes tinkling in his father's glass. He was twenty and had called on a whim. Picked up the phone, dialed the number, the only one he had for him, but he figured he'd still be there in the boardinghouse, doing his odd jobs. Until that night all his father had ever said about what his mother had done was, *she went away.* Where'd she go? When's she coming back? *She's gone,* was all his father would ever say. He had turned seven that day.

Except in dreams, he never saw his mother again. Dreaming, she came to him. He saw her entering his room in a bright white dress. He saw her floating toward him, her skirt billowing. At seven and eight, even nine, even ten, he saw her sitting on his bed, felt her fingers running through his hair. He saw it, felt it, over and over. Always it was his birthday. Always he had just turned seven. Sheathed in radiance, she floats toward him, night after night. He can't make out her face, can't quite see her expression. He's eight, he's nine, he's ten, but always in the dream he's just turned seven. She sits on the edge of his bed, reaches out a hand, draws her fingers through his hair. Over and over. Year after year.

And then he picked up the phone on a whim one night thirteen years later and called his father and his father blurted it out.

How is that fair? No wonder he rants on a bench while waiting for a bus. No wonder he lets obscenities fly.

CORINNE

She slides out of bed before dawn. She is careful not to make any noise. She has left her husband a note. She sinks to the floor, leans against the wall, sits there a moment. She hasn't slept all night. Hasn't slept in many nights. She gazes at the ceiling. Bluish, iridescent, filtered by streetlight. Her arms and legs begin to crumble. The floor lifts her to her feet. She walks down the hall to her son's room, pauses in the doorway. She will not go in. She will not wake him. He is just a little boy and needs his sleep. He is so little she can barely see his curly head from where she stands. Her heart breaks for him. She longs to go to him, tell him she loves him, has always loved him, but she will not disturb his sleep. She knows this isn't fair. Not to him, not to her husband. They will not understand, perhaps never forgive. She does not ask for forgiveness. She asks only of her husband that he not judge her too harshly. She asks her son to remember that she loved him. Only that. Remember her love. She has failed in all but her love for her son. Her blood is turning to water. Her bones are turning to chalk. She stands in the doorway, extends a hand toward her son. She will not touch him, will not wake him. Already he seems far away. She digs her fingers into his hair, pulls out a clump, stuffs it into her mouth. She chews on his hair as she backs away from his room. She walks down the hall, past the dining room, the living room. She takes the cutoff to the kitchen. Walking faster now, silently, barefoot, her thin white nightgown grazes her ankles. She walks through the kitchen, crowded with appliances. Shining white and mammoth. Indestructible. Everlasting. Guardians to keep her son and husband safe. She chews on her son's hair as she walks to the back door, opens it, passes through. She takes the stairs to the roof. Iron stairs. Five flights up. Her son's hair is sweet as flowers in her mouth. Strands of it twine around her teeth. She climbs one flight, then another. Five flights to the roof. A black tin door offers access. The sky is pale. There is no moon. The hem of her nightgown grazes her ankles. A thin white gown. She has nothing on beneath. She walks to the edge of the roof. This is hers to do. Hers alone. She stands still a moment. Space surrounds her, lapping at her feet like foam. The sweetness of her son's fair hair fills her mouth, trickles down her throat. She thinks of her son. Her precious RobRoy. She clenches his hair in her teeth. She drops her gown, steps out into the dawn.

THREE

CHRISTINE

I'm free now. On my own. Hitchhiking down the open road. Just me and my baby inside. I don't know whose he is, the son's or the father's. Makes no difference to me. He's mine. All mine. Or she is. That's all that matters. All the meaning of life wrapped up in one tiny life not even born.

I'm heading west. One town, one state at a time. No concern how long it takes. I'll get there when I get there. Stopping off along the way. Seeing the world. New Jersey, Pennsylvania, Ohio, next on my list. Indiana, Illinois, after that. Route and destination depending on those kind enough to offer me a ride. Finding jobs as I go. McDonnell's, Denny's, the local diner, pizza joint. Stay a week or two, even a month, saving up for my needs of which I don't have many. Just the basics for me and my baby. Milk and diapers. Toothpaste. Shampoo. Then move on. Jobs are easy to find if you're not too particular about the work or the pay. Requiring only food and shelter. Food's not a problem. With the jobs I find most readily food's included. Sometimes even shelter, or leads to shelter, furnished rooms, people seeking roommates on a short-term basis. I'll work one job through to its inevitable conclusion—boredom, usually, with the work or the surroundings. Termination now and then because of some flagrant misdeed on my part, my penchant for tardiness, for example, or too-frequent ill-advised remarks of which I know I'm capable, directed at a customer or even a supervisor. I'll just move on, pick up another gig, see another town, another state, always saving up for that rainy day. I'll stop to have my baby, find a good hospital, safe, clean, high-tech. That's the plan. Los Angeles is my goal. The future it dangles. The way it looks from a hill: distant and bright, glowing in the dark. Iguanas, parrots, magnolia trees. In postcards anyway. A western frontier. The movie business a perennial possibility. I'm young, pretty, thin. Or will be thin again after I've had my baby. I could catch somebody's eye. A publicist or an actor's agent.

Snag a lucky break, become a star. It's been known to happen. Why shouldn't it happen to me?

I don't in the least regret the time I spent with either the silent son or the brooding father. Don't credit the age difference between me and the father with having pushed me toward the son. The father was kind, if tending to brood. The son was just there, young, sweet, even younger than me, perpetually hanging around. It was a sort of love on my part between the son and me, more on his. Motherlove, I'd call it, in RobRoy's case. Fleeting, temporary. Not like with my baby, that's permanent unconditional forever-love. The father was a darker matter. I had pity for him. For what his wife had done. The boy didn't know the specifics. *She's gone*, he told me was all his father ever said. *She went away*. Never explicated further, never talked about it. To me at least. That explained a lot. The old man's brooding, the son's sometimes scary silence. Didn't excuse it but explained. I can look back on it now with pleasant feelings for them both. It was a mostly pleasant time in my life and left me with a bonus, the little one growing inside. Whichever one gave it to me, I'm grateful to them both.

I do feel bad for RobRoy, though, about my sudden disappearance. He'll likely be distraught. Or maybe distraught is too strong a word, but he was always going on, those rare occasions he spoke at all, about white picket fences, and I wouldn't put it past him to set out and try to find me. He never will, though. Will never see his kid, if it is his. That makes me sad. Fathers and sons, or daughters, deserve a chance at least to know one another. But not everybody gets what they deserve.

HANK

The love of my life, gone now. *My long-legged girl, my golden-haired goddess.* She climbed the iron stairs to the roof, stepped out into the dawn. My son is gone now, too. Some thirteen years later. Trailing after a girl we both had a hankering for. I doubt he'll ever find her, or that I'll ever see my son again. I wish them well, both of them, that girl and boy. But it leaves me with a feeling like empty space inside in regard to my son. Always meant to bridge the gap between us, tell him things. Things about me and his mother. Never got around to it. Maybe he wouldn't have cared, but there's nobody left now to tell them to. Dumb things.

Like her habit, before I lost my job and we still had the apartment in the city and could afford to send stuff out to be cleaned, of replacing wire hangers with satin ones. Peach-colored, tufted. She'd take my shirts off the wire hangers when they came back from the laundry, throw the wire ones away, and put peach-colored satin ones in their place. Wire hangers were good enough for me, I always told her. "No, they're not, Hank. They're not," she'd reply. He probably wouldn't have cared about a dumb thing like that, but it was something to tell him and after she left I never saw another hanger like it.

About that silence of his, his and mine, his worse than mine. I kept meaning to ask him about it, never found the time. Sure as hell hope he didn't get it from me. Leaving him with silence would be like leaving him with nothing at all.

And about Christine, the girl so giving she had room for two. She's another topic we never raised. But how could he not have known I knew? I heard her gasps, the whole series of them, through the grimy windows of the boardinghouse before I even reached the door. She gasped like that with me, too, though maybe with less force and in not such an extended series. Can't say that didn't irk me some, him eliciting a stronger response than me, but it was logical he would, being so much younger and having all that kinetic energy. Though not expertise, I'll say that for myself. He wouldn't have had that at his age. Seems expertise, however, wasn't a concern of hers, judging by her gasps. Even so, she left him. Left us both. We waited for days, weeks, for the giving girl to come back, waited without speaking of what we were waiting for. Finally, it hit us both, me first, then him, neither of us acknowledging it: she wouldn't ever be coming back. It was over, finished, like the giving had never begun. Eventually I let her go. Had to. Went back to other women. Some I'd had before. Some were new. None like what I had with Christine. And for sure nothing like what I'd had with my golden-haired goddess. After a while I got over Christine. RobRoy never did. He moped around for a couple of years, then quit school, bought a motorcycle I didn't know he had the money for, packed up, and took off after her. I hope he finds her, though I doubt he ever will. It would leave him with something, which is more than I can do.

ROBROY

I'll find her. If it takes me a lifetime, I'll find her. Before she left, she told me she didn't know which of us was the father, me or my old man, but I know in my heart it's mine. Gotta be. No way my dad could be the father. He's too old. Practically decrepit. That kid is mine. My kid, my responsibility. I'll find them and do what's right.

I've saved enough money doing chores and odd jobs like my father for a beat-up Yamaha. I'll earn more as I go, doing whatever comes along. I'm carrying her picture with me to show to people who might've happened to see her. Jog their memory. She'd be heading west. I remember what she said about the movie business and getting her big break. *A movie star's way better than a costume designer.* And I figure she'd still have that in mind, so I'll head out that way, show her picture every place I think she might've been, and track her down. Knowing she would've needed a way to finance her journey, I'll start with the local McDonald's and Denny's and other fast-food places where she might have picked up work. She's a looker and anybody who's seen her isn't likely to forget. Someone along the way will take one look at her photo and say, "Why, sure I remember her. Served me breakfast just last week," or "She was working the counter a week or two ago. Didn't realize till she stepped out she was eating for two." "She happen to say where she was going?" I'll ask. "On her way to L.A.," they'll reply. "To be a movie star." So I'll thank them kindly and hurry on out in that direction.

I'll find them, I know I will. By the time I do she will have had the kid. My kid. My responsibility. I'll swoop one up in each arm and start a new life. Me and the two of them. I don't care how long it takes.

That was then. This is now. Years pass, decades. Not everything you dream works out. I'm older now than my old man ever was. After I split from the boardinghouse I never saw him again. He's dead and gone. Gotta be. Never spoke to him after that phone call when I was twenty and called on a whim. Curious to see how he was and knowing he'd never call me. 'Course he didn't know where I was or have my number. Even so, he'd never call.

He was drunk when he answered. No surprise there. And he blurted it out. About the iron stairs and the roof, about her intention all along. Only the facts. No last words, no goodbyes.

Like I said I would, I made it to L.A. But never found Christine or the kid. I stayed forever, looking for her. Prowled the back lots, any place I thought she might've been. Even got work as an extra. No luck. No luck ever. It's like she vanished in thin air, went up in smoke. It broke my heart. Always had this vision of hooking up, starting a life with Christine and the kid. That's the way it was meant to be. Never happened. I stayed for years, roaming around, looking for them. Never happened in all those years, so I came back east where I'd started from. The kid would be older today than I was then. Never had a family of my own, never made Christine my wife. Always wondered if it was a girl or a boy.

The bus makes its turn, heads north, keeping the river on its left. It's a long, mostly straight drive uptown. After a while my head begins to nod. Chin falls to my chest, though I don't doze off. The smell of booze comes off my clothes and spirals up my nostrils. I'll be quiet on the bus, won't shout, won't let obscenities fly. A couple of gasps escape, however, despite my best intentions. Short, surprising gasps. Not a whole series of them, that's for sure. Christine is the only one I ever heard gasp like that.

My birthday party the year I turned seven comes to mind. Last party my mother ever threw for me. She popped a spoonful of chocolate ice cream into my mouth and laughed. Right there in front of my friends. Laughed her wild laugh. It embarrassed the hell out of me. Even now, the sound of it can come out of nowhere and pierce my ears.

Acknowledgments

These stories originally appeared in slightly different forms in the following literary journals:

"A Moment's Peace" originally appeared in *The Chariton Review*
"By the Pond" originally appeared in *The New Guard*
"Girl… There Was A Time" originally appeared in *TriQuarterly*
"Mistaken Identity" originally appeared in *Literal Latte*
"Special Needs" originally appeared in *Notre Dame Review*
"Stalking" originally appeared in *The North Atlantic Review*
"The Piano Room" originally appeared in *The Cumberland River Review*
"The Walk" originally appeared in *Slippery Elm Literary Journal*

author's photo: Tracy Lane

Enid Harlow is the author of four novels: *LOVE'S WILDERNESS*; *GOOD TO HER*; *A BETTER MAN*; and *CRASHING*.

Her short stories have appeared in numerous literary journals of national distinction including *TriQuarterly, Boulevard, Nimrod, The Ontario Review, Notre Dame Review, North Atlantic Review, Southwest Review, American Fiction, Quarterly West, The American Voice*, and *The Southern Review*, among others.

She has been awarded an Artists' Fellowship in Fiction by the New York Foundation for the Arts and has received two PEN Syndicated Fiction Awards. She lives and writes in Brooklyn, NY.